Defenders

Ronnie Levy

First published in 2011 by Ronnie Levy

Ronnie Levy
The Defenders

ISBN 978-0-9871786-0-2

www.theDefendersRace.com

Printed in the U.S.A

For my beautiful family. Your support and love can never be measured. Thanks for being the wonderful people you are. To everyone who has been there with advice and guidance, thanks for helping my vision become real.

One

The Nameless

Prologue

So many faces. I knew it was possible, but seeing it for the first time has put everything into perspective.

Despite the discomfort of squeezing into the lofty stands, I feel a bond as the crowd's rhythmical chants touch my soul. But it's not just their sound which unites us for I sense each person is also here to watch *my* son. Uncontrollably, his every move pumps pride through my veins, and caresses my heart with fear.

From afar, I can see his thick dark hair, just like his father's military cut, sparkle as the sun's dizzying heat sears from above. If the sweaty droplets slowly dribbling down my temple are anything to go by he, and the other participants, must be in physical distress. Knowing this, I won't wipe my face for I too want to share in every moment.

"You're gonna die!" yells an anonymous voice from the crowd.

Thankfully these agitators are small in number because their abusive taunts seem to resonate tenfold to that of our own cheers. However, despite some of the other spectators quickly putting a stop to any crudeness, the shocking words have ignited concerns for my son's safety. My only comfort is knowing the panic-stricken faces of the other participants is a fear not shared by my boy.

Standing with a calm innocence, he seems more in awe of his new surroundings than afraid of what's to come.

His breath is purposeful. His lungs exhale.

As he wrenches his neck un-naturally backward, I can see him stare in wonderment at the colossal amphitheatre surrounding him. I doubt whether he has even noticed all the people.

Even with sporadic outbursts from one of the many oversized participants, reminding him of his intimidating surroundings, my son diffuses the distraction by transforming his naive stare into a smile.

I know that look. It's a reassurance driven by his countless training sessions and a self-determined intellect. But above all else it's his passion for the *Challenge* that propels this poise; a trait inherited from his father and one which I know will elevate him above the rest.

Beep!

There it is! Not long now.

My son's smile disappears. I hope he's not losing focus.

After shaking his arms to release any tension, my thoughts ease. His legs, trapped beneath a skin-tight black bodysuit, also wobble with intent. As if tattooed on his thighs and torso, this uniform provides the perfect recipe for his heart and lungs to move in unison, allowing him to breathe as efficiently as his internal organs require.

While rotating his head, another breath inflates his pectorals causing his abdominal muscles to ripple. The protruding blood vessels, accentuating the tautness of his arms, tell me his body is screaming, ready to burst out of its imaginary cage. With his sculptured physique on display I can't help but wonder how many others are enjoying his muscular demonstration.

He has not shaved for three days. The growth has begun to show through. But as his hand brushes across a crescent-shaped scar tracing his jaw line, I can see his mind has begun to stray.

This is when my son's concentration has always come into question. His golden-brown eyes stare skyward as his thoughts shift to another time, another place.

However, in the time it took for more hollering to roar throughout the arena, his focus snaps back to another nearby participant. The disruption, yelled by this giant only a few metres away, continues.

"Victory is MINE!"

The hulk-like figure glares left, then right, daring to eye off anyone in sight. If the result was to be decided on shape alone then this man would be unmatched. In spite of knowing this, the hulk's burning thoughts are unleashed on his neighbouring participants.

"What are you looking at?! I'm gonna beat you! Beat you bad!"

As the voices in the crowd swell yet again my son, who furrows his brow, must also feel like shouting.

He must remember where he is and what he's here for. I wish he could read my thoughts. *Be patient, it's not time yet.* But as his bare feet slowly clench the ground, preparing even the finest body parts for the battle that will soon ensue, I realise it is I who requires patience.

Beep!

As another breath enters his body my son lifts his shoulders, allowing him to hold it at its deepest point.

Nothing but emptiness fills his mind.

With the slow exhale that follows, his shoulders lower, releasing any remaining anxiety.

While his eyes close, mine drift to the other grandstand, less than one-hundred meters directly in front of me and my son. The enormous chrome structure, ominously draping the entire finishing area, is a sight to behold. Its elevation is so steep that only the midday sun can peak over top.

Sometimes I marvel at our recent technological advancements. It seems like only yesterday these events were held in an eight-lane circular stadium, but as I gaze back to the starting line, beneath my stand, I am still in awe at how this new rectangular design allows every participant to race at once. Although fitting a handful of men across evenly spaced lanes may not seem like a great achievement, positioning one thousand hyperactive participants within these narrow barriers is no easy feat. But I guess that's why, when I peer left and right, the arena looks like a valley being stretched between two cliffs with nothing but barren land borders the outside lanes. Despite all that space, the adrenalin-filled men are currently squeezed between the starting line and the first row of my congested grandstand. This is not the moment to be claustrophobic.

It is with a sense of irony that, with all the modern technology surrounding them, the track's surface is speckled with loose red-brown rubble. Like an ancient gladiator stadium, our use of this dirt has been a tradition for the ages.

Since the latest beep, the crowd's chants have amplified. At first I thought it was because time had almost expired, but now I realise something else was augmenting their voices.

Beep!

As I glance up, the sea of faces that had once washed over me seem to vanish beneath a cloudy blur. Something else was emerging.

It doesn't take long for this blurry image to clear, leaving a sight I had only ever seen from afar in its place.

The planet's entire population has arrived, one billion in total.

This throng of new people, transmitting their visual support to the participants, chants with an eerie unison as the countdown to *The Challenge* is almost complete.

To add to my own anxiety the opaque cover blanketing the dirt track disappears, revealing what each participant has feared.

The hulk-like man near my son has been silenced. His face turns ghostly white.

Even though the length of the course does not seem far, negotiating these newly uncovered objects will make finishing feel like a painful eternity.

With impending hurt foremost in their thoughts, I recall that my son had once told me how these entities prey on the weakness of any unprepared participant, speaking to them in silent tongue. By the looks on some of their faces, I don't think it will be long before the weaker participants will be hearing these whispers. Until then, the secret driving these cruel objects remains concealed.

My son, unwilling to open his eyes, firms his torso. The long-awaited task, and the time for his own secret to be revealed, has arrived.

Through the chants, and following yet another beep, an official greeting is heard, instantly diffusing our voices.

"All who are in attendance are privileged to witness this Challenge. Welcome and congratulations Defenders, you honour us all."

Although the salutation sounds welcoming, the words feel haunting, leaving me on edge.

The greeting ceases.

With the entire planet seemingly silent, the lack of sound becomes painful to my ears. The anticipation is unbearable.

As if answering my own torment, the primitive sound of a gong crashes, startling myself, and those around me.

The participants steady themselves one last time. Other than a steely few, who have their eyes fixed well into the distance, most glare at the objects spread between them and the finish.

My son settles into his tightly-coiled starting position, crouching three-quarters down to the ground. He is ready to explode.

Knowing the countdown must be nearing its end, my own grip tightens. As my fingernails dig into my clammy palms I hear a subtler beep. Another then sounds, and another. Just then, the gong blasts again.

In an instant my son and the other participants launch themselves forward in unintended unison onto the track and towards the deadly objects.

The crowd around me erupts with an explosive roar.

However, in spite of all our togetherness, I still can't shake a feeling that not everything is as harmonious as the crowd's support.

I have always sensed another force has willed the participants in this direction – a power that may also be controlling them now.

I.

A strong wind blew through the arched window above five-year-old Ky's bed, slamming his door shut. The thud echoed down the hall, drawing the attention of Elric Sterling, his father, who came rushing in.

"Are you okay?"

Ky nodded excitedly and crawled to the foot of his bed. "Was that thunder dad?"

"Maybe," he said, closing the windowpane and drawing the heavy velvet floor-to-ceiling curtains. "But there could be a storm brewing in tonight's story too."

Ky smiled expectantly, slipped back under his covers and spread into the shape of a starfish. "Okay dad, I'm ready. Can you start?"

Elric took the burden off his aching feet by sitting down on the bed, causing it to sag and for Ky to curl around him. "First, I need a cuddle."

For Ky, there was no safer place to be as he awaited the nightly ritual to begin; one which started with a fairy-tale, not all being fiction, and would usually end with some meaningful life-lesson.

A few meters away Ky's sister, eight-year old Ahlis, read quietly in her own bed, hidden beneath the shadows of their shared luminous lamp. "Dad!" she asserted, as her jet-black curly hair and rosy cheeks glistened. "I'm not putting my book down until you begin."

Though her feisty tone was not uncommon, Elric giggled, recalling his childrens' antics. *"Look Ahlis,"* he remembered Ky *saying. "I didn't know this food could stick to my face!"*

Though for Ahlis, who closed her book with a thud, there would be no fooling around tonight. "Come on dad, stop day-dreaming. We've been waiting all day for you to continue last night's story."

"Yeah," Ky said, scooting to the top of the bed as the moon's fluorescent light shone through a crevice between the drapes and onto his sisters' hazel eyes.

As if sensing Elric's concern for her warmth, Ahlis pulled the doona up to her chin, poked her fingers out and grasped the covers firmly.

Elric grinned. Though he kept his eyes locked onto Ahlis, he leaned down towards Ky. "So, where were we?"

"The animal!" Ahlis said. "The animal!"

"Oh, that's right," Elric said. "There was once a time when the strongest animal of all grew so hungry that nothing could satisfy it."

Ahlis and Ky froze with anticipation.

"The animal I spoke of was man-kind, and their hunger was for power."

"What power dad?" Ahlis asked, confused.

"Kpowy x-ray vision," Ky said.

"While that may also be true, the power I meant was a desire to rule over and control every living thing."

"Why would they want to do that?" Ahlis asked.

"Because they were fuelled by yucky emotions like fear, greed, anger and hate."

"Hate is a bad word dad," Ky said.

"You're right. We try not to say it often. But for that society it was this hate, expanding like an over-inflated balloon, which was about to cause the most damage."

Peeking through the slightly open door Ky's mother, Loush Sterling, whispered. "How's the story going?"

"Dad's using his grown-up words again," said Ahlis. "Ky can't understand him."

"Yes I can," Ky said.

"I'm sure he'll be okay," Loush said, fluttering her curved lashes at Elric.

Ky grinned. "Are you going to stay with us mum?"

"Not tonight guys. I still have some work to do outside."

"But a storm's coming!" Ky said.

"Don't worry about me. I'm almost done."

"You may be small and pretty," Elric said, admiring Loush's unblemished pink skin, "but you work harder than anyone I know. No wonder people are so drawn to you."

"I only work so much because if I don't, you will and you need a break."

As a draft blew from behind Loush, the distinct aroma of freshly rolled hay, imprinted on her clothes, wafted through Elric's nose, causing him to sneeze violently.

"Dad!" Ky said. "You squashed my foot."

"Sorry my boy."

Loush chuckled, seeing a few speckles of grain fall from Elric's coarse hair.

"What's so funny mum?" Ky demanded.

"Oh, it's just your father," she replied, brushing the grains into her hands before backing quietly out of the room. "Sleep well."

The stage was Elric's once again. His children's spongy minds were ready. "I'm glad we had a laugh with mum because there's not much to smile about in tonight's tale."

Despite most stories being easy to digest, a sense of foreboding manifested from Elric's words.

"It's okay dad," Ky said, wrapping his comforter in a ball around itself. "We're ready for anything."

Elric drew a breath. "Although this story didn't occur that long ago, it is one retold many times by our ancestors."

"You mean grandma and grandpa know this story?" Ahlis asked.

"Of course," Elric said. "They told it to me. But they did so with great caution for it was one of man-kind's darkest days. It was a time when the world was swarming with people who caused much harm to others. While many knew their actions did not feel right, most had simply accepted this as the way of life."

"Did you know these men dad?" Ky asked.

"No silly," Ahlis replied. "It was way before dad was born."

"How long ago was it?" Ky asked.

"Yeah dad," Ahlis added. "When was it?"

"What do you think?" Elric said.

Ky wrapped himself tightly around his father once again and closed his eyes. Words from last night's story came flooding back, invoking the already vivid imagination of a young boy.

Bulky men, wearing overpriced suits and silk ties, shouted, *"BUY! SELL!"* at the top of their lungs. Their outcries heated their bodies to such an extent that large sweat patches under their arms were a daily sight. Not wanting to ruin their suits, jackets were draped over the back of a random chair at the commencement of each business day.

Ahlis' mind was also in full-flight. She recalled how these same men abused the dreams of others by creating envy, replacing society's ethics with greed, and using the value of money as the measure of wealth. Even with sufficient amounts of money available for everyone, no one was willing to share.

"Oh I remember exactly when this happened," Ahlis said. "They mentioned it at school when babbling on about being so different from our ancestors of only a few hundred years ago." She paused, puzzled. "But they never said *how* we actually changed."

"Ah," Elric said. "First you should understand that as the power-hungry people of that day gained an abundance of money, the poor began to build more and more..."

"Anger!" exclaimed Ahlis. "No wait. Hate! It's the balloon of hate!"

"That's right," replied Elric, seeing confusion drift over Ky's face.

"What does abundance mean?" Ky asked.

"It means a lot," Ahlis mumbled, remembering more sad stories of how the cruellest of dictators gave orders which people were forced to obey without question. "Those people should have known better. How could they be so mean and why didn't anyone take a stand?"

"It's not easy to conquer bullies," Elric said. "Back then, the people who tried were probably punished."

"But I don't get it," she snarled. "If money was the cause why didn't they just get rid of it?"

"Oh money wasn't the problem. It was only the symptom. The issue was that their society had become convinced to use money as the measure of wealth. That's where tonight's tale gets a bit scary, at a place where the hate-balloon was about to burst."

The children gripped their sheets tightly.

"As all accounts go, during one of these predictably unjust days, the sky had become dark at a time where the sun should have shone bright."

Elric's voice was heavy as his eyes intensified. "Your grandpa had told me that, in the time leading up to the balloon bursting, all the lands of Earth had become desolate. Across every landscape all that could be seen were concrete jungles or residue left over from abandoned wars."

"What about the trees and forests?" Ahlis asked.

"All gone," Elric said, shaking his head. "The lakes too had long since dried-up. All the oceans of the world were pillaged. The lives of plants and animals hung in the balance. Greed and hate had taken control while the poor and weak were held to ransom. Medicine and food could have been made plentiful, but the money needed for its development was denied. It was all too much."

A frustrated Ahlis gasped. "That place sounds awful."

Elric glanced at Ky. "What's worse was that many children were born into a slavery they were never permitted to leave. Some innocent kids were even raised as instruments of destruction with the sole purpose of harming others."

"Were these children like me dad?" Ky asked.

"Exactly like you!"

Ky frowned.

"Other infants were born into the cruellest of poverty. They would sit in silence, drinking muddied water and accepting their fate, until their pain would become unbearable. Each cried day and night until they would pass away, unnoticed by the rest of the world, while their families would go on in a shadowy daze of sadness."

"Enough dad!" Ahlis said. "No more bad stuff. Especially since we'd never let it happen."

"And why is that?" Elric asked.

"Because we measure wealth by our intellectual, emotional and physical growth, not by how greedy we are."

"Good," Elric said softly. "That's good."

Ky stared up at a crack on the ceiling. "Wasn't there anyone left to help the kids?" he asked longingly as he dragged his comforter, along with Buster, his favourite fluffy toy dog, closer to his chest.

"By that stage of human history there was no one left to care."

"*I* would have helped," Ahlis said. "*I* would have changed everything. *I* would have burst that balloon of hate."

"But instead of you, nature was there to make the change for us," Elric said. He drew another breath and whispered. "For as long as we can remember our Sun has provided us with life, but at the time of this story its golden shine had begun to disappear."

"Where did the light go?" Ky asked, enthused by the mere mention of anything to do with his passion of the cosmos. "Was the sun dying?"

"Not quite," Elric said, shaking his head. "A mysterious grey mist had emerged to blanket the entire planet, preventing much of the light from entering Earth."

"What was happening?" Ahlis pleaded.

"Humanities mistreatment of our planet had begun a chain of events which…"

"Was it the same grey sky that occurred during the Great Pre-Historic Cleanse?" Ahlis interrupted, referring to the widely discussed cataclysmic event, which ended the dinosaurs reign sixty-five million years prior.

"There are similarities in both chronicles. But only our story speaks of a fiery orange entity revealing itself from beyond the grey…"

"Entity?" Ahlis asked. "What entity?"

"Shh," Ky said.

Ahlis glared angrily. "Don't tell me to be quiet Ky! I just want to know what happened!"

Ky didn't respond, nor did he apologise. Unafraid, he sat upright and brushed the fringe of his soft dark brown hair away from his eyes.

A moment later Ahlis' focus returned to Elric, wanting to know what kind of miracle was about to save the planet.

Elric gritted his teeth. "What happened was that man-kind finally took notice. The entity, a blazing fireball shot from the Sun, broke through the grey and hurtled into Earth."

Ahlis' mouth was dry. While moistening her lips with the tip of her tongue, Elric persisted. "The fireball was so strong, and the atmosphere had weakened to such an extent, that half the planet burned instantly while the other half flooded with the melting of the icecaps. Despite only being another footnote in Earth's existence, it was complete devastation to that civilization. Like the Great Cleanse you've read about, life as they knew it no longer existed."

"What do you mean?" Ahlis asked.

Elric sighed. Ky could feel his father's stomach soften. "Only one percent of our population survived."

Although Ky, chewing his comforter, remained in a trance of silent melancholy, Elric grinned, the wrinkles around his eyes tightened.

"What's there to be happy about dad?" Ahlis asked. "So much life had ended."

"Don't think of it as an end, but rather a chance for a new beginning. Besides, not everyone who survived was saddened by the destruction."

"What?" Ahlis gasped, looking over at Ky, whose tiredness forced him to retreat deeper within his covers.

"How can anyone not be compassionate about death?" she added.

"Many of those who survived felt there were reasons this Event had occurred."

"What reasons could justify nature dying?"

"Oh nature wasn't dead. As time passed, and when the polar caps stopped melting, a renewed hope began to grow. Over the coming years vibrant gases were released, rebuilding the atmosphere and allowing Earth to become reborn. Nature had found a way to flourish, and it would be the responsibility of the survivors to never forget this story. It was the perfect time to change, to remove man-kind's bad qualities."

"So what changes did they make?"

"Well the most obvious one was out of their hands. The Cleanse had altered the physical structure of the survivors."

Ahlis glanced at her reflection in the base of the lamp. "You mean we didn't always look like this?"

"We still look similar, but with some slight differences. Each generation which followed has become stronger and more resilient to pain. It was a change which may have taken evolution much longer to achieve."

"But I don't feel any different," Ky said, tensing his abdominal muscles.

"Don't be silly," Ahlis said. "Tell us what else changed?"

"You may not have guessed it, but the survivors' biggest challenge was going to be their ability to turn hate into love and harmony."

"Why would that be hard?" Ahlis said.

"Because there will always be others who disagree with you. Though some speak with reason, those whose opinions are loud and irrational make standing up for your own beliefs much harder."

"So did they all decide to just agree?" asked Ahlis.

"Oh not at all. To stand up for your beliefs, or the rights of others, is a good thing. It means you have a zest for life. So never shy away from disagreeing. Just make sure you do so with non-violent passion."

"But Ky always gets angry, and violent."

"No I don't," Ky mumbled, his eye lids heavying.

"We *all* get frustrated," Elric said. "But non-violent passion will be your way of leading by example. It was how a small group, known as the Faction, was able to lead the people of this story away from hatred. Using a set of simple yet effective values, the life you see today had evolved."

"So, does everyone get along now?" Ahlis asked.

"I'm afraid not," Elric replied. "There are some issues which always stir up emotions, and arguments which can never get resolved. This is why that Faction invented another way to resolve conflict, one that is agreed upon to be final."

"Oh, I know the one you mean," Ahlis said.

"Shh!" Elric replied. "Let's not excite your brother, he's almost asleep."

A few seconds passed. Tiredness had also washed over Ahlis.

Elric climbed off Ky's bed and, after ensuring blankets covered both children, he moved towards the door.

Although Elric had left them with an overload of information, that was precisely his intention. "Sleep well. Tomorrow is a big day."

Ky, who had unwittingly released his grip on Buster, rolled onto his back. With his eyes still open he reached for his comforter and stared at the splintered crack in the ceiling. "Good night dad," he said.

He had learned a lot this evening, more than his young mind was accustomed to. Despite having many questions, tonight's story had exhausted him.

With a twitch of his eyelids, they closed as any thoughts drifted away. He was ready for slumber, but on this night, his sleep was not about to be one of peace.

II.

"Get away from me!" Ky shrieked, clawing at his sheets, half-awake after a night of uneasy sleep. His face, drenched in sweat, had turned a ghostly white. "Who was that?"

As the seconds of his reality washed over him, Ky's panicked breath started to return to normal. He wiped his forehead and peered around the sunlit bedroom, unwilling to recall the scary dream. Piercing through the curtains, vibrant sunshine illuminated Ahlis' vacant bed, meticulously made up.

As his eyes focused, a small piece of paper, laden with scribble, could be seen on her pillow.

Ky shuffled out of bed and grabbed the note.

Our past may tell us how we became, but our journey in the present will shape who we become...

"What does that mean?" Ky mumbled. Although only recently learning to read full sentences, he carried on undeterred.

...Each journey has a beginning. Yours may start under the bed.

"Under the bed!" Ky said, as the only words that really made sense caused him to drop to the ground.

Once lifting the obstructing sheets draping the side of Ahlis' bed, he scanned the darkened area. "There's nothing here!"

Ky threw the bed sheets back in place and plonked himself on the floor in the room's centre.

Who wrote this? Ky wondered, as a flicker from the other side of the room caught his attention. *My bed!*

Crawling commando style towards the small space between the floor and his mattress, Ky kept a close eye on the source of the sparkle. "Too dark...can't...see...anything."

He extended one arm under his bed, frantically moving it in all directions before knocking it against something – a piece of paper coarser than the note on Ahlis' bed.

Ky grabbed hold and instantly recognised it as a picture of a seldom used storage room, located at the other end of the Sterling house. A single arrow focused his attention on the artwork in the image, hung in the centre of an otherwise bare wall.

Still in his oversized pyjamas, Ky rushed into the vast hall, running the length of the house, and made his way towards the room. Half way down the hall he paused at the arched entrance into the kitchen. Its intricate wooden carvings, engraved by Elric during the construction of their home, had distracted him. However, with Elric nowhere to be seen, and Loush busy preparing breakfast, he passed by un-noticed, eager to continue playing the secret agent.

Arriving at the room's entrance, Ky grasped the door handle. *It's locked!*

He knew this task would require help.

Taking quick breaths, Ky ran back under the archway to where he could see his sister climbing onto one of the kitchen bar stools.

"Ahlis," he said, forcing his voice to whisper while madly waving one arm. "Ahlis."

Raising her head, Ahlis turned to see Ky motioning.

"Come over here," he added, beckoning her with one hand while holding his index finger to his lips with the other.

Ahlis, happy to take part in one of Ky's covert games, jumped from her seat and skipped towards her brother. "Hi," she said, arriving with a smile. "I was waiting for you."

"Me?" Ky whispered, pulling Ahlis around the corner.

After peering back to see his mum unmoved, still preparing an overabundance of food, Ky's tone elevated with curiosity. "Why were you waiting for me?"

"Why were you whispering?" Ahlis said.

"Because it's a secret and I don't want mum and dad to find out. Why were you waiting for me?"

"Because of the note."

"You mean this note?" Ky said, dragging the first piece of paper from behind his back.

Ahlis' eyes grew curiously large. "No," she said, pulling out her own piece of paper and handing it to her brother. "I mean this one."

After taking Ahlis' creased note, Ky read it silently.

Another adventure soon begins,
But there's something first you must do.
Take this key, stay with mum,
And wait for your brother to come to you.

"Key!" Ky said gleefully. "Does that say key?"

"Yeah, this one," Ahlis replied, showing it to her brother, "but I don't know what it's for."

Ky smiled. "I do," he said, handing her his note.

Ahlis grinned as she ushered Ky a few meters down the hallway. "Where did you get this from?"

"It was under my bed. Where did yours come from?"

"Mum gave it, and this key, to me. She said dad left it for us."

"So, it was dad who wrote the notes," Ky said, as a puzzled grimace appeared on his face. "Which means they already know."

"Of course silly," Ahlis said, beginning to walk towards the storage room.

"Wait! Since dad knows, shouldn't we ask him first?"

"No. He's doing the morning chores. Besides, we're old enough to do this ourselves."

Unmoved, Ky raised his eyebrows.

"Are you coming?" Ahlis asked.

Ky nodded slowly and followed Ahlis.

Arriving at the room, Ahlis drew the key and fumbled around before placing it in the keyhole. "It's turning," she said, gripping the horizontal handle and pulling it towards the floor. "But it's hard to move."

"Let me help," Ky said, also grasping the lever.

"That's it!" Ahlis said.

Slowly, the door creaked open as the dense echo of emptiness filled the children's ears.

Although reluctant to enter, both Ahlis and Ky stepped forward onto the dust covered floorboards. As if entering a lost world, the children instinctively moved closer to one another, scanning the room from where they stood.

To their left, a number of crates were piled as high as the ceiling, taking up much of the floor space.

A large curtain-less window, immediately to their right, spanned another wall entirely, allowing sunlight to illuminate nothing but the dust-riddled air.

"Still looks the same to me," Ahlis said.

"Yeah. But it's smaller than I remember."

Straight ahead was the wall Ky had always thought was bare. "There it is," he said, pointing to the artwork, a portrait hung in its centre. "Dad must have put it there."

Ahlis took a step forward, sinking her feet into a small woollen rug.

Ky followed as the pair moved towards the far wall. "Who do you think that is?"

"I don't know."

A young man, wearing a black body suit, could be seen leaping across a dirt-covered track. Although his face was blurred, his strong physique was evident. In spite of nothing else being shown in the portrait, both children felt an aura of desperation emanating from the familiar looking teen.

"So what are we supposed to do now?" Ahlis asked, taking another look at the picture on Ky's note. "The arrow only points to this portrait."

"Let me see," Ky said, grasping the note.

"No Ky," Ahlis replied, refusing to let go. "Not yet!"

"But I can help!"

Ahlis, still unwilling to let go, gritted her teeth.

Seeing the refusal in her eyes, Ky quickly secured his grip. At the same time Ahlis, who had the same thought, released it and watched as the note floated towards her feet.

As it sank to the ground, the picture twisted, exposing the flipside, before landing face-up again.

Ky looked up at Ahlis. "Did you see that?"

Ahlis bent down to pick it up. This time, however, she held it facedown.

"What do those words say?" Ky asked, pleading with her to read it aloud.

"It says '*Flip to reveal.*'"

"What does that mean?"

Ahlis did not reply, instead choosing to lift the real portrait off its wall hooks. "Look Ky," she said, gently placing the portrait face-down on the floor. "Look at that!"

"What is it? I don't understand."

"I do."

"Then tell me. Please."

"It's a parchment, and it's written in the old language."

"You mean the same language dad teaches you? The one he calls English?"

"The very same," Ahlis said, studying the words.

"Can you read it?"

"I think so, but it's a bit confusing."

Carefully, Ahlis lifted the frayed peach coloured parchment from the rear of the framed picture and laid it on the rug.

"Hmm," Ahlis groaned, as the two children sat on either side. "That doesn't make sense."

"What doesn't? Please read it to me."

"Okay. Okay," Ahlis said, deciphering the words beneath the title, *WHO ARE WE*, aloud.

"I don't understand," Ky said.

"I know. It just sounds like a set of rules."

"Rules for what?"

"I think it may be the set of values dad mentioned last night. You know, the rules the Faction created."

"Are you sure? Do you understand every word?"

Keeping her eyes fixed on the parchment, Ahlis stared at the bottom of the scripture. "The Constructor," she whispered.

"What did you say?"

"Do you remember what dad also told us last night?" Ahlis said. "He said that if all else fails there is another way to agree upon an outcome."

"And?"

"Well I think I remember hearing that the Constructor is this other way."

"So what's a Constructor?" Ky asked.

"I have no idea. Maybe it has something to do with what

grandpa..." Ahlis jumped to her feet. "...Let's go Ky. I think it's time we spoke to someone else."

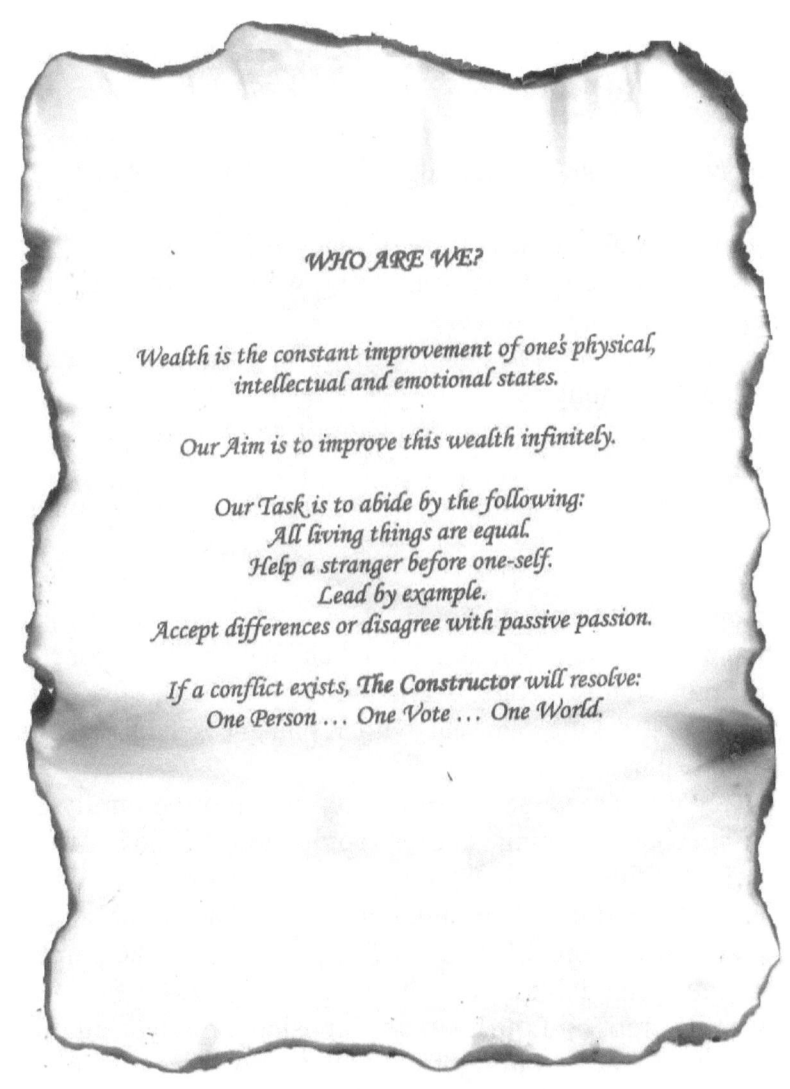

WHO ARE WE?

Wealth is the constant improvement of one's physical, intellectual and emotional states.

Our Aim is to improve this wealth infinitely.

Our Task is to abide by the following:
All living things are equal.
Help a stranger before one-self.
Lead by example.
Accept differences or disagree with passive passion.

If a conflict exists, The Constructor will resolve:
One Person ... One Vote ... One World.

III.

"Mum! Mum! Mum!" hollered both Ahlis and Ky, bursting into the kitchen.

"Did you know about the picture of that guy?" Ahlis said.

Unmoved, Loush continued to mix egg whites as the crackling of omelettes simmered on the stove.

With the smell of slightly burnt toast wafting through the air, Ky's senses tingled. "I'm hungry."

"I'm sure you are young man. Why don't you take a seat?"

"But the picture," Ahlis said, "and the parchment?"

"Uh-uh," Loush said, pointing to the dining room adjoining the kitchen. "Sit."

"Muuuum!" Ahlis replied.

"First breakfast, then chat."

As the morning sun blanketed kitchen, steam rose from a pie perched on the window ledge. Ahlis' mouth watered, subduing her urge for answers. Taking her seat with Ky at the sandalwood table, both children began to eat.

"Dad!" Ky exclaimed, seeing Elric step up onto the family porch. With his rigorous morning chores complete, the joy of eating breakfast with his family had arrived.

"My beautiful children," he said, opening the back door.

"What are these things?" Ahlis asked, placing both the parchment and the portrait on the table.

A wry smile crept on Loush's face, exposing a rarely seen missing tooth she had lost after falling from the family's rickety old hay-grazing machine. "Sit Elric," she said. "Then you can give your answers."

"Only if you join me my dear," Elric replied.

"Very well," Loush said, flicking her wavy brown hair back over her shoulders.

"Now we're all seated," Elric said, brushing his hand across his stubbly chin, "Perhaps I should explain your treasure hunt."

"Treasure?!" Ahlis said. "This isn't treasure."

"Oh but it is. This parchment is the treasure our society is built on. After the Cleanse from last night's story, the Faction, whose members remained concealed, unified man-kind with these values, ensuring old habits would not be rekindled."

"But they seem more like rules than values," Ahlis said.

"Rules are created to be followed," Elric clarified. "These values were never forced upon anyone."

"What your father means is that people decided to follow these values for themselves. After seeing the world becoming beautiful once again, the majority knew it was the right thing to do."

"Oh I see," Ahlis said, underlining a single word from the parchment. "Then what does this mean."

"Ah. *The Constructor*," Elric said. "As you know by now not all group decisions can be agreed upon. In order for the values to work, a method had to be devised to resolve these differences."

"So in their wisdom," Loush said laughing, tying her hair into a ponytail, "the same small group which created the parchment also created a forum. It was a place where every person could have a say, and use their vote, constructively. A place we call..."

"The Constructor!" Ahlis said. "But why is that funny mum?"

"Well my darling, although today's Constructor is a forum where people can discuss any issue with as much honesty as possible, it was discovered that not everything could be resolved by dialogue. After all, we are emotional creatures, aren't we my dear?"

Ahlis smiled.

"So instead of fighting like our ancestors of the past," Elric added, "if no resolution could be achieved within the Constructor then another, final method was devised."

"The Challenge!" Ahlis said, her face beaming. "The one grandpa had mentioned."

"Exactly," Elric said, nodding.

"Challenge?" Ky said. "What's that?"

"Finish your breakfast Ky," Loush said. "You'll find out soon enough."

"But there's so much food," Ky said, pointing to the kitchen counter. "We can't eat all of this."

"Oh that's for later," replied Loush. "We're having company."

Without saying another word, Ky and Ahlis slurped their cereal.

"Slow down," Loush said. "We have plenty of time before it starts."

Elric gazed out the window with an uneasy sense of curiosity. Despite knowing it had been almost two hundred years since the values on the parchment were put in place, Elric had a reason for the timing of last night's story and this morning's treasure hunt, for today was no ordinary day.

A Challenge was soon to take place. Everyone on Earth would be there to watch as, like the Constructor, this Challenge had become part of humanity's fair, just and moral system.

Others, however, would also be watching. Although feelings of being secretly observed were foreign to Elric's generation, an eerie claustrophobia had begun to whisper its way through the people of this new world.

Legend had it that a similar presence existed during the Great Prehistoric Cleanse many millions of years ago. Likewise, chronicles mention an awareness of mystical guardians as Earth, and the Faction, rebuilt itself from its most recent destruction.

Today, as the Challenge fast approached, Elric's senses tingled as the same feelings, described in these stories, had now beset his own thoughts.

IV.

"I've finished!" cried Ahlis.

"Me too!" Ky said, dropping his spoon into a half-eaten bowl of cereal.

"Agrh, you're so messy Ky."

"But I'm in a hurry. I just want to know what this Challenge thing is all about."

Elric grinned. "Well you've already seen it on your treasure hunt."

"The portrait!" Ky said, staring in wonderment at the thorough-bread of a man whose body covered most of the artwork. "But who is he?"

"He's one of many who participate in the Challenge," Elric replied. "But you'll see that soon enough."

"Really? When?"

"Why don't you go to the lounge and find out."

With the portrait tucked under his arm Ky stood and walked towards the Sterling's vast living area.

"Come on!" Ahlis said, flinging herself into the corner of one of the three weathered couches.

"Nice leap," said a wide-eyed Ky. Instantly he sped up, portrait in hand, and sprung his little body enthusiastically over the same couch where he burrowed in next to his sister.

"Impressive," Ahlis said. "Now give me some room."

No sooner had Ky shifted to the other corner, allowing Ahlis to also spread herself across the middle, than both children heard the front door slam open.

"The cousins!" Ahlis said. "I forgot they were coming."

Ignoring the disturbance, Ky re-gripped the portrait, tucking it into his lap, and lowered his eyes for another look.

Seconds later, three energized children, who lived only a few kilometres north of Ky's family estate, burst into the living room.

"Come on! It's time!" screamed Lenny, the eldest of the Sterling cousins.

"Leonard Doyle Sterling!" yelled his mother in hot pursuit. "Sit yourself down!"

"But mum, I don't want to miss it!"

"No buts. Show your manners or I'll send you back home!"

"Aw!" grumbled Lenny, as the teenager plopped himself on the floor and furrowed his thick black eyebrows. Lenny knew his usual disobedience had to take a back seat as more important things awaited.

"Don't despair my boy," croaked Lenny's grandfather, ducking awkwardly under the archway. "The Challenge hasn't started yet."

While Lenny's parents, and the Sterling grandparents, took their usual seat on the large couch adjacent to where Ky and Ahlis sat, Lenny and his siblings crammed themselves on the weathered woollen rug draped across the living room's polished floorboards.

A smaller couch, placed opposite the Sterling grandparents, awaited Loush and Elric.

"Come on dad," Ky said, glancing back to where the dining table met the food-laden kitchen bench. "Everyone's ready now. Can I please see the Challenge?"

"Ah slow down," Lenny said, curbing his own enthusiasm. "Can't you see it's not on yet. Besides, you're too young to understand."

"No I'm not," Ky said.

"Don't let him get to you," Ahlis said.

"But I just want to know what's gonna happen," Ky whispered. "Do you know?"

"Nope," Ahlis said, also looking at the portrait. "I have no idea."

"Well I do," Lenny said, puffing his cheeks in and out while paddling his stomach to some random drumbeat playing in his own mind.

Ky rolled his eyes.

"Behave yourself!" shouted Lenny's mother again, glaring at her son. With her threatening words from breakfast still ringing in his ears, Lenny began to slow his movements mockingly until his arms ceased and his mouth once again came to rest.

Donovan, who was Lenny's father and Elric's brother, grimaced with embarrassment as Lenny's two siblings hopped up on the couch to snuggle in between Ahlis and Ky.

"Fine!" Lenny said. "I wanted to sit by myself anyway."

Donovan shrugged, chuffing sarcastically. "As you can see, Lenny runs the house now."

"Come on guys," Ky said, looking back at the archway where Elric and Loush were speaking with forceful whispers.

"It'll only take five minutes." Elric said. "I'll be back before it even begins."

"Don't you put one foot out that door Mr Sterling." Loush affirmed.

"But I would have finished by now," Elric pleaded.

Although his parents often joked around, Ky could see his mother raise her left hand. "Elric. Are you staying?"

"Nope. I'm going."

In an instant Loush drove a stinging slap into Elric's bare right bicep.

Ky's jaw dropped as the whack drew the attention of the entire family.

"Mum!" Ahlis said.

Although Loush was known for saying *it's not a slap until I remove my hand*, this blow was different as Loush moved it immediately, leaving a shiny red hand print behind.

"What did you do that for?" Ky asked.

A moment later Loush lunged towards Elric's left bicep, pinched a small pocket of skin and whispered cheekily. "Don't worry everyone. This'll take his pain away."

"Ha! You haven't done that one in a while," Elric bellowed, breaking the tension in the room.

"Oh mum," Ahlis said.

"Don't '*Oh mum*' me. It's your father who wants to leave."

"Dad?" Ahlis said.

"Okay. Okay," Elric said. "The chores can wait."

With Ky's parent's sinking into the brown suede love seat, Lenny groaned. "Well that was a waste of time."

"Lenny!" said Donovan. "Enough is enough."

Lenny closed his mouth and shrugged his shoulders. "What? Doesn't anyone have a sense of humour around here?"

"Perhaps not the same as yours," Elric said, waving his hand across an invisible beam. "But maybe now's a good time to see if the

Challenge has begun."

Immediately, the attention of the group shifted to the far wall opposite to where Ky and Ahlis sat. A borderless grey screen, positioned at eye level above the Sterling's fireplace, had begun to flicker.

"Right on time," Elric said, staring at a white standby circle growing in the centre of the screen.

Activating the latest technology, this screen's supple shape transformed a multi-dimensional simulation of images into life-like realism. Being a luxury contained within most households, those who watched were able to feel as though the events on the screen were actually occurring in front of them.

"You should get the T26 model uncle E," Lenny said, as his own eyes froze in a mesmerising trance with each flickering pixel.

"Maybe one day. But I like to think that time is always on the side of the patient."

"Now what does that even mean?" Lenny taunted.

"It means there's no need to rush. That's something the Challenge has taught me over the years."

"Aw! Not again uncle E!" pleaded Lenny. "We don't need to hear about the olden days again. We just want to watch *this* Challenge."

"Leonard Sterling!" shrieked his mother. "What did I tell you?!"

Lenny avoided eye contact with his mother, instead choosing to gaze up at the ceiling.

"You told him to behave!" said Donovan. "Ahlis and Ky have never seen a Challenge before so they deserve to learn as you once did."

Raising his hand to his mouth, Lenny slowly gestured zipping his lips closed. He grabbed the cushion jammed next to Ky and shuffled himself closer to the screen. After reclining on the floor, hands clasped behind his head, he stared at the screen again as the white dot changed into a sky blue. "Finally, saved by the Challenge."

"Lenny," Elric whispered, "you're never too old to learn what the Challenge has to teach, especially knowing the important decisions which hang in the balance."

"Ah! They should just let me decide," Lenny said.

Elric chuckled, glancing at Ky. "But with Lenny not available in every situation, a reliance on the Challenge had developed."

Ky grinned. He yanked the cushion away from Lenny, placed it on his lap, and carefully positioned the portrait on top as his upper body sank deep into the couch's soft padding.

"With the dependence on the Challenge growing," Elric added, "the people selected to battle, representing the views of their chosen party, were becoming more and more revered. But there was good reason for this adoration."

"Boring," Lenny muttered.

"In order to be victorious these participants..."

"They're called Defenders," Lenny said.

"Yes they are," Elric replied. "To win, these Defenders would have to overcome their own physical, intellectual and emotional limitations. The one who could do this would be honoured, and their own view of the specific debate be accepted by all."

"That's a lot of power to have," Ahlis said. "Can anyone become a Defender?"

"Anyone can try. But in order to take part in the Challenge, a Defender would have passed the most severe of simulated tests. It's a hardship not many could handle."

"Go on uncle-E," Lenny said, egging him on. "Why don't you tell him about the blood?"

"Blood!" Ky said. "Is there gonna be blood?"

"Yeah dad," Ahlis added. "I thought that kind of combat was considered too barbaric?"

Elric nodded, "Normally that would be true, but the Challenge is held in a *controlled* environment."

"So what?" Ahlis said. "Blood is Blood."

Elric grinned. "True. But the alternative is to have an unresolved issue which, as the Faction have inferred, would lead to an *uncontrolled* conflict."

"I don't like that Faction," Lenny huffed. "They don't even show their faces anymore."

"It's true they're not seen very often," Elric said. "But it's thought they are less vocal because they see we all have faith in the parchment."

"Faith?" queried Lenny, pointing to the portrait on Ky's lap. "What makes you think I have faith in that thing?"

"Maybe you don't," Elric said. "But I know you have faith in something."

"Oh really. Like what?"

"Do you believe in the Challenge?"

"Of course I do."

"Do you accept the Challenge's outcome as final?"

"Yes," Lenny said sceptically, his cynicism giving rise to Elric's smile.

"Then your belief in this process gives you a faith in fate."

"Huh," griped Lenny. "I love the Challenge but I don't trust the Defenders."

"He's right," Ahlis said. "Can't the Defenders be influenced by others?"

"That's a good question. The Challenge does not turn out well for those who don't give everything they have. Their misplaced effort will be obvious and their lack of honour punished by the course."

Lenny turned sharply towards Elric. "Then what if someone, like myself, can dominate each Challenge? Then that person's side will win every time. Where is the fate in that?"

"Too true," Elric said. "But not one person has ever, or probably will ever, dominate. Not even you Lenny."

"Why not dad?" Ahlis asked.

"After a Challenge, Defenders are weakened to such an extent that they do not normally regain their same physical abilities. This degeneration is not permanent but we are still yet to see anyone be victorious more than once."

Lenny snickered. "Who really cares who wins anyway? I just wanna see pain, like in the Rhea Challenge a few years back."

"Rhea Challenge?" Ahlis said. "What's that?"

"Oh that was an interesting one," Donovan said, his husky throat coughing as he spoke. "The Rhea Challenge determined which of Saturn's moons would be host to the first human settlement. Deciding between Titan, and the more favoured Rhea, would come down to a triumph by mere seconds as the winning Defender, pain throbbing through every muscle, was embraced by the pro-Rhea leaders. But as fate would have it, a series of lethal gas particles on Rhea, only detectable once we landed, vaporised the first human vessel and stopped any further attempts – until now."

"Why now?" Ahlis asked. "Is this another Challenge to see if we should land on Titan?"

"No. This is the Challenge of Enceladus," Donovan replied. "It has arisen because..."

"Enough chatter dad," Lenny said. "I just wanna know who's gonna die today?"

"Lenny!" shouted Donovan, giving him a sullen glance.

Ahlis gasped, as Ky took another peek at the portrait. The face in the picture appeared clearer than before as the familiar eyes of the young man stared back at Ky.

"It's okay Ahlis," Elric said, as the screen began to hiss. "Never mind Lenny's words. It's an honour to take part and should never be seen as a duty. The Defenders know that."

"But you didn't when you Defended," said grandpa, much to the chagrin of Elric.

"What!" Ahlis said. "You were one of them?"

"Once upon a time."

"Why didn't you tell us?" Ahlis asked.

"Because he wasn't a very good one," Lenny said.

"True. But I also didn't want to influence what you thought of the Challenge."

Grandpa huffed. "You're their father. Your job is to influence them."

"Perhaps," Elric said, looking at his children. "But I still want you guys to decide for yourself."

Staring in wonderment at the portrait, Ky mumbled. "So this is you?"

Elric nodded.

The screen flickered. Lenny's eyes lit up. "It's beginning!"

Having already etched it into his mind, Ky carefully placed the portrait between himself and the couch's end.

Everyone's attention had shifted to the crackling screen.

"Why is it so dark?" Ky asked curiously.

"Shh!" whispered Lenny. "Keep your voice down. They're trying to connect."

"What time is it there?" Ky added persistently. "Why isn't there any sunlight?"

"Because it's the other side of the world," Ahlis said.

"How far is that?" Ky asked.

Ahlis looked up at her father. "Maybe he *is* too young."

"I agree!" Lenny added.

"Don't worry about Ky," Elric said. "Something tells me he already knows more about this Challenge than we realise."

V.

"Are we transmitting?" said a faceless man whose words echoed through every transmission in every household across Earth. "Okay. Good."

The transmission's crackling screen had finally cleared, replaced with the image of numerous groups of well-dressed people scurrying about a giant hall. Used as a forum for Constructor debates, the final stage of the Enceladus issue had just ended.

Not located within the hall, the unseen speaker cleared his throat. "Welcome. As we are aware, our planet's average temperature has risen quite dramatically of late. Despite the failure of colonising Rhea, a new Constructor permitting the settlement of Enceladus, another of Saturn's moons, has been going on for over a year. Though today marks the official end to this debate, yesterday's voting has kept this issue deadlocked."

"What does that mean?" Ahlis said.

"It means we couldn't agree on the outcome," Loush whispered, as the monotone voice of the speaker persisted.

"Without a conclusive result, a Challenge will take place on this day. It is the last resort, and its result will decide the outcome once and for all."

With the same words spoken before every Challenge, the speaker concluded his proclamation with an historical explanation of the Challenge.

"In its infancy, the Challenge was designed as a test of courage. Only the physically toughest would prevail. Beginning with the return of the ancient one-hundred-meter dash, time has seen it slowly evolve into the most celebrated and important decision making tool in history.

Participants, who pass a series of rigorous tests, are chosen to represent their debating party's views.

Running with nothing between them and the harsh surface below, these combatants must be at their peak in order to be victorious. In Challenges of today, however, it is not just physical abilities that count. If the participants cannot use their intelligence, if they cannot take charge of their emotions, they will not overcome the obstacles set in front of them.

Despite having one-hundred entrants, representing two possible outcomes, only one will be victorious.

We are privileged to witness the Enceladus Challenge. Welcome and congratulations Defenders, it is you who honour us – Let the event begin!"

Ahlis frowned. "But it doesn't seem right to make a decision this way. The burden would be too much for those Defenders."

"That's right," Lenny said snidely.

Ky jumped off the couch and crawled closer to the screen. "There they are!" he shouted, pointing to a floodlit stadium which suddenly appeared in front of him.

"It can't be," said Lenny. "It's too early."

Although the people had vanished, Ky was sure they were Defenders for they looked the same as the portrait of Elric.

With the track's surface becoming illuminated jagged knife-like objects, scattered randomly across most of the ground, could be seen.

"Dad, is that what you had to run over?" Ahlis asked.

"Yep. It's the ultimate test for any Defender."

"And is that why you limp?"

Elric nodded sheepishly.

Ahlis covered her eyes. "I don't like it," she whimpered.

Lenny smirked. "Then you don't want to see what happens when the objects' poisons are injected into the Defenders."

"Dad!" Ahlis said. "What's gonna happen? Are they gonna die?"

Elric hesitated.

"Go on," Lenny said. "You can tell them."

"It's true some Defenders have died," Elric said reluctantly. "Some may not have been ready while others could have had a bad reaction to the toxins. In either case, fate had chosen them for a reason, a destiny that was theirs alone."

In seeing how much of the track was lit, the bright festival lights caused Lenny to raise his eyebrows and point to the numerous toxic objects on display. "So tell me uncle-E, what does fate have to say about that?"

"Wow," Elric said. "I don't remember there being so many."

"Wait!" Lenny said, as the last remaining darkened area illuminated. "Here they come!"

Ky smiled. Confirming his initial sighting, one hundred soldier-like men crouched side-by-side. Like cheetahs waiting for prey they froze in anticipation.

Moments later the countdown concluded and the Defenders unleashed themselves onto the track's surface. Like their predecessors, they too represented mankind in a life-changing debate. As pride coursed through their veins and hurt pulsated from their eyes, each surged as fast and as far as they could. Their pain, which would only dull once their bodies stopped moving, lingered for their desire to prevail did not allow them to cease. But in spite of their greatest efforts, only a handful would finish with most never truly recovering.

The broken bone of one man, which had pushed its way through his skin, was shown throughout all the transmissions. Battling to move, long after the toxins had been injected into his system, this Defender's heavy and lifeless legs had landed on each object with a massive thud. As onlookers witnessed the soles of his feet rip open, those who watched knew he would never walk again.

While he was carried off the track, and the bloody stains were being cleaned from the surface, the speaker arrived to crown the victor.

Shuffling onto a makeshift podium, which hovered over the middle of the arena, the heavyset man was about to announce that the colonisation of Enceladus was to go-ahead.

One-billion people watched as the speaker, wearing a brown jacket, rubbed his arms in the cool night air. After adjusting his tie, and with the cognisant Defender's watching from the stadium's edge, the speaker received the green light.

With one side of this new rectangular hybrid stadium containing only barren land, the speaker turned his back to the void, faced the largest of the three remaining stands, and cleared his throat.

"Congratulations," he uttered, as a ghostly mist drifted into the arena from the empty space behind him. A low rumble, seemingly originating from within the mist, caused him to turn.

As the rumble distorted itself into a high-pitched screech, the calmness of the night changed. A circular wind spread the smoky mist. Though blanketing the entire stadium, it dissipated before anyone had time to utter words of confusion, leaving something else in its wake.

Every transmission shifted to the void, and as the whole world watched, a dozen human-like figures began to make their way towards the speaker.

While the new arrivals approached the podium, the stationary speaker, along with those watching from afar, could see a single outline, taller than the others, emerge as the group's leader.

The speaker's hands trembled as he took an instinctive step back.

Appearing to be a middle-aged man, the large figure, whose hair had begun its transformation from brown to grey, towered over the stumpy speaker.

With the assistance of an unimpressive and weathered cane, the leader, standing on only the second of four steps, gently leaned over the speaker, touched him on the shoulder and nodded politely.

Although intuition told the speaker not to let this man address his audience, he found himself moving aside, enabling the older gentleman to elevate himself onto the platform and, more importantly, granting him access to the eyes and ears of the world.

"Good people," said the new arrival, allowing the pleasant drone of his voice to wash over the crowd. "I bring news to all Hominidae on this most wonderful day."

Although allowing a moment for the listeners' bewilderment to settle, the anxious crowd remained quiet.

"We are here for one purpose only. To inform you that..."

His eyes encircled the stadium. Staring deep into the transmitter, a soulful depth crept into the man's voice.

"...you have been chosen."

VI.

"Order must be restored," spoke a deeply disturbed voice originating beneath the shadowy side of a giant rock wall

"Yes!" demanded another equally chilling individual, calling out from the same side of the jagged barrier. "We've let it go for too long. They've just been informed."

"Chosen," chimed in dozens more in unison.

"The time has come to resume," added the first voice, "What say you, Grand Elder of all the Nholls."

As silence followed, the many in attendance on this low side of the purposefully placed obstruction remained unmoved as a single voice, stemming from the other side, growled.

"Agreed."

VII.

A long time prior to the existence of *Challenges*, the wheels of destiny, leading to its evolution, were being set in motion by the most unlikely of events.

Although not around to see it, some of Ky's more baffling dreams had become entangled with visions of this past. Even now, as a twenty-one-year-old, he would regularly wake only to find his dishevelled hair mimicking his confusion. Fortunately, last night saw some of the nicer images from that history float back into these dreams.

It was a time where joyful shrieks of children resonated and happiness was in abundance. Ky's visions were so real that he could almost feel a slight breeze, carrying a hint of eucalyptus across acres of open fields.

Yellow leaves, nestling among treetops, whistled as a welcoming party was gathering.

Ten million more would arrive on this day.

The oxygen levels engulfing Earth were at an all-time high. Carbon dioxide, expelled by humans, was replenished ten-fold by the air returned from nature.

Earth was ready for its new human inhabitants and this region, being one of ten host locations, would add its one million, bringing the total human population on Earth to five-hundred times that number.

Apart from a small cluster of puffy white clouds, a majestic blue engulfed the sky. All would have seemed perfect had it not been for an in-perceivable grey smudge on one of the clouds.

The midday sun had come and gone. The time was near.

With only minutes remaining, Panu and Arna anxiously awaited the arrival of their daughter. Having not made the previous journey, due to excessive brain swelling, she had finally been declared safe for travel.

Panu, her father, stood with shaky legs. Plagued by the guilt of their own mandatory departure, his thoughts flooded with the day their eleven-year-old was forced to begin her lengthy quarantine stint. The first task, of the only treatment option remaining, was to shave her wavy-brown hair. But as the silky locks floated to the ground the pre-pubescent teen never even shed a tear; her protective shell had already formed. Though Panu was uncertain when she would recover, he felt this isolation would as least eliminate the taunts she'd regularly endured for being so intellectually advanced.

A short while into her treatment saw a breakthrough, after the medical staff used a radical surgery to alter her brain's limbic system. Following a series of lengthy tests, and believing the treatment had been a success, she was given the all clear. However, unbeknown to the doctors, the change also left her with an overdeveloped emotional capability rarely seen in people.

Watching her exit, more than a year after her arrival, some of the doctors commented on how she had changed. Though her emotional and intellect differences were not evident on the surface, it was clear she had grown taller with her hair, once again, draped over her broad shoulders.

As the voices surrounding Panu grew, his thoughts dissipated, leaving only the last image he could remember of his little girl.

With most wild life roaming the plains, unaware of the forthcoming arrival, a few animals scurried away with a sense of urgency.

"It must be time for the Clearing," said Panu.

"I hope so," replied Arna.

Allowing for the protection of those arriving, along with all surrounding life forms, the scientific advancement known as the *Clearing* would be conducted moments prior to a landing. With the protection of these life forms paramount, all precautions were taken to ensure no harm befell any one creature.

Thump! Thump! Thump!

As the wild life continued to scamper, in the distance heavier thuds were heard.

It was the marching of one of the last remaining dinosaur herds, whose sole purpose had become survival. Being on the brink of extinction, theirs was not so much a sense of urgency of this moment as it was a constant awareness of danger.

For mankind, however, a recent meteorite collision, which annihilated many of these great creatures, also created an atmospheric Cleanse. This shift in the Earth's environment enabled human settlement to take place, a colonisation that commenced around thirty years, or as the new arrivals called it, one *Neg*, prior to this arrival.

With the thuds dulling to a low rumble, Panu could see a single animal run in circles. Resembling a buffalo, with an indiscreet rhinoceros' tusk, her herd had fled the area and headed towards a distant field layered with lush grass. The abandoned creature was confused.

Should she follow the herd or trust her instincts, which told her to charge towards the coastline, a few hundred metres below?

The force of the waves crashing against the cliff base startled her.

As a burst of steam bellowed from her nostrils, confusion became annoyance and as another wave smashed, the creature dashed towards the herd, desperately wanting to catch up.

Arna and Panu's tension disappeared as they caught a glimpse of the multitude of families frolicking while they waited. But with waves crashing louder, and the day cooling faster than expected, Panu peered up at the sky to see the sun become blanketed by a growing number of clouds. As he watched he noticed the grey smudge on one break off to form a type of rain-cloud.

Panu could see light dimming by the second.

Others too soon noticed and, although climate change was known to be common during the travel of new arrivals, an eerie sensation fell over the landing area. Children's playtime had stopped. Whispers of anticipation, carried by the increasing wind, floated through Panu's ears.

The Clearing process had commenced as all wildlife in the surrounding area was instantly transported to a safe location.

Panu could no longer see the buffalo. She too had vanished.

He inhaled deeply. "It won't be long now," he muttered.

A gale-like wind began to encircle the field.

The landing area rumbled.

Speedily, the invisible wind demolished a section of the grassy area, leaving a murky haze in its wake.

"They're coming," Arna said, as a thundering boom froze her and

Panu in their tracks. Eagerly they stared as the shape of human figures materialized.

With technology working perfectly, Panu noticed a girl appear only thirty metres away, directly in front of him. "It's her," he said joyously.

Instantly the fog cleared.

"You're right," Arna replied, hearing giggles. "She's grown so much."

"Yes. But her laugh's still the same."

Despite most brightness being swallowed up by dark, Panu and Arna ran towards their daughter. Artificial light suddenly illuminated the landing area. The three embraced, leaving no space in between.

Panu closed his eyes. "Your hair's so long," he whispered.

Across the plain, and the entire planet, people were greeting others in the same fashion. Some were loved ones, while others met for the first time, greeting as strangers and leaving as friends.

As Panu's family continued their embrace, his daughter's eyes were met by a shot of light.

The brilliant glow, emerging from above the greyed sky, sent her senses into a tingling frenzy, replacing relief with fear.

She loosened her grip, stood back, and looked at her father whose dilated pupils also showed the same anxiety.

The young girl grabbed her parents again before swiftly reaching for her wrist. "Can you see the Numerals too daddy?" she stammered.

Panu peered over his shoulder, in the same direction, and squinted at the hovering glow. But after feeling his daughter's grip tightened, he suddenly realised what her vision really meant. Though he reached for her trembling hand, it was too late.

In an instant, another flash engulfed the entire sky. The result was immediate.

On that day, almost all life on Earth had been incinerated. The heat emanating at that one moment burnt every moving creature, turning it to ash. The few who out-lasted the immediate obliteration died soon after.

The tiny number of life forms who managed to remain alive had their mental capabilities reduced to that of the simplest un-evolved creatures.

Remnants of life, from the smallest atomic structure to the largest skeletal remains, were left scattered across the planets' lands and oceans. Earth had become a fiery mass, charred beyond recognition.

In a distant expanse, tears of helplessness were shared as the knowledge of the annihilation, and the end of an Age, was learned.

Not all, however, would feel sorrow.

It would take millions of years of evolution and resolve to return Earth to its former self, but, as Ky's eyes shot open, waking from the folklore of the Great Pre-Historic Cleanse, some of Elric's words came flooding back, allowing him some peace.

Don't fret Ky, for time is always on the side of the patient. All that is needed for life to continue is a survivor.

After spending a moment contemplating his father's words, another thought quickly jumped into Ky's head. "I'm late!"

VIII.

The scent of new paint permeated throughout *Flip's* classroom.

Although one of the cream-coloured walls was partially comprised of open windows, allowing the smell to fade, another was decorated by painted canvases of the human anatomy.

A third was designed as the room's access point, while the fourth wall had tiny lasers randomly speckled throughout which could, on command, transform itself into a giant transmission screen.

Located in the bottom corner of Flip's room, between the windows and the large transmission screen, sat a mangled human brain encased in a jar filled with formaldehyde. Even though identical classrooms packed the hallways, each containing fifteen screen-facing seats, this was the only one displaying such a thought-provoking item.

From the outside, this learning facility, similar to many in the vicinity, was layered with four levels; each containing hundreds of such rooms. However, unlike most constructions, which were created from the latest silicon based technology, its foundation was brick, giving an appearance similar to the schools of old.

With Flip's room having derived its name from the boisterous teaching style of its Educator as being the flip-side to the tedium of her subject matter, that of *advanced mathematics*, students would sit with trance-like stares as she, brain-jar under her arm, strutted in at the start of each schooling year.

Commencing by splattering the brain on the floor, she would systematically dissect it with her fingers in an attempt to pin-point the exact location to where emotional areas of humans could be controlled with a better understanding of maths.

After shoving the distorted organ back in the jar, she would intentionally allow her lush black hair to drape alluringly over her neckline. This heightened the attention of the males as they watched her long eyelashes flutter and rosy lips mouth her opening words. By repeating this at the start of her second, and now third, year as an

Educator, she quickly became one of teaching's favourite instructors.

Day two had arrived and her curved body and golden complexion, resembling an ancient Egyptian queen, remained masked behind a bulky turtle neck jumper and faded pair of jeans. While her scuffed boots raised curious murmurs throughout the class, she peered inquisitively across the hall to where a newly decorated room, boasting a variety of plant and wildlife murals, could be seen.

Drawn by his students, this colourful class saw their Educator teach with a sharp wit that, at times, was hard to distinguish between seriousness and humour.

Although having just started in Education yesterday, it had only taken a short while for Kynan Sterling, and his students, to transform this room into a vivid masterpiece. But, by the manner in which he encouraged his students to unleash their creativity, you would never guess his subject specialty was *Earth and the Cosmos*.

In line with this expertise, Ky's weathered hands and broad physique suggested he was used to physical exertion. Slight wrinkles on the outer corner of his eyes, though hidden by taut sun-bleached skin, hinted at his love for the land.

Unintentionally masking his temperate demeanour, he wore a white T-shirt which highlighted his dark facial growth. While the top would loosely fit most men, his muscular body stretched the fabric to its limit.

Well-fitted jeans rolled over a pair of worn brown boots with both items still showing the remnants of his daily trek from his nature-filled dwelling to this, the most populous education district on Earth.

With the excitement of his first day not subsiding until his pillow greeted him in the dead of night, Ky's second day also began with a flurry from the moment he woke.

"I'm sorry I'm late," he panted, rushing into his class.

As the bell for the start of class rang, his scruffy hair, and sleep deprived eyes, drew curious stares from even the most care-free of pupils.

"Sir?" said one of them, fidgeting. "You look, um..."

"Yes, I know" Ky said sarcastically. "But I did sleep alone last night. So you can stop staring at my glorious hair."

While only the females laughed at his intentionally humourless joke, the males of the class kept quiet in sceptical admiration.

"So my young learned pupils," he continued, with his back to the room's monitor, "since we're all back for more let's begin by..."

Ky paused. Something across the hallway had caught his eye.

Quickly, he shifted his focus through his glass entrance and towards a strange jar in the room parallel to his. *Is that a brain?*

"Are you all right Sir?" asked another of his inquisitive students.

"Sorry," he said, shaking off the distraction. "Today we will continue from where..."

There it is again!

Ky snapped his head back towards the bizarre item but was side-tracked by the room's Educator who was looking in his direction.

Despite being flushed with embarrassment, he couldn't look away. His heart trembled; a quiver he hoped she shared. With the moment lingering, he smiled reluctantly.

While much of his class began to chatter among themselves, happy for more personal time and disinterested in the reason for his silence, Ky's thoughts jolted back to reality. *This has to stop.*

His smile disappeared and turned to his students. Though uncomfortable, he tried to maintain some authority. "Okay guys," he joked, "we don't have all day!"

As time passed, and lunchtime neared, the students were becoming restless. Though the upcoming break was their chance to play, as adolescence do, the Educators too waited for their reprieve.

A very quiet beep chimed its way through each class, opening the semi-opaque doors to each room. With that, the students exited like a stampede of boar, leaving Ky, and the Educator from Flip's room, both entering the corridor together.

"Hi," she said jovially, "You're the new Educator, right?"

With the morning's proceedings having worn away any perfume she may have been wearing, her natural aroma floated into Ky's nostrils. This familiar smell of freshly picked lilies floated through his senses as his own eucalypt scent permeated from his skin, swallowing the pair with an overwhelming sense of deja-vu.

With no reply forthcoming, she persisted. "I like what you've done with your room. Very artistic."

Ky's silence aroused a rare shyness in her. Though blushing, she persevered to rouse him out of his frozen state. "My name is Nibatoo," she whispered. "But my friends call me Nibby, and so should you."

Ky knew he'd lost any chance to appear sophisticated, and to make matters worse, he felt compelled to stare.

"What are you looking at?" Nibby said, raising one eyebrow.

"Oh. Um...I just..." His head slumped, unsure as to why those words came stumbling from his mouth. "What I mean is that...I really like your hair."

Nibby smiled. "I like yours too – the messy look, right?"

Ky smiled, re-connecting his eyes to hers.

"So, what's your name?" she asked.

"Oh. It's Ky."

"I like that name."

"Thanks. I didn't mean to stare before. It's just that I felt something. Um, what I mean is..."

"Are you hungry?" she asked.

Feeling his stomach grumbling, Ky nodded.

Nibby grinned. "Good. I don't have any more classes so, if you're also done, I can show you around."

Ky nodded again.

"Oh, and don't worry," she said, beckoning Ky to follow. "I felt it too."

Although Nibby meant it, the sense of deja-vu gave her cause for concern for despite the familiarity, she knew any previous meeting would have been impossible.

IX.

Prior to eating, Nibby led Ky towards a cluster of trees bordering the east wing of the school.

"Here's a good spot," she said, sitting next to one of the smaller shrubs. "We'll grab our lunch later." After a lengthy exchange of childhood stories concluded, the midday sun had already begun its descent towards the horizon.

Ky's stomach growled again, followed by an involuntary shudder of his torso that sent a flutter into the pit of Nibby's belly. "Why did that happen?" she asked, dawdling her words to halt any flirtation.

"Oh, it's nothing. Too much energy I guess."

"But your twitch reminded me of…an older Educator who…"

A sombreness washed over Ky.

Nibby's eyes widened, realising her hunch may have been correct. "Oh no. Your dad's Elric Sterling. I'm so sorry. I shouldn't have…"

"Nah, it's okay. I'm sure everyone's heard the story by now."

Nibby shook her head. "Not me. The other Educator's avoid talking about it. Besides, I'd rather hear it from you, if that's okay."

Ky sighed. Though appearing indecisive, he stared into her eyes. "It was almost one year back now. My dad and I were grazing hay on a portion of our land full of thick woody shrubs. We'd always neglected this area because the land was so sloped."

"Did you have one of those fancy new self-guiding tractors?"

"I wish. We just used our rickety old A500 model. It wasn't too bad though because while one of us drove, the other stood on the side rails, just like you would on those old wobbly roller-coasters."

"That sounds like fun."

Ky giggled childishly. "Yeah. Not much beats it." he said.

Nibby's eyelids fluttered. "I know this must be hard, so just take it slow. We're in no rush."

Ky nodded and slowed for a deep breath. "As I drove, with dad on the side rail, a wild deer ran in front of us. I swerved before I had a chance to think. Then, in the blink of an eye, the tractor tipped, taking us down the slope and crushing dad's chest under the machine. A better vehicle would have regained control, and a better driver would never have avoided the deer in the first place."

"Oh no. You don't blame yourself, do you?"

Ky gritted his teeth. "Even after the initial crash I still had a chance to save him, but it took me ages to drag him free that by the time I did, it was too late."

"I'm so sorry."

"He had taught me so much growing up, preparing me to handle situations like this. So how could I have been so useless?"

"I'm sure you did all you could."

"That's what everyone keeps saying, but if I could have controlled my fear on the tractor, and not swerved so suddenly, my best friend would still be alive."

Nibby grasped his hand. "Did you get hurt?"

"Not really. Just this thing," Ky said, pointing to a scar on the left side of his face. "It'll always remind me of what I was too afraid to do. It's a mistake I will never make again because there'll come a time I will make him proud again, where ever he's watching from."

"Your dad was a good man. If you're anything like him, you'll have already made him proud."

"Thanks," Ky said, wiping a tear. "Did you know him well?"

"Not really. We only chatted a few times. But I remember he was really kind, as if he was my own father. I can see why the two of you were close."

Ky wiped his eyes again. "Can we talk about something else, something happier? I mean, fate sucks for what happened to my family, but then it went and introduced me to you."

Nibby's mouth curled and cheeks raised. "Then let's talk about how you become an Educator."

"Okay then," Ky sighed. "Well as soon as dad passed, the Elder's pestered me to take his place. But everyone knew that, apart from being too soon for me, no one could teach the way he did."

"Yet here you are."

"You can thank my mum for that. She talked me into it."

"Good thing."

"Yeah, but no matter how much I convinced myself, I knew I'd struggle to teach about the Cosmos. Farming was all I knew."

"Wasn't there any way to…"

"No! Farming's my life."

"I didn't mean to..."

"I'm sorry," Ky said, subduing his tone. "I guess I'm still not used to all this talk of dad…And the Cosmos is still so strange for me to teach others on. I mean most of these students probably know more about the stars than I do!"

Nibby snickered. "You're probably right."

"Very funny. But you know what, there is something else I'm pretty good at, something I also learned from dad."

Nibby scooted a little closer. "Don't you dare keep me guessing."

Ky smiled. "Well I've always been pretty good at mock races."

"You mean the ones the Defender's practise on?"

"Yeah. And even though I could probably teach a class on it, I haven't done any of late. In fact, I try to avoid the topic because it was the one thing we always did together."

Nibby's eyes became teary. "Hearing what happened to your father makes me realise how similar our pain must be."

"But how can that be unless..."

Nibby nodded and dotted her tears away. "Both my parents died when I was young. But please, let's not go there. We've dragged up enough emotions for one day. Besides," she said sniffing, pulling him to his feet, "you said you were hungry, right?"

Ky nodded, enjoying the touch of her hand. "Shouldn't I be the one taking you out somewhere?"

"Trust me, we're not going anywhere special. You can save that for our first date."

Ky grinned. "So where *are* you taking me?"

"Just my normal eating place, so you can wipe that smile off your face Mr Sterling."

After arriving at the Educator's dining hall, Ky could see dim light mimicking the mood of the empty tables. He did not like its ambience and was saddened at the thought of Nibby eating here all alone. He was beginning to sense that she was less of an extrovert than he first thought.

Nibby slouched with melancholy. Suddenly, a flurry of all the places she did not want to remember, and of people she would never see again, came flooding back.

"You may live on campus," Ky said, seeing her sadness, "but it doesn't mean we have to stay. Let's get out of here."

Nibby nodded.

As the two exited, carrying two salad sandwiches, a container of dips and a variety of breads, they walked past a small group of students waiting for their outdoor class to begin.

"Hi Flip," giggled one of the young girls.

Nibby smiled and urged Ky to hasten his steps towards, what she hoped would be, their still deserted pasture.

X.

"Not a cloud in the sky," Nibby said.

"Yep. It should make for a nice sunset."

"Do you expect me to stay with you that long?"

"Um," Ky said, fumbling with his sandwich wrapper.

Nibby giggled shyly. "I'm just kidding," she said, tying her heavy-set jumper around her waist. "I think you know I have no other plans."

Peering down past her low-cut sleeveless shirt, Ky caught a glimpse of what appeared to be the corner of a clover shaped tattoo. A sheen of sweat that layered her neckline sent a flutter through his body. Quickly, he averted his eyes, embarrassed by his own lengthy stare.

However, with the pleasant feeling of twilight fast approaching, the same shiver soon turned into a rush of contentment. "It is a bit late for lunch," he said. "Maybe we should call this dinner."

"Dinner eh?" Nibby said, pulling the jumper from her waist and laying it neatly by her side. "Then I guess this *is* a date."

Ky smiled awkwardly. As a chime sounded, he caught sight of hundreds of students scurrying in all directions. "I wonder what class they've come from?"

"I think it's the one on *Human Evolution.*"

"Whoa. Why is it so popular?"

Nibby shrugged. "Could be due to our deep-seated desire to better ourselves."

"Huh," Ky squinted.

"Just look at their faces," she said. "It's not every day you learn about the precise moment your civilization was chosen to join the *Knowledge Base.*"

As Nibby explained how that class would have revealed intricate footage of the moment Earth humans were chosen, Ky's own recollection of that day was overrun with the memory of his parent's scepticism of the events which followed. "But wouldn't the students have already been told that the Knowledge Base is basically a union of the universe's most evolved civilizations?"

"Of course, but this is probably their first actual encounter with a Polmarian."

"You mean they actually get to meet another human civilization in person? I thought that was forbidden for most of us, at least until we're older."

"That's not entirely true. Didn't you get to meet one at school?"

"Nope. As soon as the Polmarians announced Earth humans had been chosen, my parents started home schooling me."

Nibby was taken aback. "But you must have learned something about the Knowledge Base. Do you know what Obzoovers, Aramats and Nyrolacs are?"

"Um. Let's see. A Nyrolac is the collective term for all species in the Knowledge Base."

"Obviously. Go on."

"I also know the Obzoovers are an advanced species, and the creators of the Knowledge Base. They are rarely seen because it is said their high intellect would prevent other species from reaching their own potential."

"Impressive," she grinned. "So, what's an Aramat?"

While Ky scanned his brain for any kind of response, three students, chatting loudly as they passed by, interrupted his train of thought.

"So, to have been chosen," said the elder of the two young male pupils, *"we, as Earth humans, needed to achieve a certain level of intellectual, physical and emotional advancement?"*

"That's right," said his female friend. *"It's what the Obzoovers call our EALF rating."*

"Our what?" asked the younger boy keenly.

"Weren't you listening?" griped the elder boy. *"Next time you should pay attention like us."*

"I did. I just..."

"Okay then smarty. If you were really taking note, why don't you recite the true definition of the Translator for us."

The younger boy stopped, glanced across at his friends before proceeding to enunciate the following statement.

The Translator, is a technology allowing spoken words and expressions to be interpreted and vocalized in the language of the listener. Though sometimes audible, messages can also be sent directly between thoughts.

"How did you know that?" asked the elder boy.

"I guess I was paying attention."

Ky snorted with amusement.

"Shh," Nibby said, subtly knocking his leg.

The elder boy glanced over to see Ky staring at him. Hastily, the embarrassed students shuffled off.

While he tried to hold back further laughter Ky was glad that these young students still used their voices, despite the translator making spoken words obsolete. "Good to hear they're talking about what they learned, which is more than I can say about my students."

"Oh, I don't think so. Even my students were whispering about your first class."

"Really? What did they say?"

"First, tell me why you winced when that girl mentioned the EALF rating?"

"You saw that?"

Nibby nodded. "Couldn't miss it if I tried. It was as if you were appalled by it."

"Precisely. Just because being a so-called *Expert in the Art of LiFe* is what the Knowledge Base holds in high regard doesn't mean I should. It can't describe a person's determination. It won't tell you how kind someone is, or what drives them to achieve greatness. All it does is measure certain capabilities. It has nothing to do with who we really are."

"But it's this rating which resulted in the Earth human civilization being chosen."

"I know. But shouldn't there be more to what we are than just a rating?"

"Hmm…yeah, I see what you mean," she grinned. "So, since you seem to know everything, I'm sure you've finally remembered what an Aramat is."

"Oh, right. I read somewhere that Aramats have restricted access to some Knowledge Base technologies. I just can't seem to recall who they are."

Nibby giggled. "An Aramat is you silly, the youngest of all evolved life forms."

"Oh, then it's not just me, you're an Aramat too."

"Oh," she said, hesitating while sensing Ky's dislike for all things Knowledge Base related. "I thought you would have realised by now."

"Realise what?"

"That I'm not like you…I'm a Polmarian."

XI.

The origin of Polmar began with the explosion of an isolated neutron star in the Emelez sector of the Andromeda Galaxy. As the shock waves dissipated, a smaller star, known as Nechor, emerged.

Within a short while this new stellar system matured, attracting a single, but gigantic, rock-based planet into its gravity. While Polmar, as it's now called, and its Earth-like conditions aged, so too did the evolution of its humanoid inhabitants; over ten thousand Ages earlier than Earth itself was even created.

Enness, the most populous landmass on Polmar, was home to its advanced humanoid culture. Despite its ruggedly picturesque outskirts, the centre of Enness was lush, giving who ever stepped onto its grassy surface a feeling of cradled warmth.

Home to hundreds of thousands of man-made structures, its leafy downtown area remained a thriving nature-filled haven as the greater part of most buildings were built underground. Above ground, flora and fauna intertwined as yellow daisy-like clusters, scattered throughout the fields, were gobbled up by oversized herbivores. However, although being chosen, all of this would remain concealed from Earth humans as only a select few were permitted to travel – the remaining interactions between the two cultures would take place solely on Earth.

Moreover, those who did step foot on Polmar were forbidden from interacting with the majority of Enness locals. But with this placid Polmarian population approaching one-hundred billion, contact with this seemingly flawless society would be inevitable.

Back on Earth, broadcasts made it clear it was these Hominidae, a term used for humans, who had pushed for the Earthlings' selection into the Knowledge Base. It was a selection which, as Earthlings were discovering, prompted a dramatic growth in their own intellect. Yet, unlike their advances in times gone by, this new progression would not go unnoticed.

XII.

"Is it true? Is it true?" shouted the younger male student, running back towards Nibby. "Are you a Polmarian? Are you really one of them?"

Nibby smiled uncomfortably at the boy before turning to Ky. "Yes. But Earth is my home."

Following in close pursuit, the two elder students caught up. "Sorry miss. Our parents said we're not supposed to ask you questions like that until we're older, but our little friend here never seems to listen."

"Oh, it's okay."

While the youngster was being dragged off, Nibby looked into Ky's eyes. "Are you surprised by my ethnicity?"

"No. Should I be?"

"It's just that you don't seem too fond of the Knowledge Base."

"Yeah, but I'm fond of you. Isn't that what counts?"

Nibby grinned, relieved her tension had been disarmed. "So why are you so against the Knowledge Base anyway?"

Ky shrugged. "I guess I never liked being prevented from meeting the other Knowledge Base species. What's worse is that you Polmarians are our ancestors and yet hardly any of us get to travel to, and learn from, Polmar herself."

"Yeah, that's a stupid rule."

"I'm glad you agree," he said, hesitating. "But seeing you this close has actually confused me."

"And why would that be?" she asked.

"Don't take this the wrong way, but since your people have already shed many of our unnecessary intellectual and physical drawbacks, why do *you* still look and act so similarly to us."

Nibby jumped to her feet, momentarily regretting she'd revealed this much already. "Um...I'm not sure...I mean..."

"It's okay. Just sit back down. You don't have to say anything."

"I want to tell you. It's just that..."

"Please. Sit."

After crouching back down, he grasped her hand. "Now you're the one who's nervous."

Though she appeared resolute to keep her secret, it did not take long for her to shuffle closer and whisper in his ear.

"But how?" Ky said, confused.

"It's true," she nodded. "I was born a long, long time ago."

"But you can't be that old. I'm sure you're younger than me!"

"Actually, I'm around twenty of your Earth years old, but my birth occurred long before yours."

Ky stared blankly, knowing the time for humour was over. "How could that be?"

"I didn't have the most normal childhood growing up," she said, as tears welled in her eyes. "My parents may be gone but I can still see their faces as clearly as I see my own."

Seeing her sadness, Ky reached behind her and placed his hand on the small of her back. As she leaned into him a salty tear trickled down, marking his sleeve.

Unsure of what Nibby was trying to say, he carefully wiped her jittery face. "It's okay. You can tell me anything."

"How...how," she stuttered, inhaling deeply to settle herself. "How much have you read on my people's colonisation of Earth? You know, during the Great Pre-Historic Cleanse sixty-five Ages ago."

"Not much," he said, as his most recent dream started to simmer in his head. "Only what I've heard in stories."

"Well, nine old-years ago I was also one of those Polmarians chosen to populate Earth."

"Huh?"

Nibby stared blankly. "I was finally allowed to see my parents again."

"Your parents?" he said, masking a shiver running down his spine. With his mind having been thrown into a spin, no longer could he keep his jumbled thoughts at bay. "My dad used to tell me about a similar story he called the *Traveller*, but I thought it was only fiction."

"I know. That's what *they* tell people."

In seeing his bewilderment Nibby knew she had a choice to make; walk away now or explain everything. Even though it was a secret she had only told a select few, there was something about Ky that made her feel at ease, that made her want to stay.

XIII.

Nibby took a deep breath. "I don't know why I'm telling you my history, but for some reason I feel like I have to, or maybe I just want to."

"It's okay," Ky said, as both curiosity and confusion draped his words. "Take your time."

"Okay then," she said, exhaling. "Maybe we should start with *Lest* technology."

"Lest? You mean the way in which Knowledge Base Nyrolac's travel?"

Nibby nodded. "What do you know about it?"

"I'm no expert, but I've read a bit."

Despite his words, one of his self-taught interests involved Lest and how it broke matter into small atomic forms, known as quarks. Once separated, Lest would transform these elements into speedy neutrino particles which can be instantaneously swapped with any other non-living energy source in the cosmos. After being reassembled, the subject would have suffered no loss of time no matter what universal destination was selected. Soon after Lest was perfected colonisations of previously uninhabited galaxies was the first item on the Knowledge Base agenda.

"How old did you say you were when the Polmarian colonisation of Earth occurred?"

"Twelve," Nibby replied.

"But it can't be, unless..."

Nibby sighed, nervously clasping her jumper. "I know this is a lot for you to take in so please don't think I'm crazy."

"No it's okay. But just so we're on the same page, it *is* time travel you're talking about, isn't it?"

"Yes. But that only occurred *after* my arrival on Earth. What I mean is that the teleportation worked fine. I even got to hug my parents. Then..."

"Then what?"

"Then I noticed something looked different."

"What was it?"

Nibby gazed up to the safety of the stillness above. "The sky. It was filled with both dark and light. Then, in an instant, I was no longer holding my family."

"But how? What happened?"

"The *Reversal*."

"What's that?" he said curiously.

"It's a device which allows the Lest traveller a small window of time to be reversed to their place of origin."

"I've never heard of it."

"I know," she said, explaining how, due to its unstable nature, it's only permitted to be used during colonisations. "The Reversal sensor was placed on my wrist. If triggered, I should have been sent back to Polmar. But for some reason, mine had other ideas."

"Hmm. So what triggers it?"

"Normally, if having arrived in the wrong location, a person can manually activate it. But if certain stress levels are detected then the sensor can do it automatically."

"I see. So did the creepy sky cause you to activate yours?"

"No!" she barked. "I mean I did reach for my sensor. But it was only to disable it *before* the Reversal decided to send me back. I couldn't be separated from my parents again."

"That's quick thinking."

"Not quick enough. Other than the screams, the last recollection I have is of the Reversal initiating."

"I'm so sorry," he said, wriggling closer to wipe her watery eyes.

"Oh it's okay, really. I'm actually handling the memory of that moment better than I used to. You see, I used to get quite angry."

"You? No way," Ky sniffed, as a cool breeze drifted across his face. "Why did the Reversal sent you to this time, so far into the future?"

Nibby shrugged. "That's the key question, and one I don't have the answer to. But there are others who are trying to find out."

"That's good, I think. How many of them are helping you? Actually, how many others have you told?"

"Apart from you? Only one."

"Wow. Thanks for confiding in me," he said sheepishly. "So how often does this person keep you updated?"

"Not often," she hesitated, arching her eyebrows. "Actually, it's not just one person but rather a small group of Polmarian Elders who I had told."

"Elders?! Why do people always trust anyone with the title of Elder?"

"Oh Come on," she said, "you know they're the wisest of all people. Besides, each Elder assured me my secret wouldn't leave their inner circle."

"That's a great deal of faith you have in them."

"What choice do I have? I must believe this Faction can discover why I travelled through time."

"Faction?" he said, wondering if they were linked to the same reclusive group from his father's stories.

"Ky? Is everything okay?"

"Um. Yeah. Of course. What were you saying?"

"I was about to say this Faction had theorised that the massive Cleanse, combined with the power of the Reversal, affected the teleportation, sending me through time."

"Oh right, only an Elder could have told you that."

Nibby laughed. "You know sarcasm is the lowest form of wit."

"Yeah I know, but it made you smile, so it can't be all bad."

"There's that flattery again."

"Would you like me to stop?" he said smiling.

"Nah, I think you should..." Suddenly, her body tingled. She had an overwhelming urge to examine the surrounding fields. They were deserted, with no one else in sight.

"Is everything okay?" he asked.

"Um, sort of. It's just that ever since the Reversal sent me here I sometimes sense that I'm being watched."

"Watched by whom?" he said angrily, clasping both her hands. "The Faction?"

"Maybe," she said, still quivering as his soothing touch warmed her cool skin.

"Well no one's gonna hurt you while you're with me."

A hint of eucalyptus, the same scent her father had engraved into her soul during their final embrace, drifted into her nostrils. "How do you make me feel so safe?" she said, pressing her waist to his.

As Ky secured his body against hers, Nibby's eyes closed as a child-like vulnerability emerged. She tilted her head, placing it into the curve of his neck. "I can't put a finger on it, but you have a strength that's so familiar."

He leaned down and pressed his lips gently on top of her soft hair. The sweet smell filled his senses. Despite knowing they would soon have to leave this grassy haven, he too closed his eyes, as each moment seemed to slow. "For the first time in a long time I'm glad Earth humans were chosen," he whispered. "Otherwise we may never have met."

"Don't be so sure about that," she said, as they both drew their heads back and opened their eyes. "Ever heard of fate?"

Despite wanting to kiss her, he restrained himself; content just to look upon her beauty with a stare that, unlike their first glance between classrooms, lasted much longer.

However, despite his promise of safety, her body tingled yet again, overriding any pleasurable feelings.

At that moment, a movement flashed past the pair.

Ky sprung to his feet as a masked assailant swiped down at Nibby.

With the attacker fleeing towards a group of trees, Ky took off in pursuit.

"No Ky!" Nibby shouted. "Let him go!"

Despite hearing her plea, he didn't stop. Instead, as the assailant leapt swiftly over and under the low-lying branches, Ky, like a monkey, speedily climbed the tallest tree he could find. With a clear line of site to the cluster of trees the attacker ran towards, he kept his head still and scanned the surroundings using his periphery. Though he tried to catch any movement, a scattering of nearby students made it difficult to focus.

Feeling his uncomfortable perched position had begun to strain his muscles, he adjusted his body but immediately froze as he saw the assailant, draped in a full-bodied black shin obi uniform, stare back at him from afar.

The standoff lingered. After some time Ky was shaken from his trance by a diamond-like sparkle that flickered from the narrow eye slits of the masked man. But as the assailant slowly backed away Ky's thoughts shifted elsewhere.

Nibby!

In an instant, he jumped down to the ground and returned to where she stood.

"Are you okay?" he asked, forcing his voice to sound calm.

"I think so."

"What the heck did that guy want?"

"I think he was after this," she replied, exposing her wrist.

Ky noticed a drop of blood oozing from Nibby's skin. "The bastard cut you!" he said, holding her hand carefully before wiping it clean. "Well, at least he didn't steal anything."

"Yes he did. He took my DNA."

"Why would he want that?"

"I don't know. They never told me."

"Who never told you?"

Nibby hesitated, sensing Ky's protectiveness was teetering on anger. "The Elders, from that Faction I told you about, conducted a number of tests on me when I first arrived."

"I knew they couldn't be trusted."

"Don't worry. I was adamant for them not to touch me again and, after learning about the painful memories from my childhood quarantine, they agreed to leave me alone."

Ky's eyes widened in rage. "But they broke their promise."

"Not until now."

"Then why now? What happened for them to..." Ky froze, his voice lowering to a whisper. "Could they be listening to us? Would they be angered if they learned you had told me about your past?"

Nibby shrugged.

Feeling tense, Ky took a calming breath. "If it was them, do you think they can still be trusted?"

"What other choice do I have but to rely on them?"

"Yeah, I know. Well at least he didn't hurt you."

She smiled. "That's because *you* moved so fast."

"Yeah, but he was faster."

"Maybe, but I can see why you could be a..."

"Please don't say it. There's too much emphasis on being a Defender these days. There's got to be more to life than just that."

"Well, at least we're safe now."

"Sure," he said, as the pair embraced, "but for how long?"

XIV.

As the sun began to set, an orange glow over the horizon had brought with it a promise of excitement for a group of students scurrying to make their last outdoor class on time.

Looking on, hidden behind a bushy apple tree positioned half way on top of a hill, stood a grey-haired Polmarian. Despite being past middle age, the manner in which he leant under the tree's shadow caused his hair colour to appear darker, making him seem younger than he was.

He glanced towards the summit of the hill. There was no one to be seen. Surrounding him was a field full of rolling lush grass. Even though the classrooms were only a short distance behind him, the Polmarian felt far removed from the rest of the world. Slowly, he shifted his gaze back down the hill. The roaming animals, beautiful flora and distant sounds of play dulled into the background as his focus sharpened on the handful of seated students, barely at their pubescent years, waiting in a circle for their Educator to arrive.

Time passed. Though the Polmarian knew the students shouldn't misbehave, for risk of losing the freedom of open-air schooling, he could see them begin to fidget.

Just then, Ky and Nibby hurried past the class without any interaction. The Polmarian slid back behind the tree, ensuring he was concealed. But after hearing footsteps he turned suddenly to see the masked assailant, within an arm's length, staring at him.

"Did you get it?" demanded the Polmarian who knelt as the masked man reached behind his back and into a hidden pocket stitched beneath his silk-laced belt.

Carefully, the masked man pulled out a vial of blood.

"Good," said the Polmarian, tucking the sample away safely. "Now go. Your time will soon come."

The assailant was unresponsive.

"Those children won't sit still for much longer," said the

Polmarian, pointing to see if the lure of the grassy playground had been too great for the class to resist. "I must go and..." As he turned back, the masked man had vanished.

After returning his eyes to the class, the Polmarian saw one of the male students uncross his legs and stand. Instantly, the eldest female student grabbed hold of the boy, forcing him to sit once again.

Immediately, the Polmarian plunged his new shiny black bamboo cane into the ground for the time had come to begin his silent approach.

XV.

"Look!" exclaimed one student, "It's him!"

Having been elevated to the sought-after role of Elder, soon after informing Earth humans of being selected into the Knowledge Base, the grey-haired Polmarian arrived at the foot of the student's circle. With his intimidating shadow engulfing much of the group, some youngsters began to cower like prey hiding from their attacker.

"Good day to you children," he said.

"Goooood day sir," replied the older children enthusiastically.

"If it is all right with you, I will be teaching your class on Evolution."

These older children had heard rumours that the tedium of everyday class would be replaced when taught by him. Unable to hide their smiles these same older children nodded, giving the Polmarian Elder his answer while providing the youngsters with the comfort they desperately sought.

Hastily, the children made room in their circle. The Polmarian shook the fatigue out of his legs and stepped forward. His silky pale full-length robe scrunched as he sat.

From cheekbones to chin, he slowly stroked his thick beard to its end point. Following this, a deep sigh and slow inhale caught a gust of wind as the scent of fresh cut grass wafted into his nostrils.

Although most of the pre-teen students still remained quiet the eldest, and most self-assured girl sitting to the Polmarian's right, stared as the smallest boy seated opposite who was poking his tongue at her.

"Young man," said the Polmarian authoritatively, stunning the cheeky boy. "Clearly you have much on your mind, but do you think you could spare some thought to what I'm about to teach?"

The boy's face turned beetroot red but nodded just the same.

"Good. Though some of you may have heard this from your parents, I would like to start by showing you the universal way we, as

Nyrolacs, determined our chronological place in history."

"What does that mean?" asked the small boy.

"Simply put, this is how we tell time."

The Polmarian's eyes circled the group. He was quick to explain that, after being chosen, the Earthling's method of using a planet's revolution around its central star, often referred to as *old time*, was replaced by deriving its measurement from the average reproductive age of all known Nyrolacs.

Though the average age an Earth human can begin to reproduce is around thirteen Earth years, the Nyrolac average begins at twenty-eight. In the Knowledge Base this was known as one *Neg*. Another example showed how Earth, taking twenty-four old hours to complete a single rotation, is now represented as taking eight *Clicks* and sixty-four *Ticks*, or 8-64, to complete the same cycle.

Following this example, the Polmarian proceeded to circulate a tattered sheet of paper labelled *Universal Time Measurement*. It outlined this new metric system, where by groupings could be used to represent any chronological point, and was the same document given to each generation of children so that when they became adults, they would know nothing else.

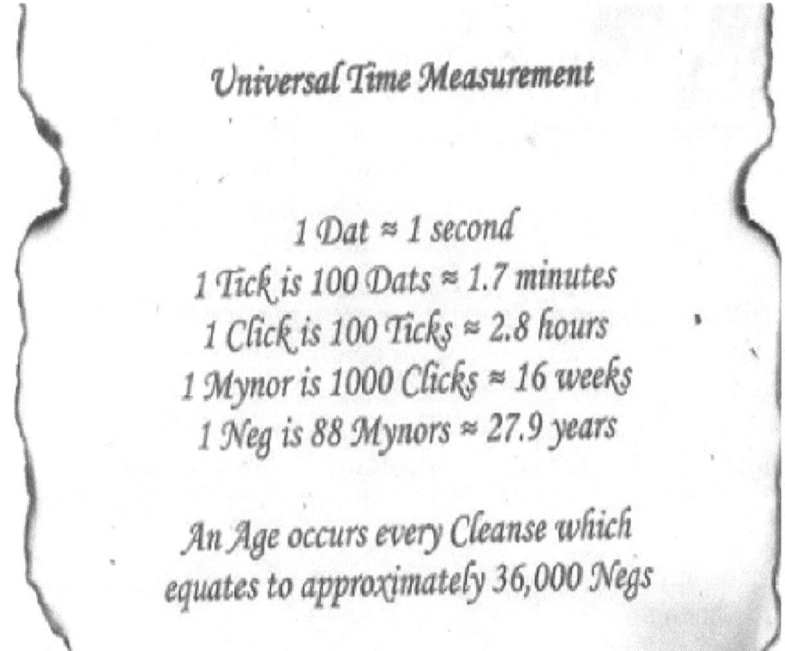

Universal Time Measurement

1 *Dat* ≈ 1 *second*
1 *Tick* is 100 *Dats* ≈ 1.7 *minutes*
1 *Click* is 100 *Ticks* ≈ 2.8 *hours*
1 *Mynor* is 1000 *Clicks* ≈ 16 *weeks*
1 *Neg* is 88 *Mynors* ≈ 27.9 *years*

An Age occurs every Cleanse which equates to approximately 36,000 Negs

"Excuse me sir," said the self-assured girl politely.

The Polmarian glanced down and raised his eyebrows. "And what is your name?"

"I'm Katie," she said proudly, as her piercing blue eyes sparkled like the crystal lakes of Earth's calmest waters.

"Okay Katie. What would you like to ask?"

"Well, I kinda get all this, but my mum gets angry when I mention it. She doesn't know why we had to change in the first place."

"Ah. Your mum is a traditionalist. But what she fails to realise is that this method of time keeping, together with any given universal coordinate, provides us with a map of the cosmos."

"So what?"

"So this map, when combined with Lest technology, allows galactic travel to any place we wish to go. Even sticklers for an unchanged lifestyle can't ignore the beauty of space travel."

Katie frowned. "They wouldn't if they were allowed to travel."

"Oh that will come. It's only a matter of time before Earthlings achieve the next Knowledge Base level and are permitted to visit other regions."

"But we've heard so many stories about these other places. It's just not fair to keep us away."

"Agrh," said the small boy. "Who needs to see them anyway? We have everything we need here on Earth."

A wry smile crept over the Polmarian. "Indeed you do."

"We do?" Katie said, surprised by the Polmarian's response.

"Of course. Although you didn't teach it to us, there's one striking similarity between your Earthling and other Knowledge Base civilizations."

"What?!" demanded the small boy. "What is it?"

The Polmarian groomed his beard again, "Mathematics."

"Do you mean like one plus one?"

"That's right! But there are more secrets than addition you know."

"Secrets?" Katie uttered. "How can maths have secrets?"

"Ah!" chuffed the Polmarian, "That's what I'm here to show you, but are you ready?"

Katie, the small boy, and the entire class all nodded.

"Good. Then let's see how ready you are."

XVI.

Katie's eyes flickered like a flame. Although she found mathematics boring, the lure of a hidden secret intrigued her enough to sit quietly. After gazing at each child, the Polmarian Elder spoke enthusiastically. "Mathematics is the most powerful concept in the Knowledge Base. Its discovery gave your ancestors the decimal system."

Arriving late, another boy came rushing towards the group. He plonked himself down next to Katie. Being the eldest of the boys, he thrust his hand in the air with confidence.

"Yes?!" said the Polmarian. "And who are you?"

"I'm Jack. What did I miss?"

The Polmarian gave him a scathing glare. "We were talking about the decimal system and..."

"What's the decimal system?"

The Polmarian grumbled. "For those of you who don't know, the decimal system is an ancient mathematical term used to denote our method of counting and is one widely used among all advanced species."

Jack looked puzzled.

"Allow me," Katie said, clearing her throat. "The decimal system is counting using your fingers."

"Oh yeah," said Jack. "That makes more sense."

Katie puffed out her chest. "Don't worry," she whispered. "Some of us need more help than others."

The Polmarian frowned. "Then I suppose he doesn't even know why *eighty-eight* is seen as a special number within the Knowledge Base?"

Katie shook her head. "Probably not."

Behind his grey beard the Polmarian chewed the inside of his lip. "For the benefit of those new to this class, you should learn that the number eighty-eight represents our infinite growth potential."

"What does that have to do with this subject?" Jack said.

The Polmarian stroked his beard. "Ah," he said contemplatively. "That is the question every student before you also asks."

"Yeah. We know. But they're sworn to secrecy about what they learn so I just wanna know when you're gonna tell us?"

"Oh, I'm not going to tell you, I'm going to show you."

"Show us! You think you're gonna be able to show us how to reach our potential by using maths?"

"Yes. It's a secret which began with the discovery of another decimal-based system, one you are already familiar with."

"Huh," Jack scowled, as his pointy shoulders and self-conscious tilt exposed his early teenage awkwardness.

"Excuse me sir," Katie said, showing herself to be the leader of the group. "I think I'm with Jack on that one. How do numbers help us achieve our potential?"

The Polmarian peered down at Katie and whispered loud enough for all to hear. "If used correctly, this alternate counting system will prevent us from making wrong choices unnecessarily. And, in case you are unaware, making correct decisions is what reaching our potential is all about."

"So can it help me become a Defender?" Jack said.

"Hey yeah," followed some of the younger boys. "Will it turn us into Defenders?"

"Ah yes, a Defender." The Polmarian hesitated. "I can't see why not. A Defender uses these same lessons to grow. But..."

"But what?" asked Jack.

"Well, while many Defenders use this alternative system to base their decisions on, there are a few Defenders who use it in an entirely different way."

"What way?"

The Polmarian shrugged. "This is something only that Defender will know."

"So what's this mysterious system?" Jack said. "Are you gonna show us already?"

"Yeah, what are these values?" pleaded Katie. "Can you tell us now? Please."

A grin washed over the Polmarian as his eyes circled the children again. "Numerals!" he boomed, "The alternate system I talk of is what your people have labelled as Roman Numerals."

"How can that be?" Katie said. "That system was discovered by *our* ancestors, not yours!"

"Oh no," chuckled the Polmarian. "You have it backwards, for it was your Romans who learnt this technique by stumbling upon *our* clues."

Blank stares swept over Katie and the children. "What are you talking about?" she asked.

"One of our early efforts in assisting your people into the Knowledge Base was to leave hints, by means of numerical blueprint, throughout the night sky. Although your ancient Romans were the only group of Earthlings to notice, it didn't take long for them to develop its entire sequence into what you know today."

"But we don't use these Numerals anymore," argued Jack. "And I have never seen you guys use them either."

"You're right. But not using the Numerals has only been for the benefit of Earth human integration. That is why this class exists, to expose you to them once again."

"Ah that's crazy," Jack snapped. "They're only useless Numerals."

Placing her hand on Jack's knee, Katie raised her index finger. "What Jack wants to know is *how* these Numerals can help us make decisions."

Jack nodded, unable to resist the charismatic charms of Katie.

"I certainly have a head-strong class today."

"We know," said Katie, "but that doesn't answer my question."

"Very well," grinned the Polmarian, his oily hand pulling out a small device which instantly transformed into a large sketchbook. "What I'm about to show you must not pass beyond this group for every child should only learn from the mouth of an Elder, not a peer."

Whether they intended to keep the secret or not, the class nodded.

The Elder began to draw what appeared to be an insignificant set of Numerals. "Although the Romans saw the sequence in order," he mumbled, while scribbling *I V II X III IV V...LXXXVIII,* "they were never able to see its true meaning."

The children who, at one time were ready to pounce with a plethora of questions, sat deadly still as the Polmarian Elder finished his design.

"I must be a Roman," said Jack, "because I can't see anything either."

The younger children giggled.

"Give it time," replied the Polmarian. "Most of you may take your whole lives before seeing what your Roman ancestors could not."

Although the result was not immediate to most, the pattern glaring at the group quickly imprinted itself into the mind of one student.

"I think I can see it," Katie mumbled.

"What did you say?" asked the Polmarian Elder.

"I see something. But how do I know what it is?"

The Polmarian's eyes widened as he took a breath. "When you truly see it, you will just know. But I'm afraid deciphering the magic of the Numerals isn't that easy."

"Maybe you're right. But it's telling me something, I just have no idea what."

While the other children remained glued to the symbolic patterns, the Polmarian exhaled. "But don't give up."

"That's fine for you," Jack said, craving sympathy. "I can't see anything except letters. What are we supposed to be looking for?"

"That I cannot answer for it appears differently to everyone. Some say it's like looking into your own soul. But those who have begun to untangle its meaning all agree it could be the key to reaching our true potential."

"But how?" Jack demanded.

"Hmm. I guess you could say that when choices appear hazy an awareness of the symbols may guide you in the right direction."

"Can *you* understand the Numerals?" Katie asked, hoping for an explanation that would enlighten her.

Although the Polmarian nodded, his tired eyes washed with a heavy glaze that suggested at how much of his own life must have been spent trying to interpret what these young children now sought.

"So what *can* you see?" Jack pleaded, eager to join Katie in gaining any bit of insight.

"Nothing that would make sense to you. But don't fret young man. Your answers, and your wisdom, will come in good time."

"Huh," said a gruff voice buried a few students away from Jack. Having remained quiet all class this male student, wearing a multi-coloured pair of sunglasses, scooted over and clasped Katie's arm. "If it really does help Defenders, I'm sure I'll see it soon enough."

Jack cringed at the sight of the sly teen draping himself all over Katie.

The Elder raised his eyebrows. He scooted out of the circle to improve his vision of the boy. "So, you also wish to be a Defender?"

"Yeahhh," he slurred.

"Although many of you will one day see the pattern, and some of you may even earn the honour of becoming a Defender, a true Defender will never see the Numerals."

"What!" exclaimed Katie, shrugging off the arm of the sly teen. "But you said..."

"Oh don't worry. Defenders can also see what you see. But despite most of us needing to see the pattern in order to guide us through our difficult choices, those truly born to protect us will also feel the Numerals. That sensation can unlock emotional energy to help push them beyond their normal limits, which is why Defending is *their* destiny."

Though the sly teen snickered, and Jack smiled at Katie's rejection of him, the other children sat quietly. As each kept their eyes focused on the Numerals, some of the dreamers imagined the newly formed pattern would reveal itself and turn them into a powerful Defender.

"Katie!" yelled a lady storming towards the class.

"Mum! Class hasn't finished yet."

"What's he teaching you?" Katie's mother exclaimed.

"Nothing you don't already know," replied the Polmarian Elder, quickly hiding the sketchbook. "Besides we're just finishing up."

With the help of his cane, the Polmarian Elder stood. "Thank you for your attendance."

As he hobbled off, his sleeve lifted, exposing a clover shaped mark engraved on his left wrist.

"The symbol," Jack whispered, trying to get Katie's attention. "So he is a Faction member."

The Polmarian turned to see Katie being dragged off by her mother, as a look of longing lingered in her eyes.

He knew scepticism of the Knowledge Base ran deep through pockets of the Earth humans. It was clear much of this older generation remained protective of their over-run civilization. They did not take easily to change, and had many reservations about what their children were learning. But with the youngest generation openly accepting this new world order, not even they could overlook the countless Knowledge Base advancements.

One of which, known as *Massine*, was about to gain more attention than any other.

XVII.

At precisely the same moment as Katie was being dragged away, a gathering of the most senior Polmarians had ended with a public directive issued via instant transmission to every household on Earth.

Massine; is a technology that can control explosions of any size by harnessing and releasing energy emissions found flowing through the universe. Importantly, it has just been listed as one which you, as Earth humans, are now permitted to obtain an understanding. Your vote on whether or not to accept this technology will soon take place.

Three Mynors, or almost one year later, two distinct views had taken shape. And as the relationship between Ky and Nibby grew, so too did the heated Constructor debates.

"Order! Order!" yelled the chairperson, as yet another forum had begun in an unruly fashion. "Order! I know these Massine debates have dragged on, and we have not yet voted on the matter, but we all need to be patient. So as has been our custom, our head Educator for the acquisition of Massine shall now be heard."

As silence eventually descended on those in attendance, Mr Spencer Regent, a senior Educator, removed his top hat and stood.

A throw back to his past ancestors, he methodically placed one hand over the middle button of his pin striped suit which hung loosely over his slender body. The other clasped a bunch of papers he had memorised as his beady eyes scanned his surroundings. "We can't ignore the benefits of Massine," he declared. "If we light small fires to thwart bigger ones, why wouldn't we use Massine to prevent unstable solar-systems from exploding?"

"But the risk is that Massine itself is unstable," replied the opposing head Educator, jumping at the chance to rebut the pompous Mr Regent. "Its volatile nature can also result in the complete annihilation of the targeted areas."

"We have all heard the rhetoric," replied Mr Regent, firming his steely glare at his new adversary. "This is one of the oldest technological innovations held within the Knowledge Base. Its good far outweighs any bad."

"But we're not ready to acquire this knowledge. Just look at our history. Remember how destructive we were, not so long ago. That's why most people want the harmful exploits of Massine suppressed, at least for now."

"Agrh! Why can't you leave all that in the past? Our sudden EALF rating increase indicates we are more intelligent than ever. After all, that's why the Knowledge Base leaders have permitted us to acquire the technology."

"Just because the information is there, doesn't mean we should obtain it."

Mr Regent grumbled. "Well, that's just your opinion."

"It's more than my view," replied the anti-Massine Educator, pointing to a large screen draping one of the walls in the forum. "Let me draw your attention to the view of the populous as captured in a paper labelled *The Sharing of Knowledge*."

The piece, written by Loush Sterling, was fast becoming one of the more publicised documents on the debate.

"We have all heard her sermon," Mr Regent said, as an icy chill washed over his words. "Loush Sterling is no more than a Knowledge Base hostile who refuses to integrate with society. She doesn't even deserve the title of Educator."

"How can you say that?" replied the anti-Massine Educator, gazing up while the large screen illuminated an excerpt of Loush's words. "Many of us feel she has a great deal of insight into the subject."

"Then maybe you lack the same vision she does," uttered Mr Regent.

The anti-Massine Educator huffed. "You're entitled to your opinion. But here's Loush's view, an opinion shared by the majority."

It is true that, for hierarchies of class systems and power mongers to exist, ignorant and uninformed people must also exist. Only providing information to dissolve ignorance will such hierarchies be dismantled and will lead to the complete sharing of knowledge among all Nyrolacs.

An exception to this is prematurely learning deadly technologies which, due to our self-destructive past, may share us knowledge no more. In other words, until we learn that destroying any part of nature will inevitably lead to our own destruction, we should not seek to acquire the knowledge of Massine.

Loush's published material was born out of nightly debates with Elric. But while she went on to become one of the public voices opposing Massine, Elric commenced Educating students impartially, in his class on *Earth and the Cosmos*, where he alluded to the consequences of obtaining Massine knowledge. And while Mr Regent continued his protests, Ky and the Educators that followed in Elric's image paid respect to Loush's work on Massine via three topics.

Topic 1, Time: *The presumption no Nyrolac existed to observe anything prior to the creation of the universe caused the Obzoovers to label this singularity which started the cosmos, an event some believe to have been the first ever Massine detonation, as time zero – our beginning.*

With the present day representing 14,252 Ages and seven Negs (or fourteen billion years) after time zero, this first topic of telling time sees many students in awe of the enormity of their minuscule place in the Universe.

Topic 2, Cleanse: *There exists an event which, according to the Knowledge Base, is the only way in which the measurement of time can be altered. A Cleanse is a random cataclysmic event with the potential to wipe out an entire species. This may change the average reproductive length of all Nyrolacs and thus alter the measurement of a single Neg of time.*

In spite of its consequences, Cleanses were seen by the Knowledge Base as nature's way but, although they mainly give enough warning for the safe removal of all nearby life, caution is not always provided; this was seen with the Great Prehistoric Cleanse of Earth, sixty-five Ages ago.

Due to this lack of warning, present day facts point to a Massine detonation having caused this Cleanse, a blast large enough to eradicate most of Earth's population.

As ensuing discussions often led disgruntled students to whine about their lack of interaction with other species, Educators eluded that not all knowledge sharing between the Polmarian and Earth civilizations could be prevented.

Topic 3, Truth: *With folklore being in as much abundance as the information within the Knowledge Base, these somewhat exaggerated stories and fables have been sceptically passed down throughout the generations.*

One tale in particular, hidden within the secrecy of the Elder's oath, depicts a mythical human. With no-one ever having survived a Cleanse, legend has it this Polmarian not only survived, but transcended time.

Rumour of this mystical human began to spread within the confines of the Elders when the Obzoovers who, after witnessing the Great Prehistoric Cleanse, theorised that one Polmarian may have survived. However, although occurring during this highly publicized Polmarian colonising of Earth, no evidence of this Nyrolac was ever found.

With Knowledge Base science stating that disappearing energy must be replaced by another energy-source, this chronicle was condemned to live out its life with all the other fictitious fables.

Nevertheless, not everyone had seen it as a fairy-tale for, as the legend grew and facts disappeared, some had never given up waiting for the arrival of the one they call the *Traveller*.

XVIII.

As Ky and Nibby continued to spend their time teaching on temperate Earth, thousands of Polmarian students, whose daytime classes ended, had just enough time to feel Polmar's warmth fade away. Replaced with dusk, an evening chill quickly filled the air as the last of the students scurried home.

The main campus would have been deserted if it were not for the arrival of a single latecomer, fleeing into a seldom used entrance of the campuses main building. Joining a hand-picked group of his fellow Earth humans, the young male stumbled to his seat. Though his laissez-faire manner drew glares, the latecomer didn't say a word.

In his direct line of site, three distinguished Educators, two of whom were Polmarian, stood in the centre shadows of the giant lecture hall. They knew each student had to pass a series of gruelling tests just to gain knowledge of the campus' secret entrance where, after arriving from Earth, each would descend to the deepest of the underground rooms.

Once arrived, a set of towering steel crescent shaped doors prevented those who were unwelcome from entering. After a small sensor scanned and accepted the approaching student, the door would vanish, giving way to the enormous lecture theatre.

The dimly lit entrance had students fumble blindly until reaching their assigned seats which, unbeknown to them, overshadowed a strange rectangular surface in the room's centre. The seats, affixed with a single yellow glow, allowed only the eerie silhouettes of the others to be seen.

As the student's eyes adjusted, most peered down the rows of seats towards the unusual reddish surface. Although it was not clear, the latecomer noticed this twenty-metre long area was layered with more than just rubble.

Suddenly, bright lights illuminated the centre of the hall as the three Educators, who stood in triangular formation, glared intently at the few dozen adolescents.

While the students' murmurs persisted, the two Polmarian Educators covertly made their way to blend in among them.

As more time passed, and when the mumbles ceased, the Earth Educator, with his recognisable face, approached the front row. "Good evening," announced Mr Spencer Regent, with the sing-song influence of a gothic choir. "Welcome to your destiny."

XIX.

With the exhilaration of their first visit to the Great Polmarian Hall fresh in their belly, students sat and listened as Mr Regent spoke with his usual arrogance. "It is most certainly true that my ancestors, and I can only presume yours, worked tirelessly to improve themselves as humans. But it was not this act which attracted the eyes of the Knowledge Base."

Though many of these students were briefed that caring about one another was the reason Earth humans were selected into the Knowledge Base, Mr Regent was about to change that perception forever. "Though at the time of selection our physical, intellectual, and emotional attributes were improving, it was how we confronted and handled issues which was of primary importance."

"Learning to like each other didn't hurt none either," said the latecomer hidden among the shadows that cloaked the back row.

"Ah, don't let the words of that sceptic convince you otherwise. Allowing the result of a single Challenge to decide the outcome of any important issue is the foremost reason we were chosen and is why some of you will have the opportunity to become a Defender – there is nothing more honourable."

Most students nodded proudly. But sensing an overabundance of self-interest at becoming this archetype hero, Mr Regent frowned. "These lessons you are so fortunate to attend will teach you what it takes to endure everything the race throws at you and, most importantly, what you must do to succeed. But know that once chosen to participate, it's not just your own fate at stake anymore. In case you don't yet realise, being a Defender is the most important thing a Nyrolac could ever do for even the ultimate consequence of death is not uncommon."

The room stilled. These students knew they were selected as potential Defenders. Although each was strong, and brimming with confidence, a quiet unease drifted across the lecture hall as each felt the sudden weight of Mr Regent's words.

As murmurs traversed the class, Mr Regent noticed some students pointing to the cluster of objects spread over the surface behind him. "Ah yes. Your curiosity of these foreign objects is perfectly normal, especially since you are one of the first Earthlings ever to see them."

Dissimilar to the pin-like material used in their own Challenges, these larger jagged objects appeared chameleon-like in colour, allowing them to blend into the red-brown surface.

"I would advise averting your eyes gentlemen," said Mr Regent, as silvery lines began to swirl throughout the objects. "Gazing too long could have you fall into their trance."

"Why?" asked the only student seated in the front row, rubbing his eyes as the fatigue from his travels had begun to show. "What's so special about them?"

"More about these shape-shifters, and the harsh conditions of where you may race, will be revealed in time. For now, you must learn about this small dusty track. Normally eighty-eight metres in length, it is what every Defender before you have raced upon."

Making his way to the start of the three-lane track, Mr Regent glared half way towards the finish. Within moments, a naked human-like figure materialised. Although his holographic legs were straight, the strange looking man lurched over. His bent arms pressed up against his thighs, elbows pushed into his lower ribs. The pain on his face was evident. Despite the absence of any blood, this individual was clearly hurting.

Mr Regent noticed some students look away as the humanoid began to dry retch. "During the climax of a race, the objects you encounter will deplete much of your liquid, affecting your entire body."

The humanoid attempted to lift his leg but stumbled, scraping against one of the object's squirming blades. Instantly he began to convulse.

Somehow, Mr Regent froze the man in mid step and pointed a laser beam at his feet. "The shape-shifter's poisons have been injected into his body. They are sufficient to kill the average human. Lucky for him, he is not average. He is a Defender. But with the ability to pierce any living organism, the poisons will continue to circulate, causing unbearable pain, until he ceases any movement."

"What's he gonna do?" shouted the front row student, jumping to his feet.

"He must finish!" yelled another.

"Yes," said Mr Regent, "but how?"

"With his desire."

"That's not enough. Though he'd entered the arena with one purpose, to represent the people who believe in the same cause, calling upon that passion won't help him now."

"Why not?"

"Because his body has deserted him and only a secret, he had all but given up on, can ignite him again."

The latecomer's interest is peaked. *The Numerals.* Silence grew as similar thoughts had each student attuned, hoping to gain a deeper understanding of these magic symbols.

The humanoid staggered towards the finish. But just as his heavied legs stilled, and blood-shot eyes watered, a murky image emerged in front of him.

"The poisons are strong. His mind knows that to live he must stop. But the appearance of the Numerals provides hope. Fuelled solely on instinct, a new source of energy is found, moving his body and giving him a chance at victory."

"How can *we* use the Numerals to do that?" asked the eager front-row student.

Mr Regent glanced over at the elder of the two Polmarians. "Summoning the energy is what you're here to learn. But only a special few can actually conjure the Numerals at this point of the race – that is something we cannot teach."

Despite some minor convulsing, the humanoid quickly steadies. "Watch carefully. The appearance of his own Numerals has given him the ability to kept going, burying any pain he may feel."

With the once slothful movements appearing more graceful, the humanoid crosses the line.

"He's finished," Mr Regent said, seeing both relief and curiosity draping the students' faces. "But his efforts have come at a cost for, no matter the result, he still has to survive the poisons."

The humanoid's eyes opened wide. He falls towards the ground. In a last grasp at life, he glances back at Mr Regent. But as the deadly objects lunge for one last attack, the hologram implodes before vanishing as fast as it had appeared.

"In case you have not yet realised, his life was designed for one purpose, to win this race."

"Why does the race have to be so gruesome," asked the front row student. "Why can't we compete without the threat of death?"

Mr Regent smirked and made his way into the seating bays. "This is the powerful statement this race makes, that there are those among us willing to suffer, willing to die, in order for the rest of us to live in peace. This is why the outcome is accepted. This is why you, as Defenders, are honoured."

A noisy grumble arose from the latecomer. It drifted its way through the great hall and caught the attention of the mysterious, and older of the Polmarians. "What did you say?" he asked authoritatively, also still hidden beneath the shadowy light.

"It don't look that tough," repeated the blasé rogue apprentice, in a rarely heard Jamaican slur.

"Excuse me!" said Mr Regent, as curious eyes oscillated between him and the student. "This is no place to be disrespectful."

"It's okay," said the older Polmarian, gesturing to illuminate the back row. "The latecomer may speak."

"As you wish." With light being shed on the area above the latecomer, and whispers spread, Mr Regent's eyes widened. "Ah. Marc Drayed I see. Please stand and share more of your thoughts with us. Or better yet, why don't you tell us what makes you think you'd be so successful?"

After a shrug of his shoulders and a lift of his brow, the unperturbed student stood but said nothing.

Instantly, students turned to stare at Marc's striking figure. Long spider-thin legs blended into his firm athletic waist. Despite his entire body being hidden behind a replica of the Defenders tight-fitting apparel, provided to each student prior to arrival, his torso's rippling muscles danced proudly for all to see.

"Since your tongue is tied, I suppose I'll have to enlighten everyone for you." Mr Regent turned towards where the bulk of the students congregated. "Squandering his youth, Mr Drayed spent most of his life swapping between the shipping docks he calls home, and the juvenile detention centres which protected that community from his uncontrolled outbursts. But since he sits here among us, I can only assume someone must have thought he'd changed his ways."

Sensing the glares, Marc rolled his eyes. "Can I sit now?"

"Not so fast. From your comments, I gather you don't think the Defenders' Race is difficult. Do you think your training ground, the one near your old wreck of a house, is tougher?"

"Hey. That's mu' home ya' talking about."

"Ah," said Mr Regent. "So now you think it is I who is rude."

Marc appeared reflective as his laid-back slur did not do justice to his intellect. But those who knew of him understood he was much more than just an anatomy class on display. Though each pupil grew up confident in their own abilities, Mr Regent was told Marc's EALF rating outshone them all.

Moments later, and maligning his initial cocky behaviour, Marc cleared his throat politely and begun to speak with a respect that surprised Mr Regent. "Sirs and fellow students, I apologise for raising my voice and for speaking under my breath. It was quite boorish of me. Maybe I need to clarify what I said earlier."

Mr Regent gazed at the older Polmarian for approval. Due to being squashed into one of the small seats, he could not help but shift his legs, causing his renowned cane to fall out of reach. Despite this, the identity of the grey-haired Polmarian Elder still remained hidden. "Go ahead Mr Drayed," he said.

Through the scornful glares, Marc spoke. "I understand the honour involved in defending. But to me, the task does not appear that hard."

"Your words reek of arrogance," said Mr Regent.

"No they don't. From my point of view it's the truth."

Mr Regent frowned. "If that's how he feels, then I have nothing more to say to Mr Drayed."

"Thank you Mr Drayed," said the Polmarian Elder. "If you can handle the track like you handle your words, then we shall all want you defending us."

Marc nodded and sat back in his seat.

With the great hall settling back to normal, and as the students once again faced Mr Regent, the Earth Educator decided to take more questions. "Yes. You again, in the front row."

"Will we ever have to compete against superior non-human Nyrolacs?"

Mr Regent took a regretful breath and answered with the pre-empted response he was instructed to give. "You should never have to compete against a superior Nyrolac."

"But what if there is an inter-species debate?"

Mr Regent smiled. "Then we have a battle on our hands."

"Mr Regent!" demanded the younger Polmarian, peering out from among the shadows. "You have been warned before. Don't force our hand."

Mr. Regent snuffed but acknowledged with an obligatory nod. "What I meant to say is that an inter-species debate is not something which will happen to Earth humans."

"Then what if all high rating EALF Nyrolacs are on the one side?" asked the front row student. "No matter what species they are."

"Then I guess that's what fate had decided."

"Yes. That's what I thought."

Mr Regent stared down contemptuously at the front row student. "As Nyrolacs, our aim is to strive for the highest EALF our potential allows, just as the Obzoovers have done. The only way this is achieved is by learning from others, and not pretending as though we already knew. This is a lesson *you* should learn."

The student peered down meekly, staring at his own feet. "Then why can't we learn from these Obzoovers?" he muttered.

"Because they no longer teach, they only observe."

"But their name is mentioned all the time. Can't we at least meet them?"

"Not in your lifetime."

As furrowed brows engulfed the great hall, sensing Mr Regent was not forthcoming with much information, another student shouted. "Can you at least tell us why there are no female Defenders?"

"Ah, now that's a good question, for in human society we all accept the male is physically stronger and with both genders equal in every other way, the male is shown to have a greater EALF potential." With all the students being male, most gladly nodded with that comment. "But this fact is solely due to our genetic birth strength. It does not exclude female humans from becoming a Defender, it just makes it much harder."

"That'd be a sight," mumbled Marc, while his mind studied the shape-shifting objects squirming on the track.

Ignoring the mumbles, Mr Regent continued. "But it's also universally accepted that it is the female of any human species which is the key to human existence. The power they harness, and summon to re-produce, is the reason why life exists. So in a manner of speaking, it is because of females that we defend. In other words, protecting them is protecting our way of life."

Although a number of questions followed, only one was important enough to draw Marc's attention.

"So what are those shape-shifters called?"

Blorm, Marc mumbled under his breath.

After a moment's pause "*Blorm!*" was also shouted by another of the studious pupils.

Even though Marc was well versed in the present-day races held on Earth, he had found ways of teaching himself about other Knowledge Base race formations. This allowed him to learn about the Blorm and, in spite of his words, know the pain they could actually cause.

Peering closely, the Polmarian Elder watched Marc's erratic demeanour. He speculated whether Marc was one of the rare Humans born with the ability to feel the energy of the Numerals, a power that can guide a successful Defender through the treacherous maze of Blorm. More importantly, the Elder pondered if he could also manoeuvre the type of race which could even do more harm than these deadly shape-shifters ever could.

XX.

In a distant place, a brutal species known as the Kryon were preparing for a Challenge of their own. *Their* Defenders, who would soon be unleashed, were currently battling among themselves.

Watching this combat in secrecy were the reclusive Obzoovers; the most evolved species in the known Universe. But despite sharing so much with the Knowledge Base, their oldest secret was yet to be revealed.

XXI.

Muffled laughter could be heard beneath a mountain of leafy foliage. Adding to the mess, Ky frantically shovelled twigs, hay and any other light debris he thought could balance on top. But despite his efforts the laughs persisted. Unable to dampen the sounds he stopped, stepped back, and observed his work.

The pile moved. Moments later, shredded objects flew everywhere as Nibby and Ahlis burst free. Although puffing, more from their giggles than their lacklustre efforts to escape, they began chasing Ky.

In the distance, barking amplified as the Sterling's' three farm dogs bounded from the house, joining the women in their pursuit.

The golden retriever, Giet, was the eldest of the three and trailed the group. Kally, the Labrador, gracefully leapt to the lead, diverting along the way to sniff upon a garden bed blanketed with carrots. Aisab, the Kelpie puppy, showed the exuberance of youth, but his clumsy legs kept him from forging ahead.

With Giet joining Kally in the garden bed Aisab was the first to arrive, pouncing on Ky and ramming him with his head. Before the young canine could get in a second shot Ky picked it up and gave it a bear hug. Seeing the affection given to the puppy, the other dogs jealously dashed over.

Ahlis, whose wavy auburn hair bounced with the breeze, arrived ahead of Nibby. Having thrown off her jumper to reveal a skin tight blouse, which accentuated her curved body and toned arms, she spared no time before rough-housing with young Aisab.

"Would the two of you behave," Nibby joked, pointing for Aisab to sit next to the obedient Giet and Kally.

Ahlis pouted. "But you have Ky as your *Flyat*. Since I still live on the farm, and will never meet someone, surely Aisab can be *my* soul mate."

"That's just gross. A Flyat should only describe a pair of Nyrolacs who declare they are each other's life partner."

"Oh I was just kidding."

Nibby grinned and meandered back towards the Sterling's ranch-style house in which she and Ky also lived. Though Ahlis followed, Ky was distracted by someone calling his name.

"Hey Ky!" shouted the voice, originating from one of the freshly mowed fields in the distance.

"Oh hey there Lenny," Ky said blandly.

Now also fully grown, Lenny's curly black hair remained glued to his head despite sprinting towards his younger cousin. The ungainly manner in which he ran caused the Sterling women to giggle as Ahlis and Nibby joined Loush on the porch.

"Wanna have a race?" said a breathless Lenny.

"You know I don't do that anymore."

"But that doesn't make any sense. You're good enough to be a..."

"Don't say it Lenny."

"Yeah, yeah. I know. It's a good thing your talent was hidden by being home-schooled, otherwise the Elders wouldn't be as easily dissuaded as me."

Seeing grey clouds begin to emerge from the horizon, Ky turned to make his way into an area of the garden in much need of care.

"Agrh," Lenny said, his voice elevating much to Ky's chagrin. "I'd probably beat you anyway. We have the same genes don't you know."

"Oh I know."

Despite hoping for some help in the garden to beat the incoming rain, Ky noticed Ahlis opening the door to the house. "Where are you going?"

"Inside to watch today's Knowledge Base lesson with mum. Do you want to join us? It's a special on Challenges and their Defenders' Races."

"Of course we do," Nibby said, knowing how Loush's grieving had previously kept her detached from anything to do with Elric's passion for the Defenders' Race.

Ky rolled his eyes and stared at the sky.

"Come on Ky," Nibby said. "Loush needs our support."

"Don't worry about him," Ahlis said, following Loush. "We all know he doesn't want anything to do with Polmarian teachings on that subject."

Nibby shrugged and also headed inside. She noticed the transmission screen had begun to flicker. "Perfect timing."

The show began by reminding the viewers that there were only a few Mynors remaining until the start of the eighth Neg at which time a Defenders' Race, one that is conducted every six Mynors, will be run to determine Earth's top Defender. This race, however, would be the first one of its kind to allow the top two finishers, not just the first, mandatory automatic selection into the next race.

"I'm glad there's so much support against acquiring Massine," Loush said. "Otherwise this next race could be used to decide the Massine debate too."

"It's good we have support," Ahlis said, "but the debate has been lingering for far too long, in spite of virtually everyone agreeing with what you've written. What happens if it doesn't get resolved?"

"Oh it will. Just give it time."

While Ahlis and Loush continued their discussion, Nibby peered out the window. She spotted Ky digging in the fields. He held a heavy iron pick in his right hand. His stroke was strong and swift. She admired how he could be so accurate with each blow. Rotating blows with a cultivation axe in his left hand, his rhythm seemed effortless as he sliced up the soil.

Nibby stood. "I'm going to bring Ky some water." After stepping off the porch she could see the sandy fur of Kally creeping closer to the right petting hand of his unaware master.

With a break in transmission, Ahlis also glanced out the window.

Having just raised the pick for another swipe, Ky's eyes shifted up to the axe. Oblivious that Kally had moved under the pick's rotation, he began his downward swing of first the axe, then the pick.

Despite Ahlis and Nibby seeing the danger Kally was in, neither had time to react.

The axe struck the ground. Ky's senses flared, causing him to freeze the pick in mid-air. With the blade centimetres away, Kally's ear twitched.

Calmly, Ky placed the axe down, followed by the pick. He knelt next to the oblivious canine and stroked his head gently. Satisfied, and as if the incident never occurred, Kally trotted away while Ky lifted his tools and continued to work.

From afar, Nibby stared as her breath began to regulate. Ahlis, who had run out to join Nibby, also watched silently as the pair tried to digest what they had just seen.

XXII.

"I can't believe what just happened," Nibby said. "Kally would have died if...if Ky..."

Ahlis nodded. "I know."

"But how did he react so fast? I mean, you guys always said how he wanted to be a Defender growing up. He certainly has the skills, as he just showed, but I've never really thought of him in that way."

"I know. It seems crazy he gave up his dream, but I guess he still blames himself for dad's death. At least mum and I think that's why he hates hearing anything about the Defenders' Race."

Nibby pondered Ahlis' words. "Um," she mumbled hesitantly. "I think I have something you and Loush should see."

"What is it?"

"Stay here," Nibby said, gesturing for Ahlis to sit on the porch. "I'll be right back."

After a short while, Nibby returned with a tattered, half torn, piece of paper in hand. "Did you know Ky keeps a journal?" she said.

"Yeah, I remember him tinkering away in some little book."

"He rarely writes anymore, but here is one of the pages."

"Why do you have it? And why is it torn out?"

"He gave it to me soon after we met. It was his way of showing me why, as you say, he gave up on his dream."

"Oh," Ahlis said, reading the first line. "This was written just after the accident!"

Nibby nodded, as Ahlis continued to read the remaining words.

Journal Entry #124

A hospital bed isn't the most comfortable place to write from but I needed to say a few things. With no one around, this old journal of mine will have to do.

It's been a while since I've written, but things haven't been so good of late. I guess that's an understatement. I mean with dad dying and all, I'm just lost for words. I know I haven't spoken much to anyone, let alone my family, but I just don't have the strength to hear what they have to say.

One thing I am sure of is that I don't want to train anymore. In fact I don't want to do much of anything. I have already been asked to teach in dad's place, but I don't think I could ever face that. A class full of students, wanting to learn from me, now that would be a joke.

I know people say it wasn't my fault, but I can't see it. My dad is gone because of what we did and I cannot bring myself to do anything which he would have considered special. I mean how can I without him here to see it...he was, and always will be, my best friend.

A tear rolled down Ahlis' cheek. "That's really sad. But I'm glad you showed me for it confirms why his adoration of Defenders had stopped."

"Yeah, but maybe it's time he started again."

Ahlis grinned. "Maybe you're right. Let's show it to mum and see what she thinks."

XXIII.

Loush, who was unaware of what had just happened with Kally, was in the process of learning many new aspects about the Knowledge Base; facts she had previously not cared about.

She learnt how older DNA examinations were combined with the latest in non-invasive scientific advancements to detect a Nyrolac's ideal twitch fibre, muscle density and heat rate potential. Access to neural passages determined their potential intellectual strength and when added together with their current emotional reading, the EALF rating was born.

Just then, the back door slammed open. "Mum! Mum!" Ahlis said.

"Calm down girls," Loush said, seeing a strained look on Ahlis and Nibby's face.

"But mum..."

"No. Please sit first. Did you know the Polmarians are concerned the young Earth Defenders of today are training too hard? They say our men won't be able to endure more than a handful of agonizing races, especially since Earthlings may not reach their peak EALF rating until they are around forty years old."

Still standing, Ahlis eventually caught her breath. "I think you mean one-hundred Mynors old."

Loush smiled, "Yes, of course. But did you also know that crystal-like objects, called Blorm, which have the ability to pierce any form of atomic structure, are used in most Challenges held outside Earth's borders?"

"We know mum. But we also have something to..."

"Then you'll also know they cause immediate hurt by releasing poisons into any living thing they encounter!"

"Yes mum. We know that too. The Blorm sends signals directly to our brain, creating paralysing pain throughout their victim's nervous system. And without medication, the only way to ease the pain, allowing any movement to resume, is for the wounded to surrender, stopping any physical or mental activity."

"Wow. You certainly know a lot about it. It's almost as if you were training to *be* a Defender."

Nibby nodded and laughed nervously. "That's kind of what we wanted to talk to you about."

"Okay," Loush said hesitantly. "What's on your mind?"

The three women sat themselves around the dinner table. With the greyness of dusk upon them, the glow of the house lights brought Ahlis' attention to a picture of Elric which hung on the wall between the kitchen and the lounge. She stared longingly and mumbled. "I miss him too."

"What did you say my dear?" Loush said, her eyelids becoming heavy as the adrenaline driving her excitement had taken its toll.

Without replying, Ahlis presented the journal entry, pressing the folds flat against the table.

Loush stared at the paper for only a moment. "What's this?" she said, alerted.

"Nibby and I are so happy you're embracing the Challenges and Defenders' Race. Maybe it's time for Ky to do the same."

Loush was pensive as she slid the paper back to Nibby. But after the girls recounted what they had witnessed in the field, Loush's apprehension disappeared. "I knew it! He's always had physical gifts, but his clarity of mind has definitely increased of late."

"So you think it's okay to mention it to him?" Ahlis asked.

"No." Loush said. "You know how sensitive he can get."

"Yeah, but if we handle it delicately…"

"Hmm," Loush said, as the pattering of rain began to hit the roof. "Perhaps we *will* speak with him when he comes inside."

Ahlis peeled back the hand woven curtain draping the window closest to her. "That won't be long now. He's securing the equipment."

Nibby tilted her head curiously. "Are you sure we should do this right now?"

"My dear," Loush said. "You guys may have let me grieve at my own pace, but Ky's different. It's time to give him a little push."

Ahlis glanced back up at the picture of Elric. "Mum's right. It has to be now."

"But what makes you think he'll listen to us tonight, especially since he's avoided the topic for so long?"

Loush shrugged. "We don't know for sure."

Just then, Ky entered. He grasped the door handle firmly, preventing the howling wind from slamming it against the wall. His legs were tired and hands darkened from dirt remnants and rake abrasions.

"Come and sit with us," Loush said, breathing with deep anticipation.

"What's going on?" Ky said suspiciously.

"Ky," Loush said tenderly, "Your physical strength has always been something that amazed your father and me."

Ky blushed. "Thanks mum."

"Your reactions, well, we've never seen anything like it. I'm so proud."

"I know mum. You've told me a thousand times."

"You also demonstrate strong mental calm with an emotional clarity second to none."

"Yeah! Yeah! I'm just like you mum. But why are you telling me all this?"

"Because there is something else I, we, want to say to you."

Ky squinted. A nervous flutter shot through his stomach.

Despite his reluctance Loush persisted. "In recent times you have retreated behind an invisible barrier, protecting yourself from a painful truth, one from which I too had hidden."

"And what would that be mum?" Ky said sceptically.

"Your father is dead Ky."

"Gee. I didn't know that!"

"Ky!" Loush repeated. "Your father is dead, and it was not your fault! Nor was it mine!"

Ky shot his gaze up at Elric's picture. "Why are you talking about dad?"

"Because he always said that if someone has the power to protect others then they should do so."

"Oh no. Not this crappy Defender talk again!"

"You have an ability most can only dream about. Why don't you share your skills with the world?"

"Why are you bringing this up now?"

"Because of what just happened with you and Kally in the field.

And because I read the journal entry your wrote in hospital."

"What!" Ky said through gritted teeth, as his turbulent eyes shot daggers at Nibby. "Why did you show them?"

"Because you have a gift," Nibby said. "I just never realised how great it was."

"Ky," Loush whispered. "If you have the potential to protect others then wouldn't it be an honour to do so?"

"What about Ahlis!" barked Ky, his chest inflating with each heavy breath. "You're letting her run away to join one of those nomadic Polmarian tribes who have links to the Faction!"

"We're talking about you Ky! Not your sister."

"But that's not fair!"

"No Ky!" Loush said, raising her voice. "What's not fair is that you refuse to use your gifts because you think it honours your father, when all you are really doing is disrespecting him. It's time to let go of the pain. It's time to trust us again."

Ky grimaced. His internal torment was finally taking its toll.

XXIV.

Ky remained quiet for what seemed like an eternity. He suddenly felt exhausted, not from the outdoor work nor the confrontation, but from a lifetime of fighting his destiny.

Hoping time would defuse the air-filled aggression, Loush was also silent.

As time passed, during the occasional exchange of chit-chat between Ahlis and Nibby, Ky's breathing returned to normal. A slow exhale put the women at ease. "So why now?" he asked.

Loush smiled warmly. "Because you're ready. We see how you've kept your abilities hidden from the world. We know you don't want to boast, choosing to keep the insecurities of others concealed by avoiding your own potential. But now it's time to step out of the shadows and shine. Believe me Ky, it will give those around you permission to do the same."

Ky sat back in his chair pensively. Lacking the will to argue any longer he stared into his mother's eyes. His heart instantly softened. Soothed by the ticking of an old wooden clock, hanging precariously on the wall, he stroked his face and squinted. "But dad…"

"I know," Loush said, melancholy trapping her voice. "But your father believed in you Ky. Above all else, he knew you would make a better Defender than he ever was."

"So what do you want me to do mum?"

"Look into your heart my son. You'll find the answer."

Ky peered up at the portrait of Elric yet again. He stood slowly. "I think I'm hungry," he said, with any defensiveness having vanished. "And I guess I have a decision to make."

As he left the room with a peeled banana, it was only then did the women begin to contemplate what his decision may actually mean. For Ky, however, this moment was a turning point; one from which there would be no going back.

XXV.

Following last night's rain, the sultry morning sunlight broke through Nibby's window, waking her to see a half empty bed. This was nothing new for Ky had never stopped his dawn workouts. This session, however, would be different.

A makeshift running circuit allowed him to train his physical skills while randomly scattered debris tested his mental reactions to the terrain.

One more! he pleaded, pushing his emotional tolerance to the limit.

After leaping over the last crop line, and grabbing a branch four meters above the ground, he swung down by means of a backwards somersault.

Good! he thought, completing the workout.

In making his way back to the house, the crunching scrub beneath his feet caused the chirping birds to stop. Suddenly a slight wobble caught his limbs. An out of place step caused him to stumble on a twig hidden beneath foliage. He stopped and glanced skyward. The sunshine had disappeared, covered by a thin layer of rain clouds.

If I have the potential, then it may be my destiny to protect those who need me. Maybe it's my duty.

Ky always liked to believe in choices, but at that moment he drew back to a word from ancient times; one often spoken by Elric. *It is a mitzvah to maximise your potential.*

He grinned as endorphins tingled through his body. His decision had been made. "Yes. It's both my choice and my obligation."

A droplet of rain fell on Ky's temple. He wiped it away and looked up again. The clouds had thickened and drizzle had begun.

He found his thoughts drifting to the portrait; the one he and Ahlis found when they were young. Although once gazing upon it nightly, since Elric's passing he had kept it locked away.

It's time for the portrait to be reborn, he thought. *It's time to look upon that Defender, my father, once again.*

Ky raised his arms, enjoying the coolness striking his bare chest. With the rest of the world unaware, he had begun to accept his future and the importance of what the race stands for. Although it would take much training, he was going to become a Defender.

XXVI.

Elsewhere, and within just a few Mynors following his now famous Defender's class with Mr Regent, Marc Drayed was training more ferociously than ever.

From deadly silence to screams of anguish, Marc's grasp of his own goal was within reach. His widely watched training sessions gave onlookers proof he was a genuine contender. And with Earth Elder's also watching, Marc's aggressive glares showered them with reasons to doubt even the most veteran of Defenders.

However, unbeknown to Marc, there were more than just Earth humans interested in his progress. For, in as much as his extroverted assurances were helping him achieve his own potential, it was this same trait that had attracted the interest of others, setting Marc on a path beyond his control.

XXVII.

As more time passed, and with the Massine debate reaching boiling point on whether Earth humans should acquire its destructive powers, Mr Regent approached a small and seemingly unoccupied stone building.

Gargoyles, perched on either side of the entrance, stared down. Carved from black diamonds, their deformed eyes and elongated mouths sent a chill through his body, causing his heart to beat rapidly. After being scanned by a beam from the intimidating creatures, Mr Regent kept his slender frame respectfully upright, and entered with caution.

Moments later, he'd made his way through the darkened passage and into a seemingly empty room where streams of light illuminated circulating dust particles. As his eyes adjusted, a large figure took shape out of the corner of his eyes. The grey-haired Polmarian Elder, the caller of this meeting, was here.

The Elder glared down at Mr Regent, studying his face thoroughly. Though unable to maintain eye contact, Mr Regent noticed the Elder was covered with facial hair, more so than when they last met. Though unable to completely disguise his rapidly aging skin the growth crawled well past his throat and joined the fake-looking chest hair that emerged from his light green robe.

The Elder sat in one of two chairs in the room's centre as his wrinkly hands motioned Mr Regent closer. Obligingly, he sat opposite, dwarfed by the Elder, in the only other chair in the room.

In spite of the room's eerie feel, this Polmarian meeting place had been used by past Elders to discuss events that have potential to endanger their community.

With security paramount, the building outside camouflaged itself into both the adjoining structures. Even if this secret location was found, its thick steel and lead walls were said to be impenetrable.

Distracting him from thoughts of his own peril, Mr Regent noticed the Elder's bamboo cane, which now boasted a rarely seen crystal perched on top of its handle, tucked securely under his chair. *The gemstone,* he thought. *They've made him a Grand Elder.*

Trying not to stare at the glowing gem, he gazed up at the Grand Elder, elevating his head sharply. However, instead of being ready to deliver the information as requested, his eyes fixated on an abrasion, slowly trickling blood, beneath the Grand Elder's ear. Whatever was happening to the Elder, Mr Regent had not been privy to. What's more, after seeing the blood blotch the Elder's beard, he could not help but wonder how this seemingly fragile man was the same strong Polmarian charged with informing the Earth humans of being chosen.

"So," grunted the Grand Elder, bringing Mr Regent's attention back.

"Oh. Of course," said Mr Regent. "The debate is balanced on a knifes edge. We're at a crucial juncture."

The Grand Elder remained silent.

"The Constructor," continued Mr Regent, "is to have its ninth sitting on the Massine debate."

"Don't you mean the Massine Challenge. I hope you remember the Debate is not the outcome we want."

"Sorry, Massine Challenge. We've been insisting the issue be declared a stalemate, that it be turned into a Challenge. But my Earth Elders remain adamant a debate *will* solve the issue. None of them want Massine. Although we have pushed for it to be declared a deadlock, this result is becoming more and more difficult to achieve."

"To the majority, your voice may be seen as unreasonable, but there is rationale behind our actions. Massine technology must be understood by your people. Their future and survival will depend on it."

"So what would you have me do Esau?"

"Don't utter my name within these walls!" barked the Grand Elder, peering over at the subtly placed electronics affixed to one of the walls.

"I'm sorry. What would you have me do your Greatness?"

"Since most will always oppose us, the only way this issue can be won is if the Constructor Forum fails and a Challenge begins. We must force a Defenders' Race. The debate *must* result in a deadlock."

"But we have tried to convince them. They already know Massine can be used as a preventative to any explosion, including other Massine detonations, and still they fear the information will cause more harm than good."

"That is why we need a more persuasive argument, and our other solution, to be put into motion."

"But why can't we just tell them of your reasons for acquiring Massine knowledge?"

"Because if our adversaries learn what we know, it would already be too late."

Knowing he was not privy to the reasons himself, Mr Regent was unwilling to challenge the Elder's authority. "When would you like this plan to take effect?"

"That depends. Is the Earth's top Defender still dominant over all others?"

"Yes. His EALF rating is unmatched and is clearly the best Defender Earth has ever produced. He has won the last two Defender races and is only now starting to reach his peak abilities."

"Is there no other who shows a similar EALF rating?"

"There is another we have been watching…Marc Drayed."

"Ah yes. I can still recall his first class, all cocky and brash. He won't be of concern. I know his EALF rating is high but he is emotionally unsteady. That will be his downfall."

Mr Regent nodded. "We all agree he is not ready. He will not win."

"So it shall come to pass that Dominique Sable will prevail in the next Defenders' Race. And you will do everything in our power to convince him to represent us."

"Yes sir."

"Good. Then force the debate into a deadlock so the Constructor will fail and a Defenders' Race will determine the result."

"But how do I do that? We are still many votes short."

"We know we can get Sable on our side," said the Elder, stroking his beard. "Show your people he is pro-Massine and we will get our deadlock."

With those words the Elder stood, picked up his cane, and produced a miniature device which he proceeded to hand over. "In order to stay in contact, you will need this."

Mr Regent's face gleamed. He hoped this was the latest Translator technology, afforded only to Elders and high ranking Polmarian Educators. If it was, he would be one step closer to achieving his ambition of becoming an Elder himself.

He took the device, placed it in his ear and winced as it fused to his head. "Is it done?"

"Yes. Two taps will give you contact with anyone on your network. What's more, you now have access, albeit limited, to the Polmarian centralised source of Knowledge. This is a database coupled with much of the Knowledge Base's own private information."

"Where is the primary database kept?"

The Grand Elder didn't answer. Instead he glanced up at the mix of computers affixed to the far wall, turned, and made his way to the opposite wall where he subsequently vanished.

Suddenly, the room had become ghostly quiet. The only sound Mr Regent could hear was the hum of computers.

Despite not learning the reasons, and although feeling the Earth humans should have been told the truth, he knew the Grand Elder's orders must be followed; a mammoth task that may have consequences far beyond what he, or the Grand Elder, could foresee.

XXVIII.

Throughout most households, rumours of the pro-Massiners' growing support base circulated as the latest debate was about to commence.

"I can't believe it," uttered an elderly man, as his early morning routine began by sinking into his lounge chair where he read the daily news. "Son! Come and look at this."

"What's happening in the world this time Dad?"

"There are only one-hundred Clicks until the start of the eighth Neg. That's only eleven days away, isn't it?"

"Yes dad."

"Time moves so fast. Does that mean it's been more than fifty Mynors since we were chosen to be part of the Knowledge Base?"

"Yes dad. Why do you ask?"

"We may have been chosen because of our intelligence," he said, pointing to the front-page headline, "but we still can't agree to end this silly Massine debate."

"What debate?" interrupted Jack, the elderly man's grandson.

"And good morning to you too my boy."

"Oh sorry. Good morning grandpa," Jack said, hugging obligingly. "So what debate are you talking about?"

"Before *we* tell you anything," said grandpa, "why don't *you* tell us why you've been so distracted of late? Did something happen to you at school? Is it your *friend* Katie?"

"No! It's nothing!"

"Hmm," mumbled grandpa, watching Jack's eyes circling the floor. "Then tell me what they're teaching you these days? What did you learn this week?"

Although it had been quite some time since the Polmarian Elder explained the truth about the Numerals, Jack had since learned that in its most aggressive state the Blorm can also create, albeit unintended, a path of safety as led by the Numerals. Though invisible, the most powerful of Defenders can feel this energy, helping guide them to safety. Despite the Numerals being all he could think about, Jack wasn't ready to divulge any facts about the them. Instead, he scanned his thoughts for anything else he could remember. "Façade," he uttered.

"Speak up boy," growled grandpa.

"We were taught more about Façade technology."

"Well go on then. Don't keep me waiting, tell me about it."

Though Jack's eyes rolled, he quickly recited anything he could recall on the topic.

"From what I remember, utilizing Lest technology for its instantaneous space travel, a capability known as the Façade was developed by early Knowledge Base affiliates."

"Very impressive. It's like you've read it straight from a book. Please continue."

"Um, let's see – The Lest portion allows a person to be visually and verbally present, in a predetermined area, without ever having to physically attend in person. It's much more advanced than that flat screen technology of your day."

Grandpa furrowed his brow. "I guess you could say that. But do you know how it actually works?"

"Well I'm pretty sure it traces the targeted image," Jack said, also catching the attention of his father. "Once its shape, colour, texture and audio emissions are captured it instantly transmits these features as a hologram appearing at the Façade's destination."

"Since when did you learn to speak like that?" asked Jack's dad.

"Leave the boy alone. Remember, he's the smart one in the family."

"Well that makes one of us," said Jack's father grinning.

Jack, who was surprised at his own recollection, wondered if the exposure to the Numerals that day in class may have opened new pathways of intelligence, just like the Polmarian Elder said.

"Keep going my boy," grandpa said. "Where do we use it?"

"Well, an example is seen during the Constructor forums you and dad talk about. You know, those boring meetings lasting over a Click."

"That's about two and a half old-hours grandpa," Jack's father said.

"I know! I know!" Grandpa grumbled. "But do either of you actually know why these forums only run for one Click?"

Jack and his father shook their heads, staring at grandpa curiously.

"To be honest, I'm not really sure either, but I do remember hearing the Knowledge Base deems this time as the maximum needed for two parties to debate before any arguments are no longer seen as constructive."

"Huh?" Jack said, puzzled.

"That actually makes sense," Jack's father laughed, turning to Jack. "I guess they think it's enough time for the selected representatives to speak and for the worldwide audience, made possible by Façade, to vote on an outcome."

"Waste of time," Jack announced. "Why do so many people need to have a say?"

Grandpa frowned. "Because it's written in our parchment. '*One Person...One Vote...One World*'. It's something you should have memorized by now."

Jack yawned. "Oh that's way cool," he said sarcastically.

"Now there's the Jack we know," grandpa said, turning to Jack's father. "Still, we'd better tell the boy the most important thing of all."

As Jack's ears pricked, his father obliged. "If no resolution is reached, the forum will close and another sitting will be required."

"Not that. The other thing."

"Oh. On occasions, a Defender's Race will decide the outcome."

"What! Really?" Jack said. "Is that what's gonna happen today? Please tell me."

A wry smile crept over grandpa's face.

"Pleeeeease grandpaaa!"

"Oh don't lead him on," said Jack's father. "This Massine debate discusses our right to harness the most powerful energy sources in the universe so there's no way they'll let a Defender's Race dictate its outcome."

"Your father may be right. Besides, despite a foolish minority wishing to obtain this knowledge, most of us want nothing to do with it."

"Let's not sway the boy with our own views," said Jack's father. "He should make up his own mind."

Though disgruntled, Jack's grandpa nodded and continued

flicking through the news. "Either way, today will be the debate's ninth sitting and, according to this, is a good one for you to watch."

"Why? What does it say?"

"Let me see – It says some Polmarians may be present for they are becoming concerned with our inability to decide on, what they think should be, a simple issue."

Jack's father frowned. "Easy for them to say. They're a peaceful society so had no trouble agreeing to acquire Massine."

Jack appeared contemplative. "I don't want to disagree with you guys but if they have the knowledge what's wrong with us also having it?"

"Nothing!" griped Jack's grandfather, "as long as it's for the right reasons, which I don't believe it will be."

"What your grandpa means is that the small group of pro-Massiners have become agitated with their lack of support. Consequently, their recent outcries have us believe their motives may not be so pure."

Grandpa frowned. "Rumours have also spread that they're taking matters into their own hands."

"Now, now, there's no proof of anything more than words."

"Don't be foolish," grandpa said. "You're afraid, just as I, that they are plotting something."

XXIX.

"Is it time? Can we join yet?" cried Katie as impatient wrinkles creased her forehead.

"You know I don't care about those Constructor forums!" said her mother, standing in the kitchen.

"But it's my first one."

"Don't worry darling," said her father, "it's almost time."

Residing in a land, quite distant from the Forum, Katie sat her slender frame on the sofa next to her dad and watched as he waved his arm in front of their Façade.

Suddenly, a rustling caught Katie by surprise as Earth's main Constructor Forum, located in the sparse landmass formerly known as Africa, materialized before her. The oversized building, purpose built by Polmarians, stood more than forty metres tall. Despite its height however, the dwelling only contained a single room, causing all words spoken within to echo from pillar to pillar.

Including the impartial adjudicators who watch over these proceedings, Katie could see a total of thirty dignitaries in physical attendance. Above them, blurred faces, from the other Façade users, speckled the backdrop.

The Chairperson, entering from a small door in one of the lower corners of the hall, distracted Katie. Although most dignitaries were dressed in pale robes, his attire was dark red. Without regard for any special introduction the Chairperson hurried to a make-shift platform in the room's centre. "It is the duty of all Earth humans, in both physical or Façade attendance and who exhibit a reasonable EALF rating, to vote."

"Can I vote dad?" asked Katie.

"Of course, so long as you have a current EALF rating. I believe the schooling system takes it every season."

Katie nodded. "What about your EALF reading?"

"Except for Defenders, whose rating is mandatory, mine, like all other adults, is voluntary. But with the honour that comes with voting, I, like most people, am happy to supply my DNA when requested."

"Oh. Then what about..."

"Look!"

"What is it dad?"

"Here come the Defenders! The best ones have been asked to witness this Massine session for it may soon have to be decided by use of a Challenge."

Katie's stare was firm. "I'm going to be a Defender one day."

"See!" her mother shouted. "All that nonsense is going to her head!"

"No it's not! My EALF rating is better than most kids my age. Besides, I was the only one who could see the pattern that Polmarian Elder drew."

"Don't mind your mother. She just wants you to be safe."

"Exactly," her mother said. "Because if this, or any debate, has no resolution then those Defenders must compete in one of those dangerous Races."

"I know mum. And I think I'd do just fine."

"But are you ready to carry the burden of deciding the destiny for everyone? That's something no one person should have."

Just then, Katie could hear the Chairperson explain how this issue would only be resolved, in this forum, if more than ninety percent of the voting population agrees. If not, then another debate will be required.

Katie looked confused. "But how will the debate end if that figure is never reached?"

Her father grinned and wiped a sheen of sweat from his brow. "The only other way for any debate to end is with a deadlock. For this to occur there has to be at least thirty percent of support on both sides."

"And why don't you tell her what happens next," her mother snickered.

"After a deadlock, a second vote will decide whether or not the Constructor has failed. If the majority agree it has *not* failed, then further debates will be scheduled. Otherwise, a Defender's Race will decide the outcome."

Katie smiled. "So how many votes do the pro-Massiners have?"

"They only hold fifteen percent."

Katie looked puzzled. "That's very small."

"Hmm," her mum mumbled. "That's what *I* said when they only held eleven percent of the votes."

XXX.

Elsewhere, Jack and his family who, like Katie's clan, also appeared in the great hall's Façade, listened to the repeating arguments.

"I see what you mean grandpa," Jack said. "Why do those pro-Massiners persist with their line of questioning when everyone else is so against acquiring this knowledge?"

"Because they're a stubborn bunch. They should just concede."

Jack's father sighed. "We all believe the knowledge is too dangerous to obtain, but everyone has the right to be heard if their opinion is said rationally."

"Then luckily none of us anti-Massiners will ever switch our vote," Grandpa said.

"Look!" shouted Jack's father. "Look who it is!"

"I don't believe it! What's he doing so close to the pro-Massiners?"

"What's going on?" Jack said. "Who are you talking about? Who is it?"

"That, my boy, is Dom, the greatest of all our Defenders."

XXXI.

Appearing alongside the small number of dignitaries, and potential Defenders, stood Dominique Sable.

A tall and powerful icon to all Earth humans, he is Earth's top Defender; the first ever to do the unthinkable and win consecutive races. He is also one of the rare few Earthlings with an EALF rating high enough to match that of a Polmarian.

Using his heavy-set frame to its full potential, Dom is known to race with a stubbornness that mimics his personality; ordering his dense bones to endure all before him. Being a native of the land hosting this Constructor doesn't hurt either for his black skin and sun-bleached hair, repeatedly scorched by countless training sessions, keeps him immune to the race's normally harsh climate.

Conversely, his gruff facial features have not aged well. A large nose, sitting crooked on his face, is disguised by his enormous teddy bear smile. Despite a lifetime of experience charming his creased face with the odd wrinkle, sexy has never been a word used to describe him.

Yet despite his endearing white-teethed grin, his appearance at this forum means a choice must be made. As such, with the formalities drawing to a close, and the Chairperson beginning to call the Defenders representing each party, Dom pursed his lips, clasped his hands behind his back and made his way towards the small group of pro-Massine debaters. Though never shying away from his political viewpoints, he felt uneasy. As gasps flooded the forum, his choice had become clear.

With this one act, the anti-Massiners know they must avoid a deadlock at all costs; otherwise a Defender's Race, in which Dominique Sable will compete for the pro-Massiners, will decide the outcome.

"How could you do it Dom?!" shouted one of many voices.

"You're a traitor Sable," yelled another. "What did they pay you?!"

Time passed, and with the debate progressing well past boredom, Dom's hidden anxiety caused him to twitch involuntarily. He wondered if he'd done the right thing – questioning if any voters would, as per the Elder's plan, follow his lead.

However, as the gong sounded, indicating the obligatory one Click debate time was up, another pro-Massine supporter approached Dom.

Welcome on board," whispered Mr Regent, as clusters of whispers swamped the forum yet again.

"Looks like this has been a waste of time," Dom said.

"Oh, I wouldn't say that. We may not have an outcome today, but I'd say, after seeing you, people will follow and realise obtaining Massine knowledge is the best way to protect ourselves against any kind of Massine attack."

"But aren't you hearing what the anti-Massiners are saying? You know, that thing everyone's quoting."

"Come on Mr Sable, you're one of us now. We don't have time for any nonsense."

"Oh, that's it," Dom said, facing Mr Regent. " *'There's no difference in us obtaining Massine as it was for Earth humans to once create the atomic bomb! If this is allowed to happen, then our own demise is sure to follow.'* "

"Don't you start citing Loush Sterling. Her words have enough popularity without you promoting them as well."

Dom turned his head away from Mr Regent and mumbled. "Oh, don't worry. Your attacks on her would out-trump any endorsement I could give."

"What was that?" Mr Regent demanded.

"Nothing important. I just wonder what you really know about the Massine debate anyway."

"I know our support is now growing," replied Mr Regent, glancing up at the results of today's vote. "The balance is clearly shifting, thanks to you."

"Don't thank me. Whatever I do, no matter how it makes me look, I do it to help my drought-affected home town of Tousol, not you."

"Yes. It is a shame what nature can do."

Dom snarled. However, his concern for this new political position on Massine would have to take a back seat for the start of the eighth Neg, and the annual race to decide Earth's top Defender, was just around the corner. Although not being used to decide the Massine issue, this race was going to demand his undivided attention.

Like Dom, Ky had a vested interest for, despite not being a participant, he planned to partake using a method unique to him alone.

XXXII.

The dawn of the eighth Neg had brought with it great fervour and celebrations as the long-awaited race to determine Earth's top Defender approached.

Nibby, who had been watching the lead up from the family sofa, looked out the window to see Ky place the finishing touches on his own dirt track. After seeing it sprinkled with piles of spiky objects, which appeared to be a close replica of the pins used in actual Defender races, she could tell virtually every detail had been catered for.

In recent times, and due to the popularity of her work on Massine, Loush had been elevated to the position of head Educator. By the populous voting her as one of their spokes-people, her goal of being able to directly protect Earth humans had arrived. Despite wanting to be with Nibby to watch this Defenders' Race, her new duties had summoned her elsewhere. Like her mother, Ahlis too was missing from the Sterling household as permission to extend her Polmarian travels had been granted.

A booming sound, from the family room's screen, startled Nibby. She flung her head back to see the Defenders curl into their crouch positions as the countdown had almost expired. While waiting, the announcer concluded his reading of the latest Defender EALF ratings. He said the top ranked Earth humans had been confirmed. These one-thousand men, along with those who had won any number of official lead-up races, had all qualified at the chance to become number one.

He also reminded the viewers that, much to the relief of the Defenders, the inaugural use of Blorm had been postponed, replaced with the less harmful pins from previous races.

Suddenly the Defenders took off, as too did Ky.

Not surprising, Dominique Sable immediately stamped his authority on the race, striding to an early lead.

With twenty metres remaining on the eighty-eight-metre track, pain had become evident. Wincing with every step, the leading Defenders slowed dramatically while many of the others had already collapsed from pain caused by the immobilizing pins.

Drenched with the mix of blood and sweat, Dom struggled as a few nearby Defenders began to make ground. But with millions watching, he called upon an inner strength to increase his stride cadence. Though his bare feet squirted more blood, a final lunge saw him cross the line narrowly ahead of several others, including the first appearance by young Marc Drayed, finishing a close second.

In her periphery, Nibby caught sight of Ky. Swiftly she turned to inform him of the result but froze as she saw him crumple to the ground. Though he too had completed his circuit without any apparent wounds, his heavy panting demonstrated otherwise.

As Nibby rushed outside, the transmission showed Marc begrudgingly wait in line to congratulate the winner. Once this obligatory task was complete, he declined any further treatment and instead rushed from the arena alone.

With his duties completed, Dom stepped away from the surrounding Defenders and proceeded to raise one arm in the air, clenching his fist in the defiant tradition of his ancestors. It was a sign of his dominance and added to the growing fears among the anti-Massine supporters.

Arriving at his make-shift circuit, Nibby slumped next to the breathless Ky. "Are you okay?"

Ky nodded. His face expressionless as his breathing steadied.

"Are you sure? I saw you collapse."

"Yep. I'm fine. I just got grazed by...by that last shape-shifter."

"Shape-shifter? Don't you mean pin?"

"No," Ky said, pointing to the track.

Nibby stared at the scattered objects, which looked more like haunting images of the Blorm than pins. "But that can't be! I mean, your feet have hardly been wounded. What are those things?"

Ky wiped the sweat from his brow. "They're used to simulate the Blorm."

"Who gave them to you?"

"I contacted some of mum's connections. I didn't want to tell anyone because they're still in the testing phase and aren't even available for the Defenders to use yet."

"And you're the dummy who does?! That's insane."

"Maybe. I just needed to know what it took to cross them."

"And now that you know, can you do it again if you had to?"

Ky shrugged, giving Nibby cause to wonder what a test of his EALF rating would reveal. She reminded herself that, though selection into a Defender's Race was primarily based on this rating, Elric's home schooling had kept his un-detected. "Have you given any more thought to finding out your EALF?"

"You know I don't want to," Ky hesitated. "But maybe it's time I did."

"Good. But I'd feel better if you could tell me how you crossed over those things."

Ky stared up into the bright sunlight. "Do you remember me mentioning a dream I had? You know, the recurring one which started after dad told Ahlis and me about the Great pre-historic Cleanse?"

Nibby nodded. "What about it?"

"Well, I still hear those whispers, telling me I have been chosen and that I may die if I keep going."

"I cringe every time you tell me that. It's not something a kid should hear."

"I know. But lately I've been seeing strange images, symbols that have never made sense, until now."

"Why now?"

"Because I think those symbols just helped me feel the rhythm of these shape-shifters. It was almost like I had an insight into what they were thinking."

"Oh," Nibby wavered. "What do the symbols look like?"

"I can't be sure, but I think they're the Numerals. You know, the ones people talk about."

"Ky," Nibby said pensively, as a single belief, kept concealed for so long, thrust itself to the foremost of her thoughts. "Since you were never really taught about the magic behind the Numerals, maybe you should keep this revelation to yourself, at least for now."

"But..."

"Just trust me on this. You're on the verge of becoming a Defender and I sense there are those among them who do not take well to newcomers. So, until your EALF rating is made public, let's keep your visions a secret."

Ky raised his eyebrows, but lowered his guard as he gazed out at the tranquil backdrop. "Good session though. I'd love to tell Ahlis how I'm progressing, but it's been ages since we've heard from her."

Nibby smiled and grabbed his hand. "Hopefully she'll be back soon. Then she can see for herself."

But despite Nibby's mask of happiness, the seed of sorrow had been planted knowing Ky's emerging abilities may attract the danger she had long feared.

XXXIII.

While Dom's posse celebrated his unprecedented third straight victory, bragging how his feet were the toughest in the business, the reclusive Faction had become privy to sensitive information.

Hastily, this small group of Polmarian Elders sent a group of Educators to advise Earth humans on this latest transmission from the Obzoovers, word for word.

It is with honour we recognise the growth of the Earth humans' intellect. As such their status in the Knowledge Base is to be elevated and the following three mandatory rules adopted.

Rule 1: If healthy, the two top Defenders have mandatory selection to the next race.

Rule 2: If a Defenders EALF rating decreases, a replacement will be made.

Rule 3: Additional planetary travel has been permitted.

Despite the excitement of the Earth human's advancement in the Knowledge Base this Faction hoped it had not come too late. Their fears were based on a pair of prophecies that if found to be true would be of monumental importance to all man-kind.

XXXIV.

"If I'm excited," said Nibby, looking into the distance from the Sterling's porch, "you must be bursting."

Ky grinned. He followed Nibby's line of sight, through the dwindling sun light, to their front fence line. "It's been ages since we've seen her. The start of the eighth Neg, and especially that last Defender's Race, was so long ago. There's just so much she has to catch up on."

"And so much we need to find out about her. After all, she's been living on my home planet, without returning, for more than ten Mynors now."

Ky gazed up one of the larger trees. Although once containing a cubby made by Elric's own hands, the tree now stood bare, with the sole purpose of lining the pebbled driveway. "Do you think she'll be okay?"

Nibby shrugged. "She was housed by the Faction so I have my doubts."

"Yeah, I can't forget how they sent that sparkly-eyed masked guy to attack you. He wouldn't be able to get away from me a second time."

"I know, but I haven't had another incident since that day we met...and something's are better left in the past."

Although Nibby's words rang true, Ky's thoughts shifted to his childhood.

"Dinner time!" Loush would call, while Ky and his friends played among the tree-tops. "Everyone has to come down now."

"Just a minute mum!" Ky replied, as each child began their descent.

Although each would climb down Ky, who was usually the last, kept his acrobatics for all to see. To the glee of the other children, Ky would jump to the branch above and lock his feet between two offshoots. After a slight pause, he swiftly rolled backwards, bending his knees before flipping, landing on his feet.

"Ky!" Nibby said. "Are you okay?"

He inhaled deeply. "I may not be able to protect everyone, but hopefully this choice of mine to Defend can help keep my family safe. Thanks for helping me find my passion again."

A wry smile crept across Nibby's face. "Maybe these travels have allowed Ahlis to find her passion too."

"I hope so. I guess she *was* fortunate to have been selected by the Faction."

"And with her purpose being to teach underprivileged children the ways of the Knowledge Base, can you imagine how much Ahlis would have learnt from them?"

Ky nodded, glancing over at a teary Loush who sat a few metres away on another of the porch steps. "Don't worry mum. They chose other Earth human volunteers too. Ahlis would have made a lot of friends."

"Oh I'm not sad. After almost a year, I'm going to see my daughter again."

"Maybe it's time you learnt to speak in new-time mum?"

"You know I speak in the old tongue when I'm nervous," Loush said, standing up. "After all, Ahlis isn't usually late."

"I'm sure it won't be long now. Come sit with us."

Even though the brick foundation of the Sterling house was solid, the wooden decks, also built by Elric and Loush soon after their marriage, had begun to show its age. With the floorboards creaking, Loush hurried her steps. "I'll have to fix that one of these days," she said.

"But how will you find time if you become an Elder like the Polmarians are suggesting?" Ky asked.

"Oh they only favour me because of your father."

"Nah, they respect your paper on Massine," Ky said

Loush shrugged. "Whatever their reasons, I won't mind remaining an Educator. Besides, being an Elder is too political for any Sterling."

"So true," Ky said, as a ruffled noise in the distance sparked his curiosity. "There she is!" he cried, spotting one of the older style transport vehicles dropping Ahlis off. Quickly, she ran up the grassy path and into the arms of her mum.

"Let me look at you," Loush said, tears rolling down. Although Ahlis' recent communications hinted at the happiness she experienced during her travels, it was only after seeing her mature glow that Loush could feel at ease.

"You do look different," Ky said.

"Yes. I can see it too," Nibby said suspiciously, dragging Ahlis towards the porch. "You've met someone," she whispered teasingly, "haven't you?"

"Shh," Ahlis said, quickly changing the topic. "So I hear mum is in line to become an Elder."

"Don't believe everything you hear," Loush uttered.

"But you're meeting with them soon, aren't you?"

"Before I tell you anything, you need to tell us about your Polmarian adventures."

"Come on mum. You know you'd be perfect for the job. It's the best way you can get dad's message of peace to everyone."

Loush giggled. "That's a nice thought dear. But the Elders just want to talk. Besides, tonight is about you."

"Okay mum."

As the Sterling's spent the last remnants of sunlight hearing about some of her adventures, Ahlis began to divulge more about the Faction than they would have liked. "I was taken aback to see that, despite all the technology on offer, their existence was one of simplicity."

"What do you mean?" Nibby asked. "We've been told those living on Polmar all enjoy the creature comforts of life."

"Not the Faction. Certainly not the branch I was part of. That tribe lived by the land, refusing most of the luxuries offered by the Knowledge Base. Living this way taught me more about life than I could have ever imagined. It also helped increase my own EALF rating."

"Did you get to work with Polmarian children as well?" Nibby said, taking her seat at the dining table after hostile mosquitoes caused the group to adjourn indoors.

"Certainly did. But they weren't really like Earth kids. I can't really put my finger in it, and I know you haven't been to Polmar since you were young, but your people definitely seem more intelligent than ours."

"Then how do you explain Nibby?" Ky mumbled through gritted teeth.

"Oh you're so funny," Nibby replied sarcastically.

"Stop it kids," Loush said. "What was the most common question they asked you Ahlis?"

"Oh that's easy. They just wanted to know who else exists in the Universe."

"But wouldn't they already know that?" Ky asked. "I thought they have exposure to other Knowledge Base species."

"No way. Although they have access to some more information than us, their Elders follow orders which suppress Polmarian access to the broader Knowledge Base."

"Sounds like you should be just as sceptical of the Faction Elders as me," Ky said.

Ahlis shrugged. "With what I've seen I wouldn't get too comfortable around their Elders. I guess I just wonder if the Knowledge Base decision makers are trying to help us, or whether they have other agendas."

Ky nodded. "It also shows that, since we're all restricted in some way, Polmarian and Earth humans are more similar than we think."

"Yeah but I'm still smarter than you," Nibby said.

Loush smiled, "You guys are just like Elric and me."

"Ky and I are the only ones with a love story," Nibby said, winking at Ahlis.

"Ahlis!" Loush said. "Is there something *else* you wish to share?"

Ahlis hesitated. "Um...well...It only happened recently."

"What did?" Ky asked, staring at his sister curiously. "What's going on?"

"I met this guy. And yes, I really liked him."

"Whoa!" Ky said. "How did you know that Flip?"

Nibby smiled.

"And..?" Loush probed.

"And nothing mum. We shared a bond but our timing wasn't right. His work demands a great deal of him, and I wanted to come home. Besides, we both agree that if it's meant to be, we'll find a way. There's nothing more to say."

"Oh come on Ahlis," Ky said. "You have to tell us more than

that."

"No Ky! I don't!"

As Ky rocked back in his chair he took a measured breath, reminding himself of what he was supposed to do come morning.

"We're all a bit tired," Loush said, aware of Ahlis' anxiety. "Let's talk about something else."

"Fine by me," Ahlis said snidely. "So tell me mum, now that *he's* qualified for the big day tomorrow, don't you think Ky should have a shave?"

XXXV.

Ky's glare at Ahlis was stern. Knowing his persisting silence had created a chill in the air, he decided to break the ice. "Taking a razor to my face is the last thing on my mind. Besides, my stubble keeps me centred."

"Does that mean your focus has finally improved?" Ahlis chuckled, feeling her tension easing as the spotlight shifted away from her own love story. "From what I've heard, you're gonna have to remain head strong if you want to do well."

"Oh that won't be hard," Ky said. "Being stubborn is what us Sterlings are good at."

Ahlis laughed. But as she began to get up to speed on his training, and knowing the upcoming Defenders' Race, due to start in just over ten Clicks, will be used to nominate Earth's first ever top-two Defenders, her smile disappeared. "Is it just me, or is it more than just a coincidence this race is due to take place straight after the next Massine debate?"

Ky huffed. "It's the eighteenth sitting of this stupid debate so, to me, it seems like they're always occurring."

"But I heard Mr Regent, by using Dominique Sable and his other pro-Massine followers, has gobbled up almost one third of the vote. That tells me they could use a Defenders' Race to decide the outcome. If that happens, this could be the perfect opportunity for them."

"So what? Let's use the race to decide it. Then the debate will be over one way or the other."

"But Sable has been so dominant."

"I'm sure there are others who have a chance," Nibby said. "Like Ky."

"That's a nice thought," Ahlis said, "but this next race is too dangerous for Ky to think he can win. After all, they've replaced the use of pins with those other objects, what are they called..."

"Blorm," Ky said. "They're called Blorm."

"Oh, right. In any case, thinking someone other than Sable can win is unrealistic. I've heard his inner circle is already singing his praises."

"That proves how ignorant the pro-Massiners really are," Nibby said.

"Why would you say that?" Ahlis questioned.

"Because they've ignored Ky's EALF rating."

As the dead of night approached, the Sterlings' voices lowered to a whisper. Without them realising, their discussions had begun to resemble more of a covert meeting of the highest secrecy than a family reunion.

"Why would they ignore his rating?"

"Because his reading was not official and so has been supressed."

"Is that true?" Ahlis asked.

"Yep," Ky said. "I don't trust those Elders with my blood."

Ahlis shrugged. "But who cares if it's unofficial, it's still a reading. What was it anyway?"

Nibby grinned. "Over sixty percent. That's higher than Sable's fifty-eight percent. So as you can see, ensuring Dom's reading is the highest rating among Defenders will keep the pro-Massine voters faithful."

"I guess that makes sense," Ahlis said. "After all, Ky's rating is nine percent higher than the Earth human average and three percent higher than the Polmarian average. Is that really your rating?"

Ky shrugged. "The electronic probes which scanned me during that trial, last Mynor, were unofficial. They could have been faulty for all I know. What matters is that I've qualified for tomorrow's race without any official reading ever being mandated."

"But I don't get it," Ahlis said. "Why don't you just take the reading once and for all? It can't just be your lack of trust in Polmarian Elders."

"There's more to being a Defender than a high EALF rating. What about honour? Just look at Sable. His rating may be high, but he has been swayed by the pro-Massiners."

"Maybe we shouldn't worry so much about Sable. I've heard the EALF rating of all Earth humans have increased of late so I'm sure there are others who may pose a threat to the pro-Massiners."

"Where did you hear that?" Loush asked.

"My nomadic tribe said our EALF increase is the reason Knowledge Base leaders have been monitoring us so closely."

"Well no matter what you've heard," Loush said. "I'm just glad your tribe let you come home before the race."

"Even though they don't think Ky is a chance to even finish, they knew I wouldn't miss it for the world."

Ky pursed his lips. "Thanks, I think."

Ahlis grinned. "You may soon get to be Defender, but you'll always be my brother first. Just take care of yourself out there and I know you'll finish."

Ky stood and poured a glass of water, staring out at the darkened porch. "Thanks sis, but tomorrow we race on Blorm. No one can escape its pain."

"That may be," Nibby said, grasping Ky's hand. "But now you have to sleep."

"Take care my dears," Loush said, knowing it would be the last time she would see her son until after the race. "You'll always be my baby boy."

Ky turned for a hug. "I'll be fine mum." But in spite of his words, he knew that if the race was used to determine both Earth's top two Defenders *and* the Massine debate, the pressure would be immense and the effects of the unforgiving Blorm would increase exponentially.

Ky didn't feel tired but knew he'd have to wake early to both prepare and arrive by the concluding stages of the Massine debate. He was told that if the votes decreed, each potential Defender will be asked to represent the side of the argument that coincides with their own beliefs. At this point the top five hundred Defenders from each side, based on EALF ratings and qualification positions, will be invited to compete in the Defenders' Race.

"Tomorrow's the day," he said, peering out of his bedroom window. Outside, the moon peeled away from the clouds and, for a moment, shone onto his face.

"Come over here," Nibby said, taking hold of his shaky hands. "It'll be okay. You'll be great."

Ky leaned past Nibby, sniffing her honey-scented hair. His senses tingled, and nerves steadied, as his mind drifted to the day they first met.

Nibby looked into his eyes and quivered as their lips met. The memory of their first touch was everlastingly theirs. Though tomorrow was filled with uncertainty, tonight Nibby and Ky could not feel any safer.

XXXVI.

Countless Façades had been activated. The entire world was in attendance. The same purpose built Constructor building was once again host as yet another Massine debate concluded. This time, the number of people supporting the acquisition of Massine knowledge had grown to one third, while the anti-Massine supporters counted for just over half, leaving more than fifteen percent undecided. Though enough support for both sides had forced another vote, this one would be unique for it decides whether to continue the debate, or declare the issue deadlocked whereby a Defender's Race will decide the outcome.

Waiting in the wings of the building's opened room lobby were the potential Defenders. Famous figures like Dom, and newcomers such as Ky, had been instructed to stand on the side of the party representing their own viewpoints for all to see.

Young Marc Drayed stood three metres away from Ky. Although the two had never met, both represented the anti-Massine party.

Mumbles grew as, standing behind Dom, the Polmarian Grand Elder leaned down and whispered. Dom nodded hesitantly.

As tension filled the forum, for what felt like an eternity, the Chairperson finally approached the podium. "Quiet Please!" he said, placing his hand against his ear as he received the transmission. "May we please have quiet."

The onlookers hushed.

"The second set of votes have been finalised," he declared formally. "With a total of two-thirds of the votes it has been decided that a Defenders' Race will decide the final outcome of this Massine debate."

A splattering of conversations broke out.

"Quiet!" repeated the chairperson.

This time, the crowd continued to chatter. The Defenders, however, remained steadfast, displaying the professionalism of a group of people who knew their every move was watched. Unseen to the naked eye, Marc slowed his breathing. The anticipation of his long-awaited chance at victory was becoming a reality.

As the verbal jousting settled, the Chairperson coughed with intent. "Please," he said, raising his hand. "People of Earth and our Polmarian witnesses, thank you for your attendance. Today's voting has officially closed the Massine debate – In one Click, that's just under three hours, from now the Challenge of Defenders will begin."

As the Chairperson lowered his arm a thunderous gong bellowed throughout the Constructor, reverberating through every connected Façade. The entire planet had been informed; the countdown had begun.

Although millions cheered, happy this issue would be over once and for all, Dom's face awash over with iron determination. His steely eyes were ablaze, knowing the result of acquiring Massine knowledge, and the resulting Massine drought protection promised for his town, would come down to him.

After the go-ahead, the Defenders began to methodically shuffle out of the forum. They would not have long to prepare for the persistent countdown, ringing through everyone's transmission, was a constant reminder; this would be the most important Challenge any of them would have ever faced.

XXXVII.

At precisely the same time as Dom and the other Defenders were preparing to enter the arena, a ceremony, quite some distance away, was concluding. The participants of this event were honoured with respect; their silence a tale of their patience.

However, as the formalities finished the graciousness in their demeanour diminished, turning from humble to ferocious. With aggressiveness draped across their dishevelled appearance, and a foul stench spewing from their harsh exterior, each Kryon had begun to ready themselves for the confrontation ahead.

They are Defenders. They live for nothing else.

XXXVIII.

Eleven Clicks remain.

XXXIX.

Everything was in readiness. The preparations carried out by the industrious ground staff were almost complete. Barring two or three workmen, scurrying around the outskirts of the track surface, this perfectly designed feat of engineering was ready to host the most celebrated Defenders' Race in Earth human history.

Showcasing the grandeur of modern day technology, this gigantic stadium had been built only a few hundred kilometres east of Dominique Sable's African birthplace, Tousol. Since day-break, this normally deserted region, known as Zambia, had become a hive of activity as spectators, arriving in the tens of thousands, scuttled across her dirty primordial landscape and into the pristine setting of the amphitheatre.

After her brief meeting with the Elders, Loush, along with Ahlis and Nibby, also stepped into the stadium. Though initially astonished at the splendour surrounding them, the Sterling women quickly ushered themselves to their pre-designated area.

As midday arrived, Loush continued to cover her ears as each attempt to talk was met with loud energetic cheers from the surrounding spectators. Their joyous grins, evident mostly in the sun-reddened faces of youngsters like Katie and Jack, could not be contained. "I can't believe one of our teachers is a Defender," Katie whispered as the teenage pair stood hand in hand.

"I know," Jack said. "Did you ever meet him?"

"I wish," Katie said, as a flirtatious smile emerged, much to Jack's chagrin.

With Nibby and Ahlis inhaling the atmosphere from the fifth row, Loush scanned the crowd. "I've heard all the rhetoric, but I've never understood why the Defenders have to risk their lives."

Just then, a subtle beep sounded.

Faces, from the Façade, suddenly projected high above the stands before blending into the mass of people below, bringing the total spectators to one billion.

The crowd, whose first row elevated one metre above the track, started a chant as the Defenders, via a darkened tunnel beneath the stadium, emerged. Among them was a sluggish Ky.

"Look guys!" Nibby said. "There he is!"

Ahlis' smile disappeared. "He looks so tired."

"Don't worry. I'm sure he's subdued because of all those adrenaline-filled guys surrounding him."

"I hope you're right. It's just that if my heart is pounding, I don't know why he isn't jumping out of his skin."

As the Sterlings watched from just a few rows behind his lane, Ky marched towards his starting bay, stared blankly at his surroundings, before brushing over the crescent-shaped scar on his face.

Ahlis pursed her lips. "Did you see that? Are we sure he's ready?"

Though no response was forthcoming, Nibby grasped Ahlis' hand as the pair peered down the line of Defenders.

"Booo!" they heard one of the few unruly spectators yell. "You pro-Massine Defenders suck!"

Once again, Loush covered her ears. She fixed her sights firmly on Ky while *he* stared towards the finish, eighty-eight metres away. As the searing sun speckled his body with beads of sweat, a nervous announcer, wearing a graduation-like shawl and standing hundreds of meters away, continued his introduction from a make-shift podium hovering over the track's centre.

Though he spoke of race specifics, it was Dominique Sable, standing closest to the announcer, who drew most of the crowd's jeers and adoration. After finishing the last of his meditative mantras, from within his own starting area, Dom gazed up beyond the overflowing stands. He was quick to sharpen his focus into the Façade, to where he thought the Polmarian Grand Elder would be. *He'd better keep his promise.* Shaking away the distraction, he slapped his legs as if waking them from a deep sleep.

Though the Polmarian did appear in the Façade, from within the safety of the hidden stone building, it was not Dom he watched as two lanes away a poised Marc Drayed stood. Oozing with the same intimidation he'd exhibited since their first encounter, Marc had unknowingly caused the Grand Elder's confidence in Dom's superiority to waver.

"Drayed must not win," he whispered, turning to his long-time collaborator who remained hidden among the shadows of the room's dim lighting. "The Earthlings must have Massine. The alternative is not an option."

As the collaborator stood and slipped the Grand Elder a confidential transcript, Marc's head began to sway to his internal tempo of old-fashioned rhythm and blues. But after another beep rang violently through the arena he, and the other Defenders, stopped moving.

The sound, louder than the previous ones, startled even the announcer, causing him to halt his introduction. "Um, Uh," he stammered excitedly. "Only three ticks remain."

As he persisted to explain why the use of Blorm had become mandatory, Jack's ears pricked up. "I didn't know they were forced to run over the shape-shifters," he said to Katie.

"How could you not know? The Elders have been talking about it for ages."

"I guess I've been thinking about other things."

"Yeah. Like becoming a Defender."

"Of course. Even you have that dream. But I just didn't think I would *have* to run over the Blorm."

"Why should that make a difference?"

"Because of what they can do. Everyone knows their razor-sharp daggers can assimilate into the flesh of anything that moves. But I also read they inject their victims with toxins that, unless you stop moving, will result in permanent paralysis."

"Since when did you do so much reading?"

"I dunno. Lately, my mind's been like a sponge, everything seems to stick."

"Ha. That's definitely not you."

Jack grinned. "Yeah. I just wish I was wrong about the shape-shifters," he said, pointing midway down the track to where patches of wriggling Blorm, constrained beneath an opaque barrier, were trying to escape.

As another beep sounded, the spectator's hushed, allowing the announcer to be heard. "...Contact with the Blorm is inevitable. It is for these reasons we accept the outcome of this race, to decide the Massine debate, as final. Moreover, it is now the top two finishers who will receive automatic selection into the next Challenge. So, with the countdown almost complete, I bid you all a good race. Defenders, we honour each of you."

The announcer lowered his head and anxiously gave the all-clear to reveal the Blorm. Instantly, the podium drifted over the exposed shape-shifters and towards the opposite grandstand. Once past the elongated finishing line he shuffled off to join the other dignitaries.

With only the Defenders left on the arena, and following another beep, ungainly noises burst from a number of Defenders. Their anxiety cannot be hidden.

Just then, a loud gong crashes again, silencing everyone. The sound, still echoing through the enormous chrome amphitheatre, sends trepidation through the spectators. Although most remain silent, there are others who cannot be restrained. *"You're gonna die!"* can be heard by one heckler, yelling to anyone who would listen.

Suddenly, a screen parading close-up views of many of the one-thousand Defenders, floats over each lane. The crowd roars as the Defenders' faces, both menacing and fearful, are shown.

After pausing on the centre lanes of Sable and Drayed, a kneeling Ky, more than two-hundred Defenders away, was left undisturbed to repeat his pre-race motto. *Start fast. Gain momentum. Keep moving after impact, no matter what.*

Though his prayer was silent, he was quick to sense the hulk in the next lane turn his head. *"Victory is MINE!"*, grumbled the pro-Massine Defender.

He continued to jabber. However, with no reaction forthcoming the frustrated giant flared his nostrils, snorted and faced his own lane. He would not speak again.

Loush, who saw the episode with the hulk, watched as Ky lifted himself off the dirt. A fluttering heart had her grip on Ahlis tighten. *My son will be okay,* she prayed, *he has to be.*

Moments of painful silence passed before the announcer's final message, spoken from the safety of his viewing area, was delivered.

For the benefit of the onlookers, another gong bellowed. Ten dats remain.

XL.

Each Defender secures themselves into position, waiting for their invisible barrier to vanish.

Ky crouches. He takes a deep breath and closes his eyes.

A blurry image materializes.

His eyes burst open. *Is that...*

With his secret revealing itself, a sense of calm surfaces.

Beep! Three dats remain.

Though he freezes all movement, his body quivers.

Beep!

All Defenders recoil.

Dom twitches.

Marc's eyes widen.

Beep!

Silence envelopes mankind.

The crash of the final gong sends the Defenders exploding forward synchronously, igniting the crowd's roars.

A few Defenders, including the hulk, jump the start and are met with an invisible barrier, preventing them from entering their lane. Though most regroup to launch themselves down the track, the half-step disadvantage will be too great for many to make-up.

Landing his first stride on the pebbly dirt track, Ky uses his secret vision to reduce his downward force, anticipating the position of the clustering Blorm.

Due to this shorter first stride, he is one of the first to strike the ground, slapping his bare foot down while evading the charging Blorm. But despite his speed, this manoeuvre sees him trail the seventy-four men tied for the lead.

The crowd's voice changes, rhythmically chanting with the tempo of the leaders.

With no time to waste, Ky's fourth and fifth stride are propelled with greater force, causing his body to extend fully upright.

Just in front, twenty Defenders take the outright lead. Included among them are Marc and Dom whose strong thighs and quick tendons elevate them, and six others, even further ahead. Marc winces, charging into the heart of the attacking Blorm as his calm exterior vanishes.

Having already been exposed to numerous slashes, the poisons begin to halt his progress. But not the only one unscathed, the other leading Defenders also slow.

On his ninth step, Ky too falters in an attempt to avoid the next cluster of Blorm. Though the slip is imperceptible to anyone unaware of his flawless striding pattern, it is the inability to regain balance which sees his next step lunge towards another group of the shape-shifters.

Without time to do anything except react, Ky lengthens his stride in mid-air, drifting clear of the stabbing blades.

Though any mishap is averted, the alarm bells sound in his head. Not even one third of the way into the race and he has already been exposed to more Blorm than in his entire simulation, putting all future attempts to catch the leading Defenders in jeopardy.

XLI.

Most Defenders had learned the race can be broken up into stages. The first has a Defender accelerate fast enough to run over the first cluster of Blorm without too much damage. The second, where the bulk of the shape-shifters gather, sees a Defender move stealth-like in trying to slow the circulating poisons. If achieved, those with strong will-power can finish the third phase without permanent damage. But with none of these men ever encountering the Blorm before, much confidence had been left at the start.

The hulk, who grunts his way back into contention, sniffs an opportunity to become the pro-Massiners hero. After seeing how the surrounding Defenders are plagued by their stumbles, he knows his game plan must change. Ignoring the dangerous second phase, his next stride lands with such brute force that the ground shakes, sending him past Ky and closer to the leaders.

Likewise, his subsequent step also comes down with the same power. Though a Blorm cuts into the webbing next to one of his toes a smile, imagining himself the winner, creeps over his face.

Confidently, the hulk slams his next stride down with greater speed. Unfortunately for him, a cluster of Blorm, who are made aware of his movements, shift into action. By trading stealth for power, a few shape-shifters skewer his heel, ripping their way into the muscle. Despite his pre-race drugs providing short-term immunity to pain, it did not take long for the five centimetre-long Blorm to thrust into his bone while slicing his tendon in two. Following another injection of poison, the massive man plummets face-first on the Blorm, squealing as his body begins to convulse. The torture of punctured eyes, along with the high dose of toxins, is too great.

Instantly, a hovering camera captures the squirting blood. While gasps make their way through the stadium, and the Blorm continues to inject even more poisons into his blood-shot eyes, the giant ceases all movement.

Horrified, Loush glances cautiously at the nearby Defenders only to see many of them, lying like the hulk, sprawled across their lanes. She hopes it's not too late for their lack of movement to allow the poisons to dissipate. But even if they regain mobility she knows that, although they have travelled two thirds of the way down the track in quick succession, the last phase will take much longer and cause even more agony.

Sixty-two meters in and both Dom and Marc stagger into this last phase. Each knows the only thing preventing circulating poisons from paralysing them is to summon a new form of energy to keep moving. They have to maximise their EALF.

But seventy-four metres into the race sees Marc come to a standstill. He crouches with hands pressed hard against buckling thighs. As a number of Blorm wiggle towards him, the image of the hologram Defender, from his first Defender's class, flashes into his thoughts.

Hunched alongside, Dom writhes in pain. *Come on Sable. Keep going. I have to finish. I have to move. I have to move NOW!* Standing upright, he surges towards the finish, negating the poisons which traverse his body.

Marc catches sight of his nemesis and twitches, as if jump starting his reactions. Though he has no more to physically give, with only a few metres to go his desire to be number one kicks in. *This is my chance.*

The crowd roars.

Though these two men were two of only a handful left standing, the latest cheers are for another Defender; one they have never seen nor heard of before.

Ky Sterling, with a body dried with sweat, crosses the finish. Stopping shy of the grandstand, he turns back and stares blankly at the starting line, grimacing in the direction of his family.

The roars continue as Marc, using emotional strength to gain a renewed energy, crosses the line in second place, thus identifying Earth's top two Defenders and, more importantly, ending the Massine Challenge.

A few dats later Dom steps across the line to a standing ovation.

As the final few Defenders finish, a mass of medics stream onto the arena, disabling the Blorm and assisting the immobile Defenders to the sidelines for treatment.

Being informed of what had occurred, Dom limps towards Ky and bows, as is custom. The elder statesman unexpectedly embraces Ky and whispers. "I don't know who you are or how you finished so fast, but for your sake, I hope it was no fluke. Our future may rely on this result."

Though also making his way over, Marc is clearly irritated. *How could an unknown beat me?*

He scowls, ushers away any treatment, and kneels begrudgingly. Opening his eyes, he notices Ky's feet were free from any major gashes. With his own feet rife with dry blood from numerous abrasions, Marc will not soon forget what he has just seen.

XLII.

The crowd was still buzzing as the cognisant Defenders sat scattered beyond the finish line. They, with the spectators, stared in disbelief as the gigantic monitor flashed up an image.

Ky had completed the first ever race over Blorm in an astonishing twenty-eight dats. It was more than ten dats ahead of Marc, and four dats faster than any other Earth human had finished a Defenders' Race before.

Seeing the ground staff finish their assembly of a make-shift podium next to the disorientated Ky, the announcer straightened his shawl and stepped out of the dignitaries viewing area. But no sooner had he arrived where the Defenders congregated did another man, donned in his customary top-hat, tap the announcer on the shoulder, exposing a clover shaped tattoo on his wrist. "Your job here is done."

The announcer stared at the insignia. "As you wish Elder Regent."

Though Mr Regent took pride in his new position, in hearing the cheers for the anti-Massiners victory he wondered whether he had done the right thing in assisting the Polmarian Grand Elder in the first place.

His eyes encircled the stadium. After a glimmer of a smile he activated the external speaker of his transmission, climbed the podium, and waited for the cheers to settle.

"Defenders," he bellowed. "I would like to take this opportunity to say thanks. You have performed with honour. Your families must be so...must be so..."

"What's the matter?" asked Ky, beginning to revel in an endorphin rush.

"I don't know," he replied, placing his hand to his ear. "I'm getting some kind of interference with my transmission."

At that moment, a piercing squeal shot throughout the arena. Mr Regent dropped to one knee as the crowd became mute, covering their own ears.

One man, however, knew the significance of this disruption. Seated within the confines of the stone building, the Polmarian Grand Elder became filled with fear. "Oh no," he grumbled, "it's beginning sooner than I thought."

The lack of response from his collaborator, seated next to him, did not bode well for the Grand Elder. "I have to go," he added. "Since the Earthlings have lost the right to protect themselves with Massine, we are now all at risk."

XLIII.

"What's going on?" Dom asked, grabbing hold of Mr Regent only to see beads of sweat wash over his forehead.

"Nothing!" Mr Regent snapped, shaking himself free while brushing the speckled dirt from his silk pants. "It's probably just interference with the Polmarians."

"Don't tell me that Regent. Something's up. I can see it in your eyes."

Despite his stubbornness, an uneasy sense of deja-vu drifted through Mr Regent. "Well I guess this is similar to..."

"Similar to what?" asked Ky, standing alongside Dom.

"It's like the time we were chosen."

As Ky's memory flashed back to that childhood moment, a droning hum sounded throughout each transmission on Earth.

"This has gone too far," Dom said. "Ask him what's going on. Ask the Polmarian Grand Elder."

"I can't," said Mr Regent. "My external translator is still not working."

However, it wasn't just his, but every transmission, which had failed. Moments later, a deep mechanical voice, heard by all, began to speak.

"The Nameless have been challenged – Prepare your Defenders immediately."

After those words, the interference disappeared. With Mr Regent's earpiece re-connecting, he quickly climbed the podium. "Please stay calm and don't take any notice of those words. I'm sure it's someone's idea of a joke."

Suddenly, a tremendous thud sounded. Unlike the previous sounds leading up to the Massine Challenge, this heavy drum beat reverberated violently throughout every human populated planet.

Adding to his deja-vu, Mr Regent could see the large figure of the Polmarian Grand Elder approach. Waving off any assistance, the

Grand Elder depressed a button hidden on the side of his cane, disabling the external speaker of Mr Regent's Translator and enabling his own.

"Fellow humans," he said, as Mr Regent quickly sat among the Defenders. "I am sorry, but what you have heard is no joke."

The crowd's murmurs rose.

"There are Nyrolacs who have always disagreed with your selection into the Knowledge Base. But no matter what happens, know we are here to support you."

"Support us from what?" asked Dom.

The Polmarian Grand Elder firmed the grip on his cane and glared down at Dom. "The people of Earth have just been challenged by the Kryon."

"Huh?" griped Marc, pushing his way to the front of the Defenders. "Whachya talkin' bout?"

"We are yet to learn the details, but what I do know is that these Kryon have labelled you as the *Nameless*. It is a term given to any Nyrolac undeserved of a name and..."

"And what?" Marc uttered as the Grand Elder's hesitation ignited further concerns among the Defenders.

"...And is used against Nyrolac's targeted for Knowledge Base removal."

"Can they do that?" asked Dom.

"The respect for the Kryon runs deep, but we will all learn more about what they can and cannot do shortly. For now, please remain in the stadium or close to a transmission and I will be in touch."

A second drum sounds, even louder than the first.

"Humans," said the Grand Elder, knowing the ears of all man-kind were listening. "Ten Clicks remain."

The Grand Elder turned, beckoned Mr Regent to follow, and walked towards one of the exits discretely placed beneath the stadium.

"What just happened?" mumbled Mr Regent, as the two moved off, leaving the Defenders, and a stunned crowd, behind. "Did I make a mistake by helping you?"

"Mistake! The only mistake is that you Earthlings lost any chance of using Massine as protection."

Realising ten Clicks equated to twenty-eight hours in the old-tongue, Mr Regent hastened his words. "What's happening in ten

Clicks?"

"There's no time to explain. You'll learn with everyone else."

"Then tell me," Mr Regent said, pointing to a cluster of grey clouds approaching fast from beyond each grandstand. "What's that?"

Sensing the Polmarian's hesitation, Mr Regent lowered his head.

"Hey! There is no time to despair. After all, there is a reason I appointed you into one of the two available Earth Elder positions."

"Two?" Mr Regent contemplated. "Who is the – Oh no. It can't be!"

"Don't concern yourself with her. There is another task I need from you."

"Very well. What will you have me do?"

With the pair moving away from prying ears, the expressionless Polmarian leant down to Mr Regent and whispered.

"But why can't you do that yourself?" Mr Regent asked.

"Because my presence is required elsewhere. I must meet with them."

"With whom?"

"The Obzoovers," the Polmarian said. "I have no choice but to speak to the Obzoovers."

Glossary

Universal Time Measurement

1 Dat ≈ 1 second
1 Tick is 100 Dats ≈ 1.7 minutes
1 Click is 100 Ticks ≈ 2.8 hours
1 Mynor is 1000 Clicks ≈ 16 weeks
1 Neg is 88 Mynors ≈ 27.9 years
An Age occurs every Cleanse ≈ 36,000 Negs

The Translator: a technology allowing spoken words and expressions to be interpreted and vocalized in the language of the listener. Though sometimes audible, messages can also be sent directly between thoughts.

Massine: a technology that can control explosions of any size by harnessing and releasing energy emissions found flowing through the universe.

Knowledge Base: a membership of evolved civilisations containing species such as Obzoovers, Kryons and Humans. Many catalogued planets, like Polmar, Cril, Zordac and Earth, are home to virtually all of these civilisations.

Nyrolac: the collective term used for the members of the Knowledge Base.

Neg: the average age a Nyrolac reproduction can occur.

Cleanse: a random cataclysmic event with the potential to wipe out an entire species. This may change the average reproductive length of all Nyrolacs and thus alter the measurement of a single Neg of time.

EALF: an acronym meaning **E**xpert in the **A**rt of **LiF**e and is a tool developed by the Knowledge Base to measure the evolutionary potential combined with the current generic make-up of a single living being.

Lest: a method of swapping energy by breaking matter into its smallest atomic form. Devised by the Knowledge Base, its primary use is that of instant teleportation.

Façade: the technology allowing participants to be visually and verbally present, by hologram, in a predetermined area without ever having to physically attend.

Two

Protecting the Hominidae

XLIV.

"I should have listened to him," Loush uttered, having just received a private transmission.

"Listened to whom?" Nibby yelled, struggling to be heard in among the splattering of panicked voices.

"Yeah mum," Ahlis said. "Who are you talking about?"

"Since the day we were chosen Elric had reservations about joining the Knowledge Base. I always thought it was paranoia, but now it appears his instincts may have been right."

"We're all just exhausted from the Massine Challenge," Ahlis said, caressing Loush's trembling hand. "We have no idea what this Challenge is really all about. I'm sure it'll become clear when we get home."

"Oh, I won't be going home," Loush said, her eyes still glued to Ky, who stood in front of the far grandstand.

"You're not making any sense mum," Ahlis said. "Let's go."

"I'm sorry guys, I'm needed elsewhere."

"Mum!" Ahlis said. "What are you talking about? Are you okay?"

Loush winced. As an intense pain shot through her left forearm she gestured for Ahlis and Nibby to move closer. "The Polmarian Elders are making it official."

"Making what official?" Ahlis asked.

Loush pursed her lips and exposed the newly engraved clover shaped tattoo on her wrist. "They've made me an Elder."

"I knew it," Ahlis said, staring at the symbolic mark. "That's great mum."

"I'm not so sure," Loush said, tapping her newly modified transmission device embedded snuggly within her ear. "I've just received my first order. All Earth Elders have to assemble on Polmar, in a restricted building they call Pretta."

"Okay, so let's go." Ahlis said.

"I'm afraid I have to go alone."

"Oh," Ahlis sighed.

"It doesn't sit well with me either," Loush said. "Your father was right to feel the way he did. Come to think of it, much of my generation had felt the same way too."

"What did they feel?" Nibby asked, puzzled.

Loush inhaled, lifting her gaze to the cloud engulfed Façade on top of the far grandstand. "Elric, and the others, believed all us Earth humans were being watched very closely by those who wanted to harm us."

Ahlis placed one arm around Loush's waist. "You're tired mum. Come home and rest first. Then go to Polmar."

"The Grand Elder suggested we stay here," Nibby said. "We should wait."

"No!" Ahlis snapped. "We need to go home and stick together."

"I'm sorry Ahlis," Loush said, still staring at the mass of strange clouds. "Now's not the time for comfort. We need to learn everything we can about the Kryon."

Following Loush's line of sight, Nibby also stared at Ky. "And what about..."

Loush wiped her eyes. "He'll be taken away. My job is to find out about these Kryon. I just have no idea where to begin."

"I think I can help," Nibby said, deep in thought.

"How?"

"I think the Polmarian Elders who raised me used to tell stories, too scary for a kid to hear, which they forbade us from telling any Earth human."

"Stories?" Loush asked. "You mean about the Kryon?"

"Yes," Nibby nodded, "amongst others."

Loush cringed. "Bastards. They probably knew this was going to happen all along."

"Maybe," Nibby said. "I remember them saying the Kryon are an extremely brutal species who won't stop until they get what they want."

"Oh great," Ahlis said, sensing Nibby's trepidation. "What else do you remember?"

Nibby shrugged. "Not much else about the Kryon."

"Hmm," Loush said, sensing the growing restlessness among the nearby spectators. "I want you girls to head home. It may be the safest place right now."

"But mum..." Ahlis said.

"I'll be okay. I'm meeting someone who better have the answers. I may not know much now, but one way or another I'm going to find out."

XLV.

The Sun was fading quickly as unnatural cloud cover forced the early onset of twilight.

"Someone has to do something," shouted Marc, covering his ears from the persisting cries of young children.

"Mr Regent asked us to remain here – in the stadium," Dom said, having remained seated on the edge of the track's surface.

"But why? We need to know what's going on!"

"Marc's right," Ky said. "We all have the same questions that need answering."

"Don't speak for me, cheat!" Marc said, unwilling to dignify Ky with the courtesy of eye contact.

"Okay," Dom said, glaring at Marc. "We all want to know who these Kryon are."

"No!" Marc said. "I want to find out why they want us removed, and why now!"

"Yeah!" barked another Defender. "And what does this Knowledge Base removal even mean? I mean, do we even have to accept this Challenge?"

Dom's eyes widened. "I'm pretty sure that mechanical voice said we must accept."

"Hang on," Marc said, "Does that mean there will be another race? Look at us, we're in no shape for that!"

"Then what happens if we decline?" asked yet another Defender.

Dom shrugged. After scanning both grandstands he tapped his ear twice, activating a highly confidential frequency on his internal transmission device. "We all have valid questions, but these people are scared. They want answers too. Mr Regent may have left but the world needs someone to listen to."

He cleared his parched throat. The sound echoed through the arena and the tuned-in transmissions. Instantly, a hush fell over the needy onlookers.

"It's time for all of us to go home," he announced. "Don't be afraid, but stay close to your transmissions – We will get through this together, just like we always have."

Dom raised one arm and clenched his fist in a tradition started by the earliest Earth Defenders. "We will protect you no matter what." As his eyes encircled the crowd, he glanced up at the Façade and deactivated his transmission. "I just hope we don't have to," he whispered.

Ky waved blindly in the direction of his family. A young girl, who stood two rows in front of Nibby, caught sight of the affectionate signal. Although not designed for her, as if oblivious to the situation at hand, she blew a kiss in return.

Ky turned back to see Dom, cupping one ear while beckoning the nearby Defenders in his vicinity. "We have to go," he said. "The word has been given. Follow me."

As Dom headed towards one of many underground passages beneath the stadium, the crowd began to shuffle out as well.

Ky peered back up at the grandstand overhanging the starting line, but he still could not locate his family.

Being hurried along, he, Marc and the other mobile Defenders followed Dom whose hand still covered one ear. The darkened path, surrounded by large stones filled with mounds of mortar, was once used as an emergency access point for the workmen who created the arena. If it were not for a narrowing perspex ceiling, allowing the stadium's light to enter, the passage would be completely black.

"This way," Dom said, taking a sudden turn away from anything familiar.

"Where are we going?" Marc asked, one step behind. "It's getting pretty dark."

"We're going to the Safe Room. It's where we'll start our preparations."

"Preparations! For what? You know we need time to heal."

The lines on Dom's face tightened. Although not replying to Marc, he whispered into his transmission. "But they won't recover in time."

"What did you say?" Ky asked, following single-file down the narrow path, a few steps further behind.

"Nothing!" Dom replied, trying to decipher any cryptic meaning he may be over-hearing in his transmission. *Did the Polmarians hide this from us, or did they not know themselves?*

As lights on the stone walls began to illuminate, Dom was informed the Safe Room was near. "Look!" he said, pointing to an unassuming symbol imprinted on the wall.

"What does that mean?" grumbled Marc.

"Be patient," Dom said. "I was told to follow the lights above the symbol, and that's exactly what we're doing."

"Who told you that and why aren't they here with us?"

Dom was silent.

"Answer me Sable!"

"Shh! I'm listening to a recording. The Elders have been summoned elsewhere and your voice is distracting me."

"So, what now?" Marc added, turning to gain support from his fellow Defenders. "Are we just gonna keep walking through this maze? Some of us need serious fixing."

"We have to trust the Elders," Dom replied.

"And we need treatment."

"Marc's right," added another Defender.

Dom groaned, feeling the growing dissention, as he started into the darkened passage. "Look over there!" he said, halting his steps, causing the other Defenders to stop in line. The group could see a flickering light growing rapidly, radiating many times brighter than the dimly lit passage. Dom's sensors heightened. No longer did he need to move towards the light for as this new flame was fast approaching them.

XLVI.

The heat from Nechor, Polmar's star and source of light, seared through the Polmarian atmospheric layer. Despite some regions sweltering, the bustling hub of Enness was kept temperate, for the most part, by its surrounding mountains. As balmy conditions, together with the frigidity of Enness' soil, made underground construction favourable, the Polmarians had built their crowning jewel on the city's outskirts.

Birthed deep beneath the surface this sacred piece of Polmarian architecture, shaped like a swollen ice-cream cone, extended over one-hundred meters above ground.

Named after the Polmarian word for *guardian* this structure, known as Pretta, was designed with the ability to grow and shrink with the needs of its occupants. The expandable perspex panels, planted from a single seed, was comprised of a strengthening agent discovered during one of many reverse-engineering attempts conducted on Blorm. The constitution of these organic panels also reacts to Nechor's heat, tinting both sides of the glass and cooling those within.

From inside, each panel is embedded with a row of seating bays that concertina outward on command. Though the upper most section is reserved for Façade transmissions, the abundance of vertical and horizontal seating sees Pretta hosting the most important of Polmarian forums.

A small cave, built into its diminutive base, is the sole access point permitting arrivals and departures via Lest transportation. Although frequent visitors to Pretta can be teleported directly to their designated seat, unfamiliar guests queue for dispatch to their bays by use of a clunky old hovercraft device.

Affixed on top of the cave is a silver platform used to chair any proceedings. This, along with the cave and the vacant dome ceiling, are the only areas kept free of obstruction.

"Look at this place," said Mr Johansen, the first of the Earth Elders to arrive. "I've never seen anything like it."

Donning a wide brimmed grey hat, this plump individual clambered his way onto the hovercraft and ascended past the rows and rows of never before seen exotic human civilisations. *So, this is what our future selves look like. There must be thousands of them, and each so different from the Polmarians.*

The steadfast Hominidae sat silently, watching the seldom seen Earthling and observing how his crooked nose sat with not-so-much as a gap between it and his gaping mouth.

As another handful of Earth Elders arrived, joining Mr Johansen in his seating bay half way up Pretta, each noticed how the yellow panels near the cave became dark-green as they ascended, creating a shadowy haze in the dome ceiling.

"It must be hot outside," Mr Johansen said, "and with the heat generated from all these humans, it's no wonder the panels are changing."

"Huh?" said one of his fellow Elders.

"Well heat rises, so I surmise that the higher we are, and the hotter it is outside, the darker the panels will become."

The Earth Elder seated next to Mr Johansen rolled his eyes, not caring much for his superfluous facts.

"Who's that?" Mr Johansen said, pointing to a man emerging on the silvery platform below.

"Thank you for attending on such short notice," announced the thin, almost rubbery looking, man draped in a white cloak. "Most of us know why we are here and, since we are short on time, please excuse me if I cut through the formalities."

After taking his seat on the solitary chair placed in the platform's centre the man continued. "For those of you who do not know, I am one of the Polmarian Head Educators and will be chairing this forum."

Although the majority of the onlookers remained silent, Mr Johansen and the Earth Elders muttered among themselves.

"Earthlings," announced the Chairperson. "Being that you are new to this forum, I must ask you to refrain from any chatter unless spoken to. This rule applies to everyone and with Pretta's panels swelling to near capacity I'm sure there are many questions to be discussed –

Now if there are no objections, and seeing all the dignitaries have arrived, I shall begin."

Although the Earth human contingent hushed, Mr Johansen whispered, angry two of the twelve expected Earth Elders were missing. "Where's Sterling?!"

"Shh," said a voice originating behind his seating bay. "Your irritating voice is echoing in every direction."

Mr Johansen held up his hand apologetically.

The Chairperson cleared his throat and, after receiving a silent transmission, removed his hand from his ear. "Welcome to all Hominidae. It is noted that at least one leading Elder and Educator has arrived to represent *their* human civilisation. I acknowledge the presence of the Elder and Educator from the planet Cril, the planet in the Goliath system which shares both human and Kryon inhabitants."

Nods arose from the row of seating bays directly behind Mr Johansen, the same area containing the people who scolded him only moments ago.

"I am especially happy that the Zordacians have also arrived. Thank you."

A single unified head bow followed, this time originating from the bays opposite to the Earth Elders. Mr Johansen could see the nodding humans dwarf those nearby. He was beginning to feel the gravity of this forum.

"As we are aware," announced the Chairperson, "The Kryon issued an inter-species Defender's Race Challenge against the Earthlings. Although refusal for them is not an option, the rest of us have a choice to make. So, before Pretta's Façade is enabled, I would like to..."

The rustic sound of two large metal objects colliding echoed through Pretta as one of her seating bays grew, sinking deeper into the expanding tiles.

"Who is this latecomer?" demanded the Chairperson, enabling the hovercraft to rise. "Ah. Elder Sterling, I presume."

Embarrassed, Loush fumbled her way over the laps of the other Earth Elders and took her seat next to a frowning Mr Johansen. "You're late," he accused.

"Mr Regent was supposed to escort me in," Loush whispered to Mr. Johansen. "Where is he?"

"Shh," snapped Mr Johansen, showing little sympathy for her tardiness. "His business does not concern you."

Loush sank low into her seat. "So, have the other humans told us how to get out of this Challenge?" she asked Mr. Johansen.

"The Chairperson said refusal is not an option."

"What?" said Loush.

"Please be quiet," said Mr. Johansen. "Don't you know, we're not supposed to speak yet."

"But with so many other civilisations here surely we can come up with a way to refuse?"

Mr Johansen turned his back to Loush. She huffed, unimpressed with his snub, as gawking eyes watched her tie the loose strands of hair back into a pony tail.

"Don't give up on your questions so easily Elder Sterling," announced the Chairperson.

Loush pressed her back against the seat and eyed the Chairperson curiously.

"Don't be alarmed," he added. "Only you can hear me. So be persistent and know there are those who will support you far more than your colleague ever will."

With Loush hiding her grin, she and Mr Johansen were rocked back in their seats as a sudden thud shook the platform below. Once again, the Chairperson placed his hand over his ear.

"I understand," he mumbled before clearing his throat again. "As I was saying, before we proceed any further we must be reminded that an inter-species challenge against the Hominidae is rare. As such, I have just been informed this forum is to be opened to the public sooner rather than later. We will refrain from any further dialogue until all Hominidae is here to listen."

With that, the Chairperson tapped his transmission, activating the Façade which filled the gap between the upper seating bays and the dome ceiling. Instantly, countless three-dimensional images emerged.

Loush's eyes encircled this upper area, trying to distinguish between the sea of blurry faces.

"Good," said the Chairperson. "Dignitaries of Pretta, I present to you all Hominidae."

XLVII.

The tunnel darkened again.

"Hey!" Marc said, pushing forward. "Where did dat der flicker go? I'm sure that was a torch or flame or something we just saw."

"Be still," Dom said, holding his position at the front of the queue of Defenders.

"There it is again." Marc said.

"Yes, I see it," Dom said, seeing the unsteady light resume its approach. "It must be him."

"Who?"

"Our guide."

As their distance to the light shortened, Ky could see the outline of a man emerge. Wearing a hooded black cloak, affixed with a miniature flashlight, the man stopped just shy of the Defenders.

"Get that light out of my eyes!" Ky said, covering his face, as memories of the masked assailant resurfaced.

"Quickly," said the hooded man, dimming the glow. "Follow me."

"You?" Marc said. "Who *are* you?"

The hooded man did not answer, instead moving rapidly into the labyrinth of tunnels.

"Come on then," Dom said, following in pursuit. "Let's go."

"He'd best be taking us to the Safe Room," Marc said, favouring one of his legs. "I don't know how much longer I...uh...I mean, the other guys, can last. The poisons are still in our system."

"Don't concern yourself unnecessarily," said the hooded man, stopping at yet another Safe Room symbol fastened, at eye level, to the walls. "Those most hurt were taken elsewhere for treatment. You will be fine, for now."

Marc sneered.

The hooded man lifted his mask. Although still dark, a beam emitted from the Safe Room symbol and flashed past his retina, beginning a sequence of machine-like crushing sounds.

"This is no Safe Room," Marc said, as the wall in front of him disappeared, leaving an open-door way in its place.

"Come on! In here," said the man, hastily ushering the Defenders inside the darkened room.

"That's a Façade," Dom said, pointing to a hologram draping the entire far wall. "Maybe we're here to find out what's going on."

"But what about our recovery," Marc said, feeling his legs buckle.

"I think we may have to wait," Dom said, his bare feet shuffling across the cold concrete floor.

Suddenly, the room lit up.

"A little warning would be nice," Marc said, rubbing his eyes as the man's face became clear. "Hey! It's you."

"Regent?!" Dom added. "Why did you leave us before?"

"Mr Sable, please step away from the wall."

"What's going on? Why are *you* here now?"

"I have been instructed to assist you. Now please step aside."

No sooner had Dom moved than another crunching sound dissolved the wall containing the Façade, shifting the three-dimensional screen to another of the walls while the new room fastened itself to this one.

"Finally we see the Safe Room," Marc said, taking a seat in one of the cushy leather chairs scattered throughout.

"Looks like you really do need some help," Dom said, taking a seat and plugging into one of the regeneration machines attached to each chair.

"Yeah that's because I didn't cheat."

Ky rolled his eyes.

"Don't worry Ky. He's just jealous," Dom said, turning his attention back to Mr Regent. "Besides, there are more important things going on like knowing why Mr Regent is here, and not the medics."

"I'm here to give you information," said Mr Regent, guiding Ky towards another of the chairs. "Defenders, please plug into your regeneration machine. Your quick recovery is vital."

"Information?" Ky said. "What's going on? Are we supposed to connect to that Façade?"

Mr Regent was silent.

"Dom?" Ky said. "You must know something about this?"

Dom appeared contemplative as more thoughts of the secret communiqués held with Mr Regent flooded his mind.

"He's no closer to understanding than you are!" Marc growled, wriggling as his dirty body suit tarnishing the white leather.

"You are all about to join a forum," said Mr Regent.

"What for?" Marc asked. "I've had enough of forums."

"He's right," said another Defender. "We don't want to sit through any more meetings."

"This forum will provide the information you seek."

"Good," said Ky. "Then we'll get this drama with the Kryon Challenge straightened out once and for all."

Marc glared over at Earth's newest number one Defender. "What would you know cheat?!" he snapped.

"Settle down Marc," Dom said, as his own heavily oxygenated regeneration machine had begun flushing away the metallic taste of blood. "Let's not get angry with each other."

"Don't tell me what to do Sable!"

"Hey Mr Regent," Dom said. "I think we need some medics to calm us all down."

Mr Regent nodded and tapped his transmission. "Send them in."

With the dozen or so of remaining Defenders huddled in close proximity, a handful of medics barged in and flung down a bunch of all-purpose recovery jump suits for the Defenders to wear.

"It's about time!" griped Marc, replacing his stiffening and bloodied body suit with one of the oversized grey tracksuits. "Now give me something to take the edge off."

"He's not the only one," said another Defender. "I can't even feel my left arm."

"You will soon," said Mr Regent. "You're about to receive a special treatment, never used by any of our Defenders before."

With the medics beginning to administer doses of relaxant serum, the tension among many of the Defenders quickly eased. But as one of the medics crept closer to Mr Regent, Ky became alerted.

The medic whispered to Mr Regent and nonchalantly mingled back in among the Defenders. Moments later, Ky's eyes widened as Mr Regent began to slowly back out of the Safe Room.

"What's going on?" Ky said, standing up.

"Please sit," Mr Regent said, gaining the attention of Dom.

"But where are you going?" Dom asked.

"I have somewhere else I need to be. Just remain here and I'll be back before you know it."

"But what about this information?"

"Oh, it won't be long now," said Mr Regent exiting.

Although still attached to his regeneration machine, Ky seemed irritated.

"Are you okay?" Dom asked. "You should be resting."

Ky began to pace up and down. As new blood began to circulate through his body so too did anxiety. "I don't feel right Dom."

Marc smirked. Despite still recovering, he disconnected himself from his own regeneration machine. His heart began to pound as the pent-up frustration of not winning had boiled to the surface, causing any quiet surveillance of Ky to cease.

Marc stood, brushed away the assistance of his medic, and made his way towards Ky. The unhurried approach was not indicative of his fury. His face, however, could not lie.

Marc's lips pressed together and his pupils dilated. Lines on his forehead became prominent as he stepped closer, arriving behind his new nemesis.

Placing one hand on his shoulder, Marc swung Ky around in one motion.

Ky looked up towards the larger figure. "What?!"

Using his periphery, Marc could see the nearby Defenders pretend not to listen, while those further back raised their heads curiously.

"How did you do it?" Marc said.

"Do what?" Ky asked.

"Don't play stupid. You tricked us. You tricked me! You must have. No one could have done what you just did. It's impossible. So, I'll ask again, how did you do it?"

Ky shrugged Marc's grip from his shoulders. He stepped back and peered at the surrounding Defenders. "For those who don't agree with Marc. Thank you for your congratulations and respect."

"Answer me cheat!" Marc said, stepping into Ky who, although his forehead pressed up against Marc's nose, did not move.

Just then, the entrance to the Safe Room cracked, vanishing as it had done before.

The Defenders, who had stood, began to part. "You better stop

Marc," uttered a familiar voice entering the room.

Marc turned. "And why is that?" he said scornfully.

"Because this is neither the time nor the place," declared the heavy-set voice dripping with wisdom. "But maybe I shouldn't expect anything different from you Mr Drayed."

Ky backed away from Marc, and as Dom stood, temporarily disconnecting his regeneration machine, the Defenders watched the unmistakable figure of the Polmarian Grand Elder, bamboo cane in hand, make his way towards Marc; dwarfing the Defenders as he passed.

"What are you doing here?" Dom said, as the Grand Elder shuffled past.

"I know this is the first time many of us have met but I want all of you to call me Esau. I'm too young to be an Elder, don't you think?"

Marc laughed mockingly, clearly irritated that his chance to confront Ky had vanished.

"Young Mr Drayed," Esau said, "your race was quite impressive. It is an honour to be here with you."

"Me?" Marc said impassioned, unsure how to handle the approval he so desperately sought.

"Of course. But with that being said, I will not have any tension among *my* Defenders. You must unite if you are to be ready."

"Ready?" Marc said. "You mean we actually have to race again?"

"I'm afraid so."

"But we're all tired. We'll need more time to recover."

"Unfortunately, time is the only thing you don't have."

Marc furrowed his brow and backed away from the group of Defenders.

Dom, who had retrieved a chair, placed it carefully next to Esau. "Excuse me Grand Elder, but since you are Polmarian, what did you mean when you said *my* Defenders?"

"I meant we're all in this together, don't you agree?"

"But only us Earth humans were challenged."

"That's not how I see it," Esau said, taking his seat. "Now sit and resume your healing."

Though confused by his words, the Defenders obliged. With Marc last to abide, albeit begrudgingly, each locked themselves back into their regeneration machines.

"I'm not sure any of us understand why you think we're all in this together," Dom repeated.

"As I look among you I see much determination. Some of you even possess the willingness to die so that others can live. There is no higher honour. There is no tougher ask. But no matter the desire, you will not be successful in the task ahead without our help. It is for this reason a session of Elders has been called, one you are about to join, which will determine how much support your fellow Hominidae will actually give."

"But why would they want to help us?" Dom asked.

"Because we're all connected. Let's just hope the rest of humanity see it the same way."

Esau tapped his cane, activating the latest model Façade which had camouflaged itself on the ceiling. "Please move into a reclining position so you can see. It won't be long before the forum provides all the answers you seek."

Hiss! Crackle! Hiss!

"It's time," Esau said, groaning as he stood, making his way towards the exit.

"Where are you going?" Dom pleaded.

"I am required to join this forum in person, but Mr. Regent will be back shortly." Esau grinned. "Oh, and be sure to keep your voices down, these new Façades can be quite sensitive."

"But when will we learn about the Kryon," Ky muttered, gazing skyward.

Esau peered back inquisitively before disappearing, leaving Ky to ponder his own question while watching the massiveness of the forum materialise. The Defenders could see the Chairperson standing in Pretta's centre, mouthing words they could not yet hear.

"Where's the sound?" Marc demanded.

"Give it time," Dom said, looking intently at the blur of faces directly behind the Chairperson. "Look at all those people – I wonder who's been invited."

"I'd say everyone," Ky said, staring in wonderment as the voice of the Chairperson could finally be heard.

This was the first time Earth humans were permitted to attend such a forum. More importantly, it was the first time Earth humans were getting a glimpse of their fellow man.

XLVIII.

"Lower your voices," said the Chairperson, directing his words to the newly connected Façades. "Quiet!"

Is he talking to us? Ky thought, remaining silent.

"That's better," said the Chairperson. "The Educator from Cril may continue."

"… As I was saying," said one of the Educators seated behind the Earth Elders. "It's the Earthlings who have been challenged, why do we have to accept? There is no time to prepare."

The Chairperson huffed. "If the Earthlings must be ready to defend in less than nine Clicks then we all can."

Concealed by her colleagues Loush sank deeper into her chair and grimaced, unclear as to what this all meant.

Mr Johansen stood, "Excuse me Chairperson," he said submissively, his audacity from earlier having vanished. Setting the transmission volume of his Translator to maximum, his voice carried up into the Façade. "Can you explain why we *must* accept this Challenge?"

"That question has already been answered in the debate."

"I thought this *was* the debate?"

"No. The debate of the Nameless ended prior to the Kryon issuing their Challenge. This is the forum to decide whether or not we help you."

"What?! Then how could you have let us be challenged in the first place?"

"You misunderstand. No Hominidae was permitted to attend the Nameless debate. The announcement of their decision, which came just over one Click ago, was the first the Hominidae learnt of the outcome."

Mr Johansen frowned. "But why target us?"

"Because of your violent history."

"Come on. We're not like that anymore."

"Maybe so. But none of that concerns the Kryon any longer. I advise you to focus your questions on the specifics surrounding this inter-species challenge."

"Okay," Mr Johansen said sceptically. "Are the rules any different to what we're already used to?"

"You and your Defenders will discover that soon enough. What I *can* tell you is that prior to your inclusion into the Knowledge Base, the Kryon had insisted a number of restrictions be placed."

"Yes, we know. We weren't allowed to travel beyond Polmar. We weren't allowed to learn about other species. We weren't allowed to automatically obtain Massine. Shall I go on?"

"No need," said the Chairperson. "But there was one condition you are unaware of."

"Oh?"

"The Kryon imposed a restriction that if you were ever challenged, prior to being fully accepted, then you must accept without recourse."

"Besides," added the Cril Educator, "you are the Nameless. What else do you think you deserve?"

"You to standing up for us would be a start," Mr Johansen said sarcastically.

"That's why we're here now," said the Chairperson. "To decide whether we will participate in this Challenge with you."

"And if you don't, what happens if we refuse to participate ourselves?"

"Whether you do not participate, or turn up and lose, the same fate awaits you." The Chairperson hesitated. "… If you do not win...you will be targeted by Massine for annihilation."

Mr Johansen's legs weakened. As he dropped back down into his seat the Elder from Cril, also seated behind the Earthlings, maximised the volume of his own transmission.

"Make no mistake," said the Crilinian, with a tone gentler than his subservient Educator, "the Kryon do not see you as Nyrolacs. They do not honour you. They do not respect you. And they definitely do not *want* you to understand anything more than you already know."

"But..." whimpered Mr Johansen, as the Façade's focus shifted to the Cril Elder.

Loush gently placed her hand on Mr Johansen's shoulder. "It's okay," she whispered. "Help will come."

"But why can't they just exclude us from the Knowledge Base?" Mr Johansen quietly pleaded, comforted by Loush's support.

The Crilinian Elder sat and rolled his eyes. "You cannot simply be excluded. Knowledge Base rules decree the loser of an inter-species challenge must have their intellect devolve. That civilisation must start again."

"But that's just ludicrous," said Mr Johansen.

"Maybe to you. But they are the rules we have abided by since the Knowledge Base began, and is the reason an inter-species challenge is not granted lightly."

"Granted? You mean someone had to permit this to occur?"

"But of course."

"Which civilization has the power to do that?"

"No one. That's why it was a conglomerate of virtually every advanced species which agreed. But they, like the rest of us, didn't think you would lose the right to use Massine as protection."

Mr Johansen moaned. "So, we pro-Massiners should have won after all, then we could have protected ourselves."

"I know none of this is easy to hear," interrupted the Chairperson, drawing the attention of the Façade.

"That's easy for you to say," muttered Mr Johansen.

"Actually, Elder Johansen, if we accept then our fate will be intertwined with yours as we will face the same outcome."

"What?! If you can be annihilated too then why help us at all?"

"I can't speak for everyone, but we Polmarians feel your destruction would destroy a part of us too. Besides, if we don't protect our own kind then who will?"

Mr Johansen was quiet.

The Chairperson was alerted. He covered his ear, gazed up to the top of Pretta and nodded. "We're out of time," he announced. "We must vote to decide if the rest of the Hominidae will accept the challenge and defend alongside the Earth humans."

Instantly, Pretta echoed in noisy anticipation as the Chairperson's attention remained glued to Esau's regular seat, cordoned off in the upper most bay closest to the apex of Pretta.

Having just arrived, Esau motioned for the Chairperson to sit with the Earth Elders. After the Chairperson acknowledged him, Esau caught a glimpse of movement from above. In gazing up, beyond the Façade, he could see the panels in the dome turn black.

He squinted, trying to focus his eyes, for even on the hottest days he knew the glass should never be that dark.

Turning his attention away, he could see the Chairperson seated among the Earth humans. *Good!* he thought, as the movement above returned.

Moving his eye sight back up to the dome, Esau pressed his lips together as the abundance of surrounding noise faded out of his mind. *Go on, show yourself.*

Time began to drag. Esau's eyes grew heavy.

Suddenly, a small portion of the blackened panels lit, turning red. The unfamiliar silhouette had Esau staring keenly, waiting for the mysterious object to make itself known.

Abruptly, the reddened panel began to swell before forming a burning eye which stared straight back at the Grand Elder.

It can't be! he thought, ogling the entity. *It's impossible.*

Despite dwarfing the unaware humans below, the shadowy silhouette would not make itself known, vanishing as fast as it had appeared.

To Esau, however, that single revelation had confirmed his worst fears.

The Nholl are here. The prophesy is real.

A rumour, which had been passed down through stories and fables, had instantly become true. The species, thought to be responsible for many cataclysmic events of the past had made its presence known.

Despite being afraid, Esau remained silent, not letting the creature's arrival become a source of panic. A moment later he snapped out of his trance, knowing everything had changed. There was no longer a choice for he knew it was more than just the Earth humans who would need to prepare.

The Grand Elder was supposed to be the one with the answers. But as the mumbling within Pretta grew it was he who would need to seek guidance – he just prayed the Obzoovers would have a solution.

XLIX.

Ky's eyes welled with a tear. Hearing the consequences of not accepting the Kryon's challenge drove home how crazy everything had become since his victory. He closed his eyes, not wanting to let his emotion be known.

"Are you OK?" Dom whispered, peering across.

Ky shrugged. "None of what the Chairperson said makes any sense. Whoever these Kryon are, there's no way we can beat them on our own."

"Maybe we don't have to," Dom said, pointing to the humans chattering within Pretta. "Look at all those civilizations. I'm sure they'll help us."

Ky blinked rapidly. With the tears evaporated, he focused on one of the only clear faces in among the other Façade observers.

"Strange looking fella," Dom said, staring at the same man whose unusually long eyelashes lavished this male with a feminine quality. The purity of his light blue skin was also a shade rarely seen among male Nyrolacs. In stark contrast, a black pony tail, spanning an arm's length and perched on top of his head, fought gravity as it pointed straight up.

Maligning his girlish appearance, Ky noticed his cheekbones were flatter than the surrounding Nyrolacs, causing his face to elongate and accentuate his sunken jaw line.

"Yep. They sure look different!" Marc said, eavesdropping.

"Maybe we shouldn't say too much," Dom replied. "He may hear us."

"Who cares?" Marc said, as the entrance to the Safe Room creaked. "We don't even know the guy...or girl...or whatever it is."

"That is a Zordacian Defender," said Mr Regent, entering the room.

"A what?" Marc said, having missed the formal introductions given by the Chairperson.

"A Zordacian. They are the most evolved of all Hominidae."

"How do *you* know?" Dom asked.

"Oh, I've been quite busy since leaving you."

At that moment, the Zordacian's thin ears twitched. He turned his head to the side, allowing the Earth Defenders a glimpse of his prominent forehead which extended over his eyes.

"Their brains must be huge!" Marc said.

"Evolution, my unevolved colleague," said Dom, "evolution."

"Oh, there's far more to it than that," said Mr Regent. "That Zordacian has the highest EALF rating of all living Hominidae. He is the key to this Challenge. The key to us winning."

"Key!" Marc said, grinding his teeth. "What about me?"

"You?" Mr Regent said. "Losing will bring death to our people. We'll take all the assistance we can get."

"So, you think they'll help?" Dom said.

"No one knows. But the Chairperson's preparing the voting directives as we speak. We'll find out soon enough."

Ky rubbed his eyes. The regeneration machine was making him tired. However, as his focus returned to the Zordacian Defender he was startled to see that he appeared to be staring straight back.

What's more, a diamond-like sparkle in the eye of the Zordacian sent a shiver through Ky, as the memory of Nibby's attacker was once again rekindled. This single, but unmistakable, Zordacian trademark had Ky on alert. *The masked assailant!*

It had been a while since Ky had allowed himself to think of that incident, but because he and Nibby agreed to discard the episode as a one off, Ky knew his concentration had to remain on the Challenge.

"Can he see us?" Ky asked tentatively.

"I don't know," Mr Regent whispered, sensing a hush fall over Pretta as the Chairperson rose to his feet.

"At this time," announced the Chairperson, "I would like to formally welcome the Earthling Defenders. In their presence, I will now read the directive."

After shuffling his fingers over his transmitter, a broadcast appeared in front of the Chairperson. Following another motion, the oversized words began to scroll for all to see.

"The directive of an inter-species challenge states that, during the eighth Click before the race begins, and prior to any voting taking place, the challenged species is permitted to have any and all questions answered. It must be noted that only one representative, selected by the Chairperson of the day, is to speak on their behalf – As per this directive, I assign Elder Sterling as this chosen representative."

Mr Johansen turned and stared at Loush. "You?" he uttered.

"Elder Sterling," said the Chairperson. "Please rise."

Ky's body tingled. His arm hair stood. "Mum?" he mumbled, as an ominous feeling engulfed him.

"What did you say cheat?!" Marc said.

Ky snarled. No words left his mouth. With his surname not well known to the other Defenders, and with tension rising in the Safe Room, he thought it best not to reveal their relationship.

Loush stood and bowed her head. *Okay. Where to begin. Just stay calm. Be confident.* "So apparently, I'm not dreaming. This is indeed real. And even though I'm glad we have the opportunity to pose some questions, all I really want to do is to find a solution or at least a way we can survive this ordeal."

Marc grumbled, his face sullen. "By the way she's talking you'd think she'd have to compete herself."

"Show some respect," Ky said through gritted teeth.

"Ah shut up."

The Façade zoomed in on Loush as she seemed to stare directly in the vicinity of her son. "It is apparent to me that we need the support of all Hominidae. We need them to defend with us. But irrespective of my pleas, I sense everyone's mind is already made up."

Ky's heart skipped, returning his mum's glance, while Pretta quickly filled with eerie silence.

Loush turned, staring directly at the Cril Elder. "Knowing that the Kryon inhabit the same planet as your civilization, and given we need to learn as much as we can about them and this challenge, my questions must start with you."

Resembling a Polmarian, only with eyes set further apart, the Cril Elder nodded.

"How long have you known about their plans to remove us from the Knowledge Base?"

The Cril Elder did not reply.

The Chairperson cleared his throat. "Ah, next question please

Elder Sterling."

"What's wrong with that question?"

"The Elder from Cril will only answer what he sees fit," said the Chairperson, as Loush's knees became shaky. "Please proceed. The voting will commence shortly."

"Regardless of how long you have known, do the people of Cril feel what the Kryon have done is ethical?"

"We believe in the Constructor," replied the Cril Elder, "and as such we cannot fault their methods."

"But do you agree with them? Do you think we should be removed from the Knowledge Base?"

The Cril Elder was silent; a superior grin appeared on his face.

"So then tell me more about these Kryon, and what they really think," Loush said, becoming notably agitated.

"The Kryon believe your inclusion would bring danger to us all."

"And why would that be?"

"That information was never divulged to the Hominidae."

"Then how did they gain support from other species?"

"The Kryon are very powerful, and very persuasive. I'd say their allies would have gone along with anything the Kryon would have asked."

"Are you saying there's nothing you, the Cril Humans, can do to stop this?"

"Make no mistake Earthling; the steps for your removal had begun a long time prior to your inclusion. There is nothing you, or your unevolved people, can do."

"Please Elder," said the Chairperson. "Show some tact."

The Cril Elder grunted, refusing to look at Loush anymore.

"Are we just gonna let those Cril creeps speak to our own Elders like that?" Marc said protectively.

"You've changed your tone," Dom said, "I didn't think you respected Elder Sterling."

Ky grinned.

Marc clenched his jaw. "Oh, I don't care about her. I just want to learn more about these cowardly Kryon so we can take them down."

"Quiet please!" announced the Chairperson, directing his words at the contingent of Earth Defenders. "Our time is short, and since only the top two Defenders from each civilization compete in an inter-species challenge, if we don't agree to defend with you then the two best Earth Defenders must compete against the Kryon's top two, alone."

"But we get to choose *our* top two, don't we?" Loush said, wincing as the clover tattoo began to irritate her arm.

"No. That choice was made by the result of your Massine Challenge."

"But Ky and Marc won't recover in time. We have to be allowed to select two others."

"Elder Sterling. Our most recent transmission clearly states the top two Defenders have mandatory automatic selection into the next Defenders Race. With only two spots per civilisation allowed, our hands are tied. I'm sorry, there can be no exceptions."

"Then you must vote to help us. That way they won't have to participate, will they?"

The Chairperson shook his head. "If we help then the top two Defenders from each human civilisation will compete together, including the Earthlings."

"Do the same rules apply to the Kryon?"

"They must send one Defender for each of ours."

"Then since our guys must compete no matter what," Loush said, her eye's drooping despairingly, "maybe it's time to tell us about the race rules itself."

"Very well," said the Chairperson who, once again, shuffled his fingers. Moments later the transmission began to scroll again. "The rules of this Defenders Race are set before you. Please read them carefully."

Ky rubbed his eyes. The Healing Machine was in full swing and as drowsiness, being one of the necessary side-effects, set in, he peered across at Marc who yawned while also trying to read the wording.

"The writing's too small," Marc said squinting, unable to understand the translated language. "Besides, all that matters is that I get to race the cheat again."

"Come on Marc," Dom said. "Your attitude isn't helping any of us. You and Ky have to stick together so please read the rules."

"I don't care about the rules!" Marc said, irritated that Elder Sterling had mentioned Ky's name before his. "All I have to do is run fast."

"Then do us all a favour and stop talking," Dom said as he, and the rest of the Defender's read in silence.

Ky's eyes were drawn to one passage in particular, labelled ***The Result.***

If there is less than five dats between the top finisher from each side, the result is to be determined in the Zankar; a combat to the death between these two finishers.

"That doesn't really sync with the EALF philosophy," Ky said, also yawning. "It makes no sense that Marc and I have to do this on our own."

Dom nodded. "And are they serious when they say if there's not enough time between first and second, a fight will follow?"

"That's the cool part," Marc said. Although grinning, his tough-guy exterior was wearing thin on everyone.

"I don't know how cool it is Mr Drayed," said Mr Regent. "From what I have learnt, a physical encounter against the Kryon is something we cannot win."

"What do you mean?" Dom said. "Who the hell are these Kryon? We have to learn more about them!"

"It's clear they're somewhat advanced in the Knowledge Base," Mr Regent said. "And from what I've just been told, those from Cril, the planet where the challenge originated, have Defenders stronger than any other Kryon."

"In what way?" Dom asked.

"Their muscle fibres are extremely dense which allows them to be both strong and fast. By also using the full potential of their mental capabilities, they have the ability to unite and influence their competitor's race by penetrating the thoughts of any adversary."

"We're gonna be sitting ducks," Dom said, reclining his seat to the maximum.

"Look," said Mr Regent. "Pretta is resuming."

The Chairperson wiped his face. After repeatedly pressing his hand against an apparently malfunctioning transmitter, more beads of sweat dripped from his forehead. "I don't believe there have ever been this many people in Pretta. Due to these high temperatures, I have just been informed that only a few more questions will be allowed. Elder Sterling, I advise you to be precise with your words."

Loush stood and inhaled deeply. "Okay. It's clear the Kryon are physically stronger, but we would like to know what weaknesses they may have."

"That is a good question," said the Chairperson, "for a clue to this may lie in their own past. Despite the Kryon having extremely high intelligence many believe they, like Earth humans, were selected into the Knowledge Base prematurely. Due to this their emotional strength was never allowed to evolve in line with their other attributes. It is this lack of emotion you must exploit."

"About time," Ky mumbled, fighting droopy eyelids. "I finally learn something about the Kryon."

L.

Eight Clicks remain.

LI.

Though having briefly drifted off to sleep, a loud rustling startled Ky. Peering around, he noticed the Façade had been replaced with static interference, while the absence of any medics caused the Safe Room to resemble more of a deserted cavern than the bustling hub from before.

Leaning against one of the walls was Esau. He had returned and was whispering suspiciously with Mr Regent.

"What's happening?" Ky asked. "Is the Challenge still on?"

"The Grand Elder has only come back momentarily," Mr Regent said. "We need you to rest."

"Tut, Tut," said Esau. "He'll have time for that soon enough. But since Mr Sterling is awake, maybe it's time he shared in the latest development."

Ky squinted distrustfully. He scanned the room for the other Defenders. Although most were gone, Dom, Marc and the other few remaining were sleeping. "Go on then."

Using his cane, Esau brushed away any help from Mr Regent and sat next to Ky. "While you were sleeping, the Cril Elder disclosed to your Elders and fellow Earthlings that the Kryon may be the guardians of a universal secret; one so powerful that it forced many advanced species to side with the Kryon."

Ky stared blankly. "What are you saying?"

"Isn't it obvious," Mr Regent said, taking a seat on the other side of Ky. "Their fear of this secret is the reason why they permitted this challenge to take place."

"Good!" Ky said, sitting upright. "Then let's expose this secret and stop this ridiculous situation."

"I'm afraid we can't do that," Esau said. "The Crilinians said they've tried to uncover this secret for quite some time."

"But surely they have some more clues they can share?"

Esau shook his head. "The only other information the Crilinians provided to your Elders were details on what happens if you lose."

Ky appeared pensive. "I don't think I want to hear any more right now."

Mr Regent frowned. "You, above anyone, must learn the consequences. Just think of it as incentive."

"But I..."

"Now listen carefully Mr Sterling," said Mr Regent. "Our only hope is that the Hominidae unite and defend together with us. But if the votes don't go our way, I would hope you will use any motivation available to help us win."

Ky sat back in his chair. "It seems like I don't have a choice."

"It certainly appears that way," Esau said. "Please continue Mr Regent."

"If we lose, all Earthlings will have to return home for quarantine, at which time every Lest travel device will be removed. Once confined, a Massine explosion, with the invisible radiation of Revert technology, will be detonated. All of us exposed will devolve to the original state of humanity."

"What does that mean?"

"It means our EALF abilities will be no more and our people's evolution will have to begin again."

"Can we try and protect ourselves?"

"Without the knowledge of Massine, nothing in existence will be able to protect us."

Esau nodded. "Once the grey clouds of Massine appear there will be no escape."

"Then you must vote to help us," Ky pleaded, partially distracted by Esau's flaky skin. "Marc and I can't do this alone."

"I agree," Esau replied. "But you *will* feel better in time. As for the vote, the key will be the Crilinian humans. If they agree, all will follow."

"So how do we get them to help?"

"That won't be easy. After all, they've seen this happen to mankind before."

"What! I thought an inter-species challenge has never occurred against the Hominidae."

"It may be rare, but it did happen," Esau said, as a scratching sound startled him. "Marc is waking. We need to move." The Grand

Elder plunged his cane into the concrete floor and began to stand.

"Wait! You have to tell me more. Did the humans win?"

"No."

"What do you mean *no*? Tell me what happened!"

"No point. This race is different. All you need to know is that the same thing happened when the Crilinian humans tried to protect us, the Polmarians, against the Kryon."

"And..."

"And the result was that many Polmarian colonies were targeted in the event known to you as the Great pre-historic Cleanse."

"That was Massine," Ky said, his thoughts drifting to Nibby and her family. "And the Revert?"

Esau nodded. "To this day, that event left our Cril human brother's afraid of the Kryon."

"Hey," Marc said. "What's going on?"

"Yeah, what's happening?" Dom added.

"Nothing you men need concern yourself with," Esau said, as a group of medics came rushing back in. "Please wake the others."

"Then what about non-humans?" Ky whispered. "Have they ever defeated the Kryon?"

"Only once," Esau uttered. "But that species now lives in hiding, still fearing Kryon retribution."

"But..."

"I can tell you no more," Esau said, his voice elevated. "Your fellow Defenders will soon learn what I have told you, but for now we must all go."

"Learn what? Go where?" Dom asked, clinging to his regeneration machine. "I'm not healed yet."

"Although the time of the Earthling has arrived, not all of you need to be ready so please follow me."

In quick succession, the medics forced each Defender to their feet and connected them to a portable regeneration machine.

With Esau and Mr Regent exiting the Safe Room, each Defender shuffled off behind. Ky glanced pensively back into the hazy Façade of Pretta.

"Mr Sterling," said one of the medics. "You must hurry."

As Ky shadowed the groggy Defenders he passed Mr Regent standing in the doorway. "I thought our attendance in Pretta was mandatory."

Without even giving him a second glance, Mr Regent ushered Ky out. The door to the Safe Room sealed with a thud.

"But don't Defenders have to vote?" Ky added, confused by the havoc.

"Not our Defenders," said Mr Regent, scampering to find Esau. "And certainly not you."

LII.

We've already taken too long, thought the Chairperson, despite knowing the voting procedure had already commenced. *But there is one more question I need to ask.*

Arriving back from his seat among the Earthlings to Pretta's platform, the Chairperson glanced up at the emotionless Zordacian Defender. "Knowing what may lie ahead, it fills my heart with both warmth and fear that your presence is required. But just before we finalize our votes, can you tell us if *you* think we have enough time."

The Zordac Defender's face was resolute.

The Chairperson persisted. "Will the Earthlings be ready to defend in such a short time? After all, they had just competed in their own Challenge."

Seated next to him, a Zordacian Educator stuttered. "May I respond on my Defender's behalf?"

The Chairperson nodded. "Of course."

"I believe the Kryon's Challenge was issued with perfect timing," said the Zordacian Educator unsympathetically. "But if a Defender is worthy then it should take no more than three Clicks for the regeneration process we gave you to have restored the Earthlings EALF capabilities."

"Then do you think they will be ready for the race on Elsh?"

"Elsh!" said Loush, standing. "What's Elsh? Isn't the race going to be on Earth?"

"Unfortunately not," said the Chairperson, devoid of any sarcasm. "Elsh is the host planet of this inter-species challenge."

The Zordacian Educator crossed his arms. "If you want my advice, just pray we defend you. That way your Defenders only have to worry about surviving."

Loush's legs wobbled. She peered around Pretta. The surrounding faces were cold, unwilling to help. Focusing on the panels, she could see their darkened state had caused the artificial light within Pretta to activate, adding to the frosty feel and mimicking her sense of isolation. She slumped in her seat and buried her face in her lap.

Mr Johansen, sensing Loush's despair, placed his arm around her, providing the support she so desperately sought.

"My son," she whimpered, tears welling in her eyes.

But as the Chairperson gave the directive to finalize voting, it would not be Loush's youngest child solely who would have an influence over this challenge.

LIII.

Back at the Sterling ranch, Nibby rubbed her arms with gusto while staring aimlessly at the Façade.

"Are you okay?" Ahlis asked, sitting next to her on the large and weathered couch.

"I'm really cold."

"Yeah, you look quite pale. I'd say the unfriendliness of Pretta is catchy, but I'm guessing you find it hard to believe the Constructor has failed us."

"You could be right," Nibby said, pulling on a jumper. "But it's also the thought of that violent Massine weapon. We fought so hard to not allow it into our lives when, in the end, it may end our lives."

"Now I feel chills."

"Imagine how Ky must be feeling," Nibby said, "especially after what the Cril Elder hinted about the Kryon and their secret."

"Maybe he was just trying to scare us?"

"Or maybe he was trying to prepare us for the worst."

Nibby shrugged. "I'd say we're probably in danger no matter what the truth is."

"But you're a Polmarian," Ahlis joked. "You probably want Ky and Marc to defend alone."

"Hey," Nibby barked. "I'm a Sterling before a Polmarian so don't say that, not even in jest. The Hominidae *will* vote to defend with us, or at least they'd better. My life is with Ky. My fate is the same as yours."

"I know," Ahlis said, placing her hand on Nibby's shoulder. "I'm sure the humans will answer mum's pleas."

"We can't rely on that," Nibby said, grinding her teeth. "I have to go."

"Go where? Into Pretta?"

"No. I have another place in mind."

As Nibby moved, so too did the Façade's focus as it shifted onto the face of one Defender; the Zordacian human who was becoming more pivotal than the Earth humans had realised.

LIV.

Throughout ancient times of past, the Knowledge Base progressed without much disturbance. Although only a rare few knew its origin, species after species continued to join its growing members.

Well into its development, the Knowledge Base's first humans came from an accidental discovery. Having always been labelled as aggressive un-evolved animals, a random scan of a seldom searched galaxy revealed a small civilization of humans, residing on a planet called Zordac, who exhibited a naturally high EALF rating.

Word among the Knowledge Base spread and, in spite of much resistance, this cluster of highly evolved humans became man-kinds first to enter the Knowledge Base; long before the earliest Polmarian humans began their evolution.

As time passed, and other human civilizations joined them, this Zordacian community continued its own evolutionary rise, learning from the most sophisticated of species. Without the assistance of inter-species breeding, a practise not permitted for humans within the Knowledge Base, they also began to excel in Defender Challenges. Those in their inner circle knew it would only be a matter of time before a Zordacian was born who could challenge even the most advanced species of Nyrolac.

LV.

With medics having already chaperoned most of the Defenders into hospital, Esau ushered the remaining handful into a small damp holding area filled with mattresses scattered randomly on the floor.

"Don't touch me," Marc growled, shrugging off his medic, who prodded the Earth Defender towards one of the make-shift beds jammed in one of the corners.

Ky, still jerky from his treatment, made his own way to the opposite corner where he knelt.

"Don't worry," announced Esau, "the side-effects of the regeneration are only temporary. Once you fall asleep again the rest of the healing will take place."

"Sleep!" Marc said. "How do you expect me to sleep when I feel so jittery?"

"Oh, that won't be a problem," Esau said, taking a seat next to Mr Regent in one of the few unoccupied chairs.

Visibly uncomfortable with his confined space Marc gritted his teeth, marched past the remaining huddled Defenders and, with his back to both Esau and the entrance, stood over Ky. "Get up cheat!"

Ky sprung to his feet, unafraid to plant his smaller frame chest-to-chest with Marc's intimidating physique.

Marc raised his hand. Knowing no Elder was going to quell this antagonism, Ky balanced his body weight and prepared his defensive stance.

"Hey!" shouted a voice from the doorway.

Marc turned. "Interrupted again!" he yelled.

Ky peered beyond Marc. Although familiar, the voice was not one he could have expected.

LVI.

"Who are you?" Marc grunted, staring at the curvy silhouette strutting towards him. "Why did you stop me from...from...I mean this is no place for a... for a girl."

"That's right," said Mr Regent, seeing the kerfuffle. "Who let you in here? This is no time for visitors. We're about to get the results."

"I just thought someone may need to calm these boys down," said the female. "I guess I was right."

Esau too stared, his cane slipping from his grip.

Ky's heart pounded. "Nibby," he said, stepping out of his defensive stance to embrace her. "It's good to see you."

"This is not the time for games," she whispered. "You must conserve your strength."

Stepping away from Ky, she accidentally brushed Marc's barrelled chest.

"Pardon me," she said.

"Donchya worry pretty girl. Now you know what a real man feels like."

Ky glared at Marc, while Nibby raised a single eye-brow.

"You must leave now," Mr Regent said. "Please Grand Elder, we must control this environment."

"Hmm," Esau said, retrieving his cane. "No, let her stay."

As a high-pitched squeal sounded, causing everyone in the holding room to wince and shout distasteful idioms, Ky pulled Nibby aside.

Moments later, Pretta emerged on the Façade. The Chairperson, standing on the platform, was pointing to a bunch of numbers flashing inside a flag-like image that materialised a few meters above his head. "The customary one Tick of voting time has ended," he said. "The results are in."

A hush fell over Pretta as the Chairperson read the numbers aloud.

"It has come to pass that ninety-nine point nine-nine percent of all Hominidae have voted, with the majority agreeing to..."

The chairperson snuck another peak at the numbers, ensuring his first glance was correct. "...It has been decided we will accept the Challenge of the Nameless. All Hominidae are to defend with the Earth humans."

Cheers roared through Pretta and her connected Façades while Loush's face painted a picture of relief. "They did it," she said to Mr Johansen. "They're helping us."

The Chairperson glanced up at the Earth human contingent, nodded, and then scanned the rest of Pretta. "To most of you, please return home and comfort your people – As for those charged with preparing your Defenders, please ensure they're fully prepared for the upcoming Defender's Race; our fate is in their hands."

In the holding room, and through the murmuring among the Defenders, a congratulatory hand shake between Mr Regent and Esau was short lived. "Don't forget, we still have the task of defeating the Kryon," said the Grand Elder.

"But the Zordacians will be there to protect us, won't they?"

Esau was silent. He caught a glimpse of Marc whose flushed face and raised shoulders still showed his annoyance. "Drayed is still too angry to defend."

"Isn't there any way to get a replacement?"

"No. He must compete."

"But look at him creeping back towards Sterling. Should I sedate him?"

"No. Let him be."

"Of course, "Mr. Regent chuckled. "With the other humans

defending, it's only his own safety at risk."

Esau pursed his mouth, handed Mr Regent a transcript to read, and keenly watched the Defenders.

"Looks like it's just you and me little man," Marc muttered, jaw still clenched.

"Hey!" Nibby said, seeing Marc's pupils dilate. "We may be getting help but you guys still need to work together if you want to survive the Kryon. Don't waste your emotions on Ky, there's more than your egos at stake."

The holding room fell silent.

"Hey lady," Marc bellowed. "I don't even know you so don't tell me what to do!"

"I'll stop as soon as you leave Ky alone."

"I knew it. He's so weak he needs a girl to fight his battles. We'll just see how well the cheat does in the re-match!"

"Re-match!" Dom shouted, charging towards Marc. "The Challenge against the Kryon is no re-match. It's a battle for our survival! And stop calling Ky a cheat!"

"Look Sable. There's no way he could have raced the way he did."

Staring down at Ky, Marc cracked his knuckles and rolled his head from side to side. "How did you do it cheat? How did you beat me?"

Wanting to end the intimidation Ky jumped to his feet. He tried to create room by leaning into his rival with his shoulder but Marc's heavy frame was unmoved.

"Come on Marc!" Dom shouted. "Let it go."

"You don't have to do this," Nibby added, pleadingly.

Marc clenched his fists and grinned, wondering if another appearance of superiority would finally cause Ky to retreat. With no reaction, Marc grunted and let loose a wild swing towards Ky's face.

In an instant Ky shifted his head and caught the attacking fist in his hand. Twisting the aggressor's arm towards the ground, Ky kicked Marc in his obliques with just enough force to send him sliding across the floor.

"And you call yourself a Defender," Ky said dismissively. "I'm no cheat. Learn some respect."

Marc jumped to his feet, shook his head, and charged again.

With the other Defenders watching, Dom stepped in and grabbed one of Marc's arms, turning him around. "I wouldn't if I were you."

"You're not me," Marc snapped, facing Dom. But distracted by something in the distance Marc's arm quickly softened. "How did you find me?" he mumbled in the direction of another fast approaching person, also a stranger to this holding room.

"I followed my sister here," said the new female voice.

"Sister!" Marc exclaimed, "Where is she? You never said you had a sister."

"Then you still have a lot to learn about me."

Noticing the other Defenders perusing her curved body, barely covered with cloth from her strapless dress, Marc grumbled. "Hey! Keep your eyes to yourselves."

"Ahlis?" Nibby whispered.

"Okay. What's going on here?" Marc said.

"Come with me," Ahlis said, dragging Marc away as she winked back at Nibby.

Ky's arms were shaky. Seeing his anxiety Nibby caressed his hand. "Are you okay?"

Ky shrugged. "Drayed must be that guy she met on her travels. You know, the one she didn't want to talk about."

"Could be. But don't think about that. You should rest."

As Nibby placed Ky's head on her lap, she listened as Ahlis and Marc's loud whispering echoed.

"You're still as pushy as ever I see," Marc said.

"And you still can't control your emotions, just like always," Ahlis said.

"What? Yes I can!"

"I saw how you attacked Ky!"

"Ky! Why would you care about that?"

"Because Nibby is Ky's Flyat, you know, his partner."

"I get that. So what?"

"Well it was Nibby who I followed."

Marc gazed over at Ky as logic kicked in. "You're telling me *he* is your brother?"

"Yes, and *we* need to talk," Ahlis said, pulling Marc into the opposite corner to where Ky lay.

"How did she get into this holding area?" Ky asked, nestling into

Nibby as she ran her fingers over his hair. "I suppose you gave her one of your Polmarian security passes?"

"You know me too well."

"I'm just glad you're here."

At that moment, a loud rumble echoed through the holding room.

"Listen up Defenders," said Mr Regent, climbing on top of a flimsy table wedged against one of the walls. "The gong has sounded."

"What does that mean?" asked Dom, scanning the room. "And where is Esau?"

"The Grand Elder has gone. But he wanted me to read this transcript to you."

"Okay, but just don't fall," Dom joked.

"This is no time for humour," Mr Regent said, holding a wrinkled piece of paper no bigger than the size of his hand. With ink that seemed to have dried long before the Kryon announced their Challenge, Mr Regent couldn't help but wonder when Esau may have written, or in fact received, this note:

"Defenders, though all Hominidae may soon unite, know that the emotional growth you've experienced during recent Challenges has done more good than you realise. Use it to your benefit for it may be the only advantage you have over the Kryon."

Another gong shook the Holding room, wobbling the table beneath Mr Regent. Although he steadied himself, his legs trembled from a lack of sleep:

"No matter what you are told, understand this unique healing treatment you are receiving will not be complete until the countdown expires, so tread carefully and be cautious of everything you see. May you have good luck. You will need it."

Mr Regent huffed. "That's it?"

"Wait!" Dom said. "There's something on the other side."

Mr Regent flipped the paper. He hesitated, raising his eyebrows.

"What does it say?" Dom asked.

"I'm not sure if I should. It's confusing, and probably not meant for us."

"Just read it," Dom demanded.

Still unsteady, Mr Regent inhaled deeply. The damp air cooling his airways. "It says, '*You're being watched. The fate of the*

Nameless, and perhaps all Hominidae, depends on you.'"

The gong repeats. Mr Regent's hands felt a chill. He hopped down and folded the transcript. "The gongs indicate only seven Clicks remain. So stop fighting and get some sleep."

"But shouldn't we discuss that transcript?" Dom said. "Besides, I'm not that tired."

Mr Regent grinned. "Don't take this the wrong way Mr Sable, but *your* physical state no longer matters."

Ky whispered to Nibby. "But Dom's right. That transcript said we have a chance to win, and implied our emotional strength will be the key."

"But it also said to be cautious," Nibby said. "And that's exactly what I want you to be."

Ky grinned. With the regeneration entering the next phase, Nibby could see him yawn with more frequency.

After seeing one of the medic's gesture for Ky to sleep, she gently lay him flat on the mattress, slid a cushion underneath her legs, and knelt by his side. "So, did you see Ahlis' face? She seems happy to see Marc."

Ky turned his head and spoke groggily. "Then maybe *she* can keep Drayed calm. He'll need to keep those emotions in check if he wants to be ready."

"That's why he's lucky you're here to lead the way."

"But...but he's scared...scared of learning from anyone, let alone me."

"Hush now Ky. It's time to sleep."

A lengthy silence drifted over the couple.

"He'd better realise what's at stake," Ky added, his eyes gently closing. "It's not just his life at risk anymore."

Drip. Drip. Drip. A drop of rain began to fall.

LVII.

With the forum in Pretta coming to a close, and the echoes of departing footsteps disappearing from the vacating hall, the Zordacian and Crilinian Educators made their way down to Pretta's central platform.

"Where is he?" the annoyed Crilinian asked the seated Chairperson. "Where is your Grand Elder? Why did he summon us? I should be preparing my Defenders!"

The Zordacian nodded. "I too was summoned. We don't have time for this."

"Please be patient. It won't be long now."

The Crilinian frowned while the Zordacian's expressionless face hid discontent. The windy echo of emptiness drifted through Pretta. As suppressed fear began to overwhelm the Chairperson, a buzz, only he could hear, had him place his hand against his ear. "I understand."

The Chairperson jumped to his feet. "They're ready for us. We must leave now."

The Cril Educator clenched his teeth and snarled with disapproval. "Fine, but he'd better have a good reason."

After stepping into the cave at Pretta's base, the three men vanished.

"Where are we?" asked the Crilinian, scanning his new mystical surroundings.

"Look," said the Zordacian, pointing to a seemingly insignificant stone dwelling nestled among a group of larger shop front buildings. "Over there!"

The Crilinian squinted, "Is that..."

"Yes," replied the Chairperson, "follow me."

Knowing this residence had been used for secretive meetings over the ages, the three Educators approached with caution.

Arriving at the entrance, each gazed up at the threatening gargoyles staring down from above. Their shimmering beams, guarding the entrance, began to flicker.

After a swift manoeuvre of his right arm the beams scanned him, bypassing the others. Instantly, the entrance opened, allowing the men to make their way inside.

Although cautious, the Crilinian said nothing as he and the Zordacian followed the Chairperson into a darkened hall. Illuminated by small iridescent lights secured into the floor, the Educators froze as a shadow in one of the corners began to move.

"Sit," spoke the shadow, as the series of dim lights shifted, drawing attention to a line of chairs placed in the room's centre.

The Educators obliged.

"Grand Elder?" said the Chairperson, his eyes adjusting. "Is that you?"

Without saying a word, Esau moved beneath the brightest of the lights and sat awkwardly in his usual chair, opposite the Educators.

A tap of his cane illuminated another series of lights whose haze clouded the frustrated Crilinian's eyes yet again. "Why are we here?"

After another tap of his cane, a piercing squeal emitted from one of the corners where a Lest device was installed.

"Tell us why we're here," repeated the Crilinian, covering his ears.

Esau pointed to the Lest device, and as the painful sound cleared, the Educators could see the arrival of another.

LVIII.

"Oh my," said the Zordacian Educator, standing in awe as his own, rarely seen, leader materialized. "Greetings Grand Elder."

Shaking off the tingling sensation from his teleportation, the Zordacian Grand Elder acknowledged Esau, his long-time collaborator, before sitting in his own usual seat.

Esau stroked his beared into its triangular point. "Good you could make it back. How is your Defender?"

"Unchanged and undaunted. Did you give the Earthlings the transcript?"

Esau nodded.

Though unsure of what the Grand Elders were talking about, the Chairperson and Cril Educator stood alongside the Zordacian Educator. Together they bowed at the feet of the new arrival; it was a sign of respect afforded to the more highly of evolved Nyrolacs.

"Take your seats," said the Zordacian Elder, furrowing his already wrinkled brow.

With their seats facing both Grand Elders in a semi-circular fashion, the three Educators sat silently.

"Are you pleased all Hominidae have joined the Earthlings in support?" Esau asked the Crilinian Educator.

"Why would that please me? The vote has put us all at risk."

"But they're a part of who we are. If we let them die, how can we call ourselves human? How can we think of ourselves as evolved?"

"We had evolved long before the Earthlings."

Esau frowned. "Maybe your people have, but our history cannot be separated from theirs. You know of what I speak."

The Zordacian Grand Elder nodded.

The Cril Educator sniffed, unsure how to handle the Grand Elder's banter. He gazed over to one of the walls. It was draped with the most advanced computerised equipment the Knowledge Base had to offer.

"Are we boring you?" said Esau, snapping the Crilinian out of his trance.

"Ah. No. Well, it's just..."

Esau huffed. "Time's short! What are you trying to say?"

The Crilinian was taken aback but composed himself. "...Why have you asked us here? As I suggested in Pretta, it doesn't make sense to accept something we cannot win. The Kryon, especially those from Cril, are too advanced...too aggressive...too strong for any human."

"Oh, I wouldn't say that," said the Zordacian Educator. "Our Defender has just as much skill as any Kryon."

"Yes, but can he fight a Kryon? Can he kill a Kryon?"

The Zordacian snubbed his nose and mumbled. "None of us know for sure."

"Then how can we win this Challenge?"

"With faith," said Esau. "We have to trust our Defenders."

The Zordacian Grand Elder snickered, gazed across at his giant Polmarian colleague, and chuffed. "Do *you* have faith Esau?"

"Of course."

"Then why don't you tell the Educators why they're really here. Why don't you tell them what the Obzoovers told you?"

"You spoke with the Obzoovers?" said the Crilinian, hope draping each syllable.

Esau nodded.

"What did they say? Did they tell you how we can avoid this Challenge?"

"Go on Esau." said the Zordacian Grand Elder. "Tell them."

Esau grunted.

"Do they have a solution?" pleaded the Crilinian.

Esau hesitated. "No."

"Then *what* did they say?"

"They said what I told you – to have faith. They wanted us to spread *that* message, not just to the Earthlings, but to our own civilizations as well."

"Of course they do, but they must have said something else as well."

The Zordacian Educator stood. "What else do they need to say? Our Defender has never been defeated. The Grand Elder and I have faith in him."

"But he has never come up against a Kryon," said the Crilinian, also standing.

"Please sit," said Esau. "There *is* something else of which the Obzoovers want us to be aware."

Perplexed, the Educators sat as Esau stretched his jaw. "Word has been given that the Kryon have started to arrive on Elsh in great numbers. The top two Defenders from each Hominidae civilization must depart immediately. While we have contacted the other leading Educators, everyone knows our strongest Defenders belong to you. With this in mind, you should ensure your Zordacian and Crilinian Defenders are ready to depart as soon as possible."

The Educators nodded as the Zordacian Grand Elder's deep inhale was heard by all. "Esau," he said. "You must not delay any longer. Please tell them what the Obzoovers said about the arena on Elsh. It is, of course, the real reason why they have been summoned here."

"What about it?" said the Crilinian, flinging his arms in the air. "Isn't it ready? Because if it's not then we should be allowed to call it off. Did the medics find any abnormalities with the track itself?"

Esau stroked his beard. "The Blorm. I'm afraid the entire surface is covered with it."

"But that's never been seen before," said the Crilinian. "Which means the Kryon must be stronger than we first thought, seeing how they were allowed to choose some of the race specifics."

"Crossing the Blorm may be their strength," Esau said, "but they underestimate our Defenders. So, don't be afraid. Go and tell our people everything you know, especially the Obzoover's message of faith."

"Actually, I don't think my people need to hear me make more speeches," said the Crilinian.

"That's why you will be delivering your message elsewhere – to the small Earthling town of Tousol."

The Cril Educator grimaced. "But my Defenders..."

"Your people will be informed," said the Zordacian Grand Elder, "and you will do as you are told. Now go. My Lest device is ready to take you there."

"As you wish."

"The rest of you are dismissed."

After the Educators dematerialised, Esau leant over to the

Zordacian Grand Elder. "There's something I have not yet told you. Something I didn't want the others to learn."

The Zordacian leaned in inquisitively.

"The first prophesy," said Esau. "I saw one of them in the dome of Pretta."

"What! Are you sure?"

Esau nodded.

The Zordacian Grand Elder appeared contemplative. "So, it is coming to pass before our very eyes. If this is true, you know we cannot rely on faith alone."

Esau nodded. He pushed himself up with his cane and winced as pain shot through his aging legs. Although control of the Challenge was out of his hands, the Grand Elders' faith in their own plan was about to be put to the test.

LIX.

Drip. Drip. Drip. A silvery droplet tumbled slowly towards an unaware Ky. Originating, not from the vibrant blue sky, but the mysterious horizon, this opaque watery substance shimmered as it pursued the Earth Defender.

The drop hardened. It gathered speed, changed shape into a thin jagged blade, and advanced rapidly over the gravel floor.

Though he continued to meander, a darkness, engulfing the entire sky, captured Ky's attention. He turned and stared helplessly as the blade drove deep into, and through, his shoulder.

Peering down, he could see a bloody red spot quickly grow, drenching what was once a clean white shirt.

Despite feeling no pain, he put pressure on the wound and gazed back towards the horizon from where a mist was fast approaching. *That's not rain,* he thought, as the objects morphed into a cluster of similar looking blades.

Ky back peddled. "Help!" he whimpered, staring hopelessly towards the vacant landscape.

Nobody came.

The blades dispersed, attempting to surround him.

Turning, he tried to dash towards a cluster of faint blurred lights buried within the darkness, but found himself unable to move with any speed.

"Run!" he shouted.

Despite his plea, Ky's legs would not take heed. However, with the blades seemingly suspended in mid-flight his focus on the distant light objects sharpened.

They're faces, Ky thought, moving towards this new source of hope. "Please help me!" he repeated.

As he moved closer the faces grew in size, whispering faintly as each stared back at him.

Ky listened carefully as a single word, and the voices which resembled those of his family, became clear.

"Help us!" said the voices.

At that moment, the blades shot past Ky. "Wait!" he shouted, realising it was not he who needed saving. But as the last of the blades flew by, one grazed his leg, sending him slumping to the ground.

Dust flew everywhere. Ky rubbed his eyes vigorously, blinking rapidly as his vision cleared.

A large grotesque and overweight bald man, wearing only a loincloth around his hairless body and a mask to cover parts of his deformed face, stood over him. He held a long wooden club, with pointy spikes protruding from both ends, and stared up at the sky.

Who's this guy? Ky thought.

To the man's side, a steel frame of equal height, encased a golden gong which began to shake of its own accord.

Still wanting to chase the blades, Ky tried to stand but saw that the man had pinned one of his legs; pressing on his latest wound.

Helpless, Ky gazed up at the faces only to see they had vanished. Instead, the blades turned and melded to form a larger dagger-like blade before continuing in its pursuit of the Earth Defender.

Ky shrugged his leg free and jumped to his feet. He tried to limp away from both the bald man and the dagger but could not make any headway.

He peered back one more time only to see the dagger, held by a blood-riddled monster, hover in front of him.

Although the monster had a head on top of its shoulders, the creature had no face. Its unresponsive stare pierced deep into the Earth Defender's soul.

Ky's instinct was to grab the dagger but decided to heave his arm towards the beast instead. "Bastard!" he screamed, as his hand drove through the centre of the mysterious ogre.

Afraid of the consequence of coming face to face, Ky did not want to remove his hand from the monster. And as the creature fell to the ground he realised that he too was holding a dagger. But still fearful, he glared back to see the bald man drive his club into the gong.

With bloodied hands, Ky covered his ears to block out the gong's thunderous noise. His lack of defence gave the faceless monster the opportunity it needed as it, still holding its own dagger, drove the object towards Ky's face.

At that moment, Nibby opened her eyes to the sound of Ky who, lying next to her, was gasping for air.

"What did you say Ky?" Nibby asked.

After sitting up, Ky coughed up a small amount of blood. "Must be the regeneration," he said, sweat pouring down his face.

Although knowing vivid dreams were also a side-effect of the regeneration process, Nibby placed her hand on Ky's forehead and waved for a medic to come over. "You have a temperature. Are you okay?"

"I don't know. I think so. I mean, I had that dream again, the same one I've always had, only this time it felt so real."

"Ky..." Nibby said uneasily, never fully comprehending what his nightmares had been about, "...I was also dreaming."

"What about?"

"I dreamt I was watching you. I don't know where you were but I could only watch as you tried to protect me from...from some kind of monster."

Ky's eyes widened. "That was *my* dream! Did you see the daggers too?"

"No Ky. They weren't daggers, they were Blorm."

"Are you sure?" Ky said, remembering he wanted to grab hold of the sharp object. "No living being can hold the Blorm the way that creature did, without fatal results!"

Nibby hesitated.

"Did you hear the gong too?" Ky added.

Nibby nodded. She looked back to see what was keeping the medic but saw that the holding room was almost deserted.

"Time's running out," Ky whispered, pointing to the countdown sequence of large numbers flashing on the Façade monitor.

Despite whispering, their conversation was loud enough to draw the attention of Mr Regent who made his way towards the couple. "Mr Sterling. It's time for your briefing in the Preparation Room."

"Yet another room," Ky griped. "Why do we have to move again?"

"Because there's a lot to learn. Oh, and only Mr Drayed, Mr Sable, and yourself are coming. The others are to return home."

Nibby helped Ky to his feet. "I guess there's no point in arguing."

"Probably not," Ky said. "But I'm so glad you came. I know none of this is easy for you."

"We should all be thanking you," Nibby said, embracing Ky with such ferocity that she could feel his heart beat against her chest.

Despite wincing, Ky did not let go. "I'll see you soon."

"You better. I love you Ky."

"We must leave now Mr Sterling," announced Mr Regent coldly.

Ky reluctantly released his grip on Nibby and blew a kiss to Ahlis, who was peering over Marc's shoulder during their own final embrace.

Following Mr Regent, Ky gazed back to see Nibby and Ahlis' eyes fill with sadness. The door shut. He sighed, lagging behind Dom and Marc. Although the other Defenders couldn't tell, it was the first time Ky didn't want to go on.

LX.

Three Clicks remain.

LXI.

Ky eventually caught up to Mr Regent, standing disgruntled. "You'd best keep up Mr. Sterling!" he said, shoving Ky under a sunken entrance to another room sparsely decorated with nothing more than rows of stacked benches leant against one of the walls.

"What's this place?"

"Maybe if you had been listening, and not delaying everyone, you would have remembered what I had said."

"Is this the Preparation Room?"

"Yes. It's the entry point for all Challenges held outside Earth's realm."

"Marc!" Ky said, happy to see he was not left alone with Mr Regent.

Sitting cross-legged in one of the corners, Marc's head drooped in his lap. His silence a vast departure from his earlier outbursts.

Mr Regent placed his hand on Ky's shoulder and led him to another of the vacant corners where he sat, still staring back at Marc.

"I didn't know you knew my sister," Ky said, feeling a touch dizzy.

Marc groaned, confused by his own chaotic emotions. "And you never said you were a Sterling!"

"Should I have?"

Marc nodded, as his head and arms began to shake. "Then I would have known you were...known you were Ahlis' brother."

"Are you okay?" Ky asked, seeing Marc's disorientation.

"What were you trying to hide?"

"Nothing," Ky said, waving to gain Mr Regent's attention.

"Oh, don't worry," said Mr Regent. "His reaction to the regeneration is quite normal. Both of you have been injected with boosters to finish off the process. You too may soon feel as Mr Drayed does."

"Oh," Ky replied, dropping his head between his knees as he tried to shake vertigo.

Suddenly, the door to the Preparation Room crashed open.

"Dom!" Ky said. "Where did you disappear to?"

"Aw, my body wasn't responding to the regeneration so the medics injected some kind of sedative to assist the treatment. It hurt like hell but, since I'm due to go home any moment, it was the best way to make sure an old man like me can recover in time for teleportation."

"What! You're not coming with us?"

"Afraid not. You'll be on your own. Besides, the Zordacian regeneration seems to be working on you, so you'll be fine."

"You're not off the hook just yet Mr Sable," said Mr Regent, pointing to another of the vacant corners in the brick enclosed area. "Take a seat."

Taken aback, Dom looked across at Marc. "Why? Do you want me to take Drayed's place?"

"Both he, and Mr Sterling, are not recovering as fast as we would like. Their anxiety towards one another has been a hindrance."

"But Marc's aggressiveness seems to have gone. What do you want me to do?"

"Talk to them. Mr Drayed may be calm, but he and Mr Sterling are not united. Only then, say the Zordacians, will their regeneration truly work."

"Friends! You want them to become friends?"

"No. We just need them to unite."

"Agrh. I don't even know what that means," Dom said, beckoning Ky to his feet.

"What are you doing?" said Mr Regent. "He should be resting."

"Rubbish," Dom replied, placing his arm around Ky as he rose. "These guys are too drowsy. Movement is what they need."

Dom guided Ky to the wall farthest from Marc before pinching Ky beneath his ribs. "Whoa!" Ky yelled. "Why did you do that?"

"Just give it a chance."

"Hang on, that does feel better. What did you do?"

"Just a little trick I learnt during my training."

Ky grinned. "You're full of tricks. So, what about Marc?"

"Don't worry. He'll be okay, so long as you stick together. Despite his bravado, Marc doesn't think he can race again so soon. I'd say he needs you to reassure him."

Seeing the curiosity in Ky's eyes, Dom pulled him closer and whispered. As time passed, and with Mr Regent drifting off into some sort of meditative state, Ky took a step back. "Do you think it'll work?" he said, feeling his strength returning; a sensation not felt since before the last Challenge. "I've tried talking to him before."

"If he's not ready to defend it'll harm both of you, and that will hurt all of us. If you must try something, why not this?"

Ky nodded and sat himself down next to Marc, whose folded arms couldn't mask his shaking body.

"You may have come second," Ky said casually, "but you're probably still the best."

Marc, who was staring into nothingness, blinked rapidly. "Of course I'm the best. Everyone knows that."

Ky smiled and, risking the repercussions, nudged Marc's rib cage with his elbow.

Marc didn't budge.

"What's going on?" mumbled Mr Regent, snapping out of his self-induced coma.

"Shh," replied Dom. "You want them to unite, don't you?"

Ky braced himself and thrust his elbow into Marc's side yet again. This time, however, the big frame of Marc rocked back and he placed his own arm around Ky's neck.

In an instant Ky was trapped and Marc began to squeeze.

"Hey!" shouted Mr Regent. "Stop it!"

Dom too felt uneasy. "That didn't go to plan."

Ky, however, didn't struggle.

Marc glanced up at Dom. He raised his free hand, squeezing it into a fist as it approached its apex. A wry smile crept onto his face.

Before Dom could move, Marc drove his fist downward towards the back of Ky's head, stopping one centimetre from impact.

Mr Regent's jaw dropped.

Dom did not move.

Marc opened his hand and began to rub Ky's head playfully, as Dom's laughter hid his relief. "Good to see you're feeling better," he said.

Marc released Ky, allowing the pair to rise to their feet. "I didn't expect it Ky," Marc said softly, "I just didn't think I would lose to some unknown."

"I know," Ky said nodding. "So, you and my sister eh?"

Marc smiled. "Sure, if it were up to me. But she's a stubborn one."

Ky and Dom both grinned.

"What are you grinning about Sable?" Marc said in jest.

After a moment's silence, Dom stopped grinning. "There ya' go Mr Regent. Now these guys are ready."

LXII.

The small moon-like planet of Elsh, like Cril, hovers on the outer south rim of the Andromeda Galaxy. Due to the planet being kept under Kryon guard, transmissions have been sent to the Hominidae Elders informing them that even Lest teleportation may have its delays.

"Please," said Mr Regent, relaying the information, "you must concentrate." Having already made the Defenders listen to an Elsh history lesson, the Elder persisted with a rapid-fire of more newly received details. "Unlike the fifteen other planets within their Goliath system, Elsh's unique gravitational pull will give the Kryon a distinct advantage."

"Why is that?" asked Marc.

"Its stronger gravity makes it harder to lift your legs. This means a stronger Nyrolac will find it easier than a weaker one."

"I know we've never seen them, but how do we know they're stronger than us?"

"Don't be naive," Mr Regent said, as his famous crotchety voice re-surfaced. "You'd best assume the Kryon are less like a Nyrolac, and more like the beasts of your scariest nightmares."

"He's right," Dom added, "We can't assume they'll have any resemblance to us. That's why I'm glad the other humans are defending with us."

While images of Ky's dream rekindled, Mr Regent tapped his transmission. "I'm afraid, Mr Sable, your confidence may be misplaced."

"And why would that be?"

Mr Regent's arms dropped by his side. He stared directly at Ky. "I've just received word that Elsh's arena will be completely covered in Blorm."

While Ky's eyes widened, Mr Regent persisted. "But luckily for us, all inter-species Defender races are fitted with a Gravity Tunnel."

"A what?" said Ky.

"A Gravity Tunnel. It's an invisible cloak which alters the gravity and oxygen levels of any object. In this case Elsh's arena, and surrounding areas, will ensure all species can breathe and, more importantly, feel the same pull of gravity regardless of their size or mass."

Marc's forehead creased. "So, are you say'n weedy guys, like yourself, will be pulled down with the same force as a big dude like myself?"

"Even the lightest of flying birds will feel the crush of the tunnel's pressure forcing it down," huffed Mr Regent. "So, no matter what you are, it's best to be prepared for contact with the Blorm."

"Ah, the Gravity Tunnel," Marc said mockingly, his chest blowing out with pride. "The almighty species equalizer."

"Yes," said Mr. Regent. "You could say that. But the problem is that Elsh's volatile environment may take the Gravity Tunnel a while to kick in once you arrive."

"You mean we won't be able to breathe?" Marc snarled.

"No. It just means the nausea and heaviness from your travels may persist a little longer than normal."

"Great," Marc said antagonistically, forcing one of his rehearsed smiles to appear. "No wonder the Kryon chose Elsh."

"Stop being so negative," Dom snapped. "Don't you know by now there's more to this race than just physical strength?"

"The Blorm," Ky said pensively.

"What?"

"The Blorm is the key. We all have to cross it. The Gravity Tunnel will ensure that. So, using those objects, and finding the Kryon's emotional weaknesses, is what matters most." Mr Regent's dismissiveness gave Ky's intuition cause for concern. "What else aren't you telling us?"

"What do you mean?" said a sheepish Mr Regent, whose face twitched involuntarily. "You know everything I do."

"What are you hiding Regent!" Dom added.

"Forget it," Ky said. "He only tells us what he wants us to hear."

"But..." Dom said.

"You should listen to Mr Sterling," said the Earth Elder, tapping his transmission again. "I understand," he mumbled, looking up at the far wall of the Preparation Room.

"More secrecy!" Dom said, clearly unhappy with all the covert happenings.

"Defenders," said Mr Regent. "It's time for Mr Sable to leave us. Out that door if you don't mind."

Dom frowned. "Where am I going?"

"Home Mr Drayed. You're going home."

"Lucky boy," Marc said.

"I would have gone with you if they let me."

"We know."

"Then I guess this is it."

Ky smiled. "Keep everyone positive back home."

"Will do. And you stay focused. Remember your strengths maybe their weakness. You can survive this."

As soon as Dom exited, Marc and Ky peered around the deserted Preparation Room. A flickering fluorescent light on the far wall sent an eerie shiver through both men.

"So, what now?" Ky asked Mr Regent distrustfully.

"You don't like me very much," the Elder said rhetorically. "May I ask why?"

Interrupting, Marc laughed. "It's because you're such a %$*#."

"A what?"

"He means you're rude," Ky said.

"Yes. I have been told I can be quite blunt. But I sense there's more to it than that – Mr Sterling, please enlighten me."

Ky hesitated and huffed. "To be honest, I'm not particularly fond of Elders."

Mr Regent smiled. "But Loush Sterling is an Elder."

"She's the exception. Now don't mention my mother again. I've heard the things you've said about her."

"Ah, now we get to the truth."

"And don't deny it. Dom said you meant every word."

"It's no secret how I felt about Elder Sterling's papers on the Massine debate. But I must admit I was too harsh. I see that now."

"I'm glad you told me," Ky said sarcastically. "So now go and tell the rest of the world."

"I don't have to. Everyone saw how honourably she spoke in Pretta. She will have earned everyone's respect."

Ky nodded. "Fine. Let's just drop it. After all, we do have another matter to focus on."

Mr Regent huffed and hesitantly shuffled towards the fluorescent light where he proceeded to clap three times, causing a subtle rumble beneath the Defenders' feet. "Brace yourself," he said, as the brick wall disappeared, revealing a smaller adjoining courtyard filled with bright smoky lights.

Ky blinked, sharpening his vision, as the smoke cleared. "Esau? What are you doing here?"

"Hello Ky. I am standing inside the strongest Lest teleportation device ever built on Earth. It is what you will use to travel to Elsh."

"But why are you here?"

"To wish you both a safe passage," Esau said, stepping out of the device and into the grass covered courtyard.

"Lest transportation is safe enough, isn't it?"

"Of course. But the race is not."

"So, you think we're in danger?"

"Defenders are always in danger." Esau's face creased, smirking with his characteristically wicked grin. "Just think of this as your chance to show that Earth humans do indeed belong."

"Yeah," Marc said. "We can do this."

"Now that's good to hear," Esau said, placing his hand on Mr Regent's shoulder. "Please escort me out before you send these two brave Defenders off."

Mr Regent nodded, grabbed the Grand Elder's arm, as both exited the Preparation Room.

Ky stared back towards the Elders. "But are we fully healed?"

With no answer forthcoming, Ky and Marc cautiously approached the tiny courtyard containing the inter-galactical Lest device; a technology they would have never before dared to use on their own.

LXIII.

"It was difficult to keep it hidden," said Mr Regent.

"You played your part well," Esau said, handing Mr Regent a backpack.

"What is this for?"

"Hope. Open it after I leave. Although the instructions are inside, you should know what to do."

"But what about..."

"Yes. I know. It was important you didn't say anything. Fear already courses through their bodies and, until now, they needed to concentrate on their regeneration and on each other."

"And now their unification has occurred, don't you think they should be told? It may help them survive."

"Only their participation is important. Our hope lives with the Zordacian meaning the survival of our Defenders is not essential."

"But we need to give them every chance. I want to tell them."

Esau hesitated and released himself from Mr Regent's support. His legs wobbled as age, and fatigue from his numerous travels of late, had begun to show. "Where did Sable go? I need to speak with him."

Mr Regent pointed back towards the Safe Room which contained the regeneration beds. "Are you going to be okay?"

Esau revealed a tight smile, trying to disguise any pain. "You may return."

"So, can I tell them?"

Esau pondered for a moment. "Yes. But be specific with the facts. After all, it's not just the Kryon who await them on Elsh. *They* have sensed the occasion. They can taste the battle. They too will be there."

LXIV.

"Wait!" Mr Regent screamed, leaping in front and preventing the Defenders from taking another step further into the courtyard. "You can't enter yet. He's not ready for you."

"Who's not ready?" Ky asked.

"Agrh, never you mind. Just don't move any closer."

After beckoning the men to sit down on the lush grass beneath, Mr Regent tore open his newly acquired knapsack. He gazed up, inhaling the chilly aroma of the mist hovering in the open-air courtyard. "The skies have cooled since yesterday's race."

"It's Massine, isn't it?" Ky said.

Mr Regent nodded. "Please sit."

Marc dropped to his knees. The spongy foliage engulfed his lower limbs. "I almost forgot what this softness feels like."

Ky too sat. He bent both legs and leaned back on his heels. "It's so gentle on my legs."

Mr Regent smiled, knelt, and dug deep into his knapsack. After bypassing a bunch of crumpled papers, he pulled out a capsule. "These strands of grass are laced with a Zordacian healing serum which, together with this tablet, will provide you with the last stage of your regeneration."

Once ensuring the Defenders had swallowed the capsule, he hauled out a grey cloak, draped it around himself, and bowed ritualistically.

"Defenders," he said, lifting his head. "Despite what you may think of me, it has been a privilege preparing you for this Challenge."

Although the cloak's hood shadowed his ghostly white face, he flung the sleeves away to reveal two neatly folded and freshly pressed body suits – each with a red ribbon placed on top.

Ky was puzzled.

Mr Regent stood and tapped his transmission. He moved aside, allowing the Defenders to gaze at the far wall.

A small box-like engraving began to etch itself in its centre, drawing the Defender's attention.

"Is that..." Marc said.

"Yes. This is your direct teleportation into Elsh, and will soon be the last Lest exit point open on Earth."

"Are we leaving now?" Marc said tentatively.

"Not yet," said Mr Regent, drawing back his hood. "Please take off your jump suits, get dressed, and approach me."

In an instant, Marc's body was bare. After pulling on his knee length tights, and tossing his jump suit in one of the corners, he eagerly presented himself.

"Let this be your link to your fellow Hominidae," said Mr Regent, swaddling the first ribbon-like arm band around Marc's bicep.

"Ouch! That's too tight."

"The soreness will ease after you have adjusted to the Elsh environment. But until you do, let the pain keep you alert."

Marc lowered his arm and grasped the sore spot. "It feels like rubber, yet I can't move it."

"It cannot be removed until the task is complete," said Mr Regent, binding the second arm band around Ky, causing him to wince.

"Defenders. The track on Elsh is unlike any you have ever competed on. It is made up of two adjoining eighty-eight meter circuits."

"What!" Marc said, as his temple began to throb. "We can barely survive a single circuit. How can we do two?"

"Hopefully you will find a way. But a reprieve will come at the end of the first circuit for it is there, on a platform, you will remain until eighty-eight more dats are counted. When this time expires, you *must* begin the last leg."

"What do you mean *must*?" Marc asked.

"It means that, if you can stand on your feet, the platform will force you to begin. And being forced doesn't work so well against the Blorm."

"Then what if we're ready to leave before?" Marc asked.

"Even if you are ready, your countdown's invisible shield will not allow you to enter the second leg until this personal countdown has expired. But remember, poisons will be coursing through your body. This will be your one and only chance to recover from the first stage, so use that time wisely and don't let the poisons become permanent."

Marc's face turned pale. "How do you know all this?"

"I have been privy to the instructions for the Challenge. They are rules the rest of our people are learning as we speak."

Marc frowned. "Good idea. Let's just scare everyone by telling them everything."

Mr Regent looked sheepishly back towards the Lest engraving.

Ky huffed. "But he's not telling us everything. Are you Mr Regent..."

Mr Regent turned back and nodded. "There is another danger on Elsh."

"Are you kidding?!" Marc snapped. His fiery eyes intensifying as he placed his sweaty palms against his temples. "This is why we don't trust Elders."

"Please calm down Mr Drayed," said Mr Regent. "Your emotions are still hindering your recovery. If that continues, you may not be granted access into Elsh."

"So what?!"

"If you, or Mr Sterling, do not partake, then we are deemed to have rejected the Challenge, and our people will perish. But I don't need to remind you of that now, do I!"

"But..."

"If it's pity you seek," said Mr Regent, "just remember the Kryon will show you none."

Marc's breath had become erratic, his head clearly hurting.

"Just breathe mate," Ky said.

Marc lowered his shoulders and inhaled deeply. His arms drooped and biceps began to twitch. "I'll be okay. Just tell us about this other danger."

"Very well," said Mr Regent. "It is said Elsh can become riddled with clusters of unevolved creatures, known as *Dromes,* during inter-species Defender races."

"I guess they're not after an autograph," Marc said sarcastically.

Mr Regent frowned, clearly unreceptive to humour. "Most of them are harmless," he said, briefly describing the Rumies, a wolf-like creature commonly seen on Zordac. "But though these Rumies probably won't even know you've arrived until the race is over, I'm afraid there are others who won't be so civil."

"Huh! Who?" Marc griped. "I mean, what would they want with us?"

"The Hord, as they are called, are the king of all Dromes. While no one really knows what they look like up close, we're told they inhabit any world hosting these inter-species races. They hibernate, deep within the planet's core, and wait until their deadly obsession with the Defenders comes to pass. I guess if a Defender represents protection, you'd better think of these vicious beasts as the anti-Defender who want only to see you fail."

Mr Regent hesitated.

"Oh, don't stop now. Your words are so comforting."

"Very well," Mr Regent smirked, finally getting Marc's sarcasm. "Signified by their screeches, the Hord gain strength as the countdown nears expiry. When this happens know that, as you chase the finish, the Hord will be chasing you."

Marc pursed his lips. "So, let me get this straight. In order to protect our own species from annihilation we have to go into this foreign planet, adjust to its gravity and oxygen levels, avoid the inhabiting predators and defeat a superior species in a Blorm engulfed Defenders' Race. Oh, and this victory has to be by more than five dats or that one-on-one battle to the death will follow. Does that about sum it up?"

"Don't concern yourselves with the individual nature of the Zankar. Just stay united and try to finish. We have another Defender who can handle the Kryon."

"Gee. Talk about pressure on that Zordacian guy."

"Hey," Ky said. "The engraving is gone."

"Ah," said Mr Regent, turning his back to the Defenders. "Not long to go now."

Ky closed his eyes. Despite being half naked, he felt warm. "I think I've actually recovered."

A hiss sounded from the sky above the courtyard. As Mr Regent raised his head an immense boom sounded.

Ky's eyes shot open.

The countdown warnings had changed, resonating even louder than before.

"The gate is open," said Mr Regent.

Marc, who had been startled by the countdown, suddenly dropped to the ground. "Agrh!"

"Marc?" Ky said, seeing that one of his legs had begun to convulse. "What's going on?"

"I don't know, but my foot hurts like hell."

While cracking sounds began whipping the surrounding air, Mr Regent ignored Marc's pleas and whispered. "My Defenders, they're ready for you."

LXV.

"Ky," Marc shouted, grasping his right leg. "My foot *really* hurts, and it's getting worse!"

As another chime echoed throughout the courtyard, Ky scampered across and lifted Marc's sore foot in the air. "It's probably just a cramp," he said, fisting Marc's sole vigorously.

"Take it easy!"

Ky smiled. "You're gonna face much worse than this."

Marc grimaced. "But it hurts so much."

"Just keep breathing normally," he said, feeling the joints click into place.

"Okay. Okay. It's easing. The pain's going."

"Good. But I don't think that was a cramp."

"What else could it be?" Marc said, sitting upright.

Ky shrugged. "Dunno. It felt like your bones were shifting."

"You're right," said Mr Regent. "The re-alignment of bones is another side-effect of the regeneration. It usually occurs painlessly during your regeneration sleep, but due to your recent anxiety over Mr Sterling, your recovery was somewhat delayed. But I wouldn't worry, it's probably over now."

"Well, my foot *does* feel better. Actually, it feels great."

"And how about you Mr Sterling?"

Marc laughed. "His feet were never hurt in the first place. I'm sure he's fine."

"Look! I know people don't understand how I ran over the Blorm without being hurt, but know I'm no different to you. Anyone can do what I did, especially you."

Marc frowned and glared at Ky's feet. "But you must have known something about the Blorm I didn't. What did it feel like when you ran over them?"

Ky shrugged. "It's hard to explain. Some of them seemed to freeze, protecting me from the others."

Marc raised his eyebrows. "Maybe they're afraid of your so called high EALF."

"I don't think so."

"Then how did you know which ones to run over? Did you see the Numerals?"

Ky nodded. "They appeared just before the race. And you too?"

"I always see them. Good thing too, otherwise I would have been really hurt." Marc appeared contemplative. "Maybe you just see more of them."

"Maybe," Ky said. After a flickering drew his attention, Ky peered over at the wall beyond Mr Regent. "Look! The engravings are back."

"Good," said Mr Regent. "Are you ready Mr Sterling?"

Ky nodded.

"And you Mr Drayed?"

"I've spent my entire life preparing for this."

At that moment, a black smoke crept out from within the engraving, transposing itself against the brick wall. As Marc peered closer, he could see this new shadowy silhouette was taking on his own image before morphing into a small phoenix-like creature perched upside-down.

"Mr Drayed," said Mr Regent. "Your entrance to Elsh has been activated. Please prepare to leave as he will be waiting."

"Who will be waiting?" Marc said, jumping to his feet and pointing to the mystical creature whose folded wings seemed to be guarding the gateway. "You mean that thing?"

"No. That is the Challenge's protector and will only permit entry for those delegated to Elsh."

"Then who's waiting for me?"

"Your guide. Apart from Defenders, they are the only other Nyrolacs permitted into Elsh."

Marc gazed deeper into the shadow but jerked back as the creature's wings opened. "And what is my guide supposed to do with me?"

"From the moment we chose to accept the Challenge of the Nameless, these guides were sent to prepare Elsh for your arrival."

Marc inhaled. He pumped his fists together, causing his arm band to tighten. As dry sweat glued the silk shorts to his naked waist, he exhaled. "Then we'd better not keep him waiting."

Mr Regent smiled and stepped aside. "With their preparations almost complete, your guide's last task is to lead you to your lane."

"Is that all? Will they help us adjust to Elsh?"

"Despite being expert medics, they are not permitted to assist you until the race is over. So don't expect anything more."

Another chime startled Marc. Despite knowing the countdown, both Defenders were on edge as the decibel level of each sound, once again, seemed to elevate.

After providing a few more details about the guide's, Mr Regent peered back at the shadow. The phoenix was unmoved. "Please disable your Translators. They are not to be used until the Challenge is over."

"But how will our guide understand us?" Marc asked.

"He won't."

Marc tapped his transmission, deactivating his Translator. Beads of sweat re-appeared on his chest. His toes tapped the grass like they were playing piano. He took another deep breath, holding it in as if it were his last. *Remember to breathe slowly*, he reminded himself. *Just like Ky said.*

After seeing the phoenix lower its wings, Mr Regent knew Elsh's co-ordinates had been received. He turned back to Marc. "Au-revoir," he said, gesturing for him to move inside the shadow.

Marc moved towards the silhouette as blue and white light emerged, swirling at a pace which mimicked its gentle sucking of air.

"See you soon," Ky said, having also disabled his Translator.

Although reaching for the shadow, Marc looked back and smiled, happy he could still understand his fellow Defender.

The gravitational pull from the shadow grew stronger. The swirls gained speed. As he made contact with the image the lights began to flicker sporadically. Marc was gone.

Ky shuddered, for without a moment's reprieve the shadow changed from Marc's image to that of his own.

Instantly, the suck changed direction, blowing a wind that dried the sweat on his forehead. His body tensed and his own arm band tightened.

After Mr Regent waved him through, Ky nodded with a grin that seemed to relinquish much of the internal hostility he had felt towards

Elders.

He stepped forward. His eyes widened and nose tingled as an influx of oxygen forced him to exhale.

Here I go, he thought, as an inward gust drew him closer.

Feeling light headed, Ky looked back but quickly realised he was enclosed, surrounded by a blur of jelly-like swirls.

As the encircling colours changed to the brightest of whites, a brief moment of silence ensued.

A drum beat echoed, followed by the sound of a rumbling stampede.

The white disappeared, leaving Ky dazed, while the thunderous roars grew.

Be calm. Everything's okay, he thought. As the noise softened to a background patter, his vision, along with a flood of memories, returned.

Sitting on the front porch of his family home, Ky gazed up to watch the rain tumbling on his balcony's tin roof.

The creaking door to the Sterling's farmhouse opened. Still unsure of his reality, he peered back to see an older man approach him.

Ky rubbed his eyes. "Dad?" Ky said, "is that you?"

LXVI.

One Click remains.

LXVII.

Far away, a murky dawn surrounded Tousol, a small drought-affected village in old Africa, and the birth place of Dominique Sable.

Throughout his youth, Dom's local community had watched him evolve from a ferociously talented boy into the epitome of a Defender. Though well-spoken and rational, numerous world travels had never diminished his outspoken pride for his village.

Rewarding his loyalty, this same affection was returned by his townsfolk, despite his failure in the Massine Challenge. While Pretta's proceedings, which carried on throughout Tousol's night, peppered images of the debating Elders and their fears, the ten thousand strong residents instead chose to recount their hero's past glories. Not even glazed eyes and foggy heads prevented them from huddling around their archaic outdoor, sphere-shaped Façade of which its gigantic screen hovered over the centre of the village's only oval.

Doubling as the training ground for other aspiring Defenders, the patchy turf was left neglected by the town's lack of rain that jagged rubble had become more prominent than grass. Though uncomfortable to sit on, it was the perfect surface for Dom to have honed his famous *toughest feet on Earth* slogan.

While many of the idealistic adults continued to chatter through the breaking dawn, Sam Sable, Dom's younger cousin stared at the visiting Crilinian Educator who sat silently on the stage built beneath the Façade. Though Sam had heard the recently publicised influx of Educators into many human communities was an attempt by the Elders to subdue fears of the upcoming Challenge, Sam wondered why this strange looking human was not more forthcoming with his advice. "If you are so unwilling to tell us anything," he shouted, making his way closer to the stage, "why have you come? Dom's going to be here any moment. I'm sure he'll give us the answers we need."

The Crilinian sneered, unhappy with the predicament the Grand Elders had put him in. "I am not telling you any less than what the rest of our Hominidae are currently hearing. And your Defender, Dom, knows no more than I."

"But we all saw how secretive you were in Pretta. I know you're hiding something."

Through jeers of agreement, the Crilinian spoke. "I won't be here for much longer, so why don't you ask me something I might have an answer for."

"You mean something you're allowed to answer," Sam said, sitting.

"Don't take it to heart," whispered an older lady seated next to Sam. "Just look around. We're a proud community who believe in your cousin. We know he'll be here soon. He will know what to do."

"But that guy's so smug. We shouldn't be treated like this. I'm sure he knows something. Why else is he here?"

"Does that really matter?" she said, drawing Sam's attention to the other side of the stage. "Besides, if there's something to learn I'd rather hear it from him."

"Dom!" Sam shouted, seeing his cousin materialise to the enormous cheers engulfing the oval.

Smelling the morning's warmth toasting the crispy dew, Dom took his seat alongside the Crilinian Educator. "Please," he announced, raising his arms to hush the crowd. "No matter what has been said, this is the time to unite with all Hominidae, not to create more adversaries."

"But he's supposed to be giving us information," said Sam, standing and pointing to the Crilinian. "Every time he's been asked about the Kryon, or about their EALF rating, you wanna know what he does? Nothing! He just sits there."

Dom smiled, happy to see his feisty cousin's love for the EALF rating had not diminished with his own lack of success. "I guess you really want to know how *Sterling* and *Drayed's* EALF stacks up against the Kryons'."

Seeing it was not just Sam, but much of the townsfolk, who agreed, the Cril Educator grunted. "I don't know why you persist in thinking your Defenders have a chance against the Kryon," said the Crilinian. "The Zordacian is our best hope. Your Earthlings should focus on surviving."

"But if you want us to unite," Dom said, facing the Crilinian, "like the Grand Elders have requested of you, then you should empower us to support all Hominidae Defenders. Letting the townsfolk see the similarities between the Kryons and our Defender's EALF rating will go a long way to achieving this."

"What makes you think the Kryon's EALF rating is similar to *any* humans, let alone an Earthlings?" grinned the Crilinian, tapping his transmission to summon the latest Kryon EALF ratings; downloadable from the Knowledge Base by someone of his status. "To be honest, I held back this information to *give* you hope, not take it from you. But seeing how eager you are to learn, perhaps I should divulge this information."

"But..." Dom pleaded.

"No! It can't be."

Dom could see the traces of arrogance vanish before the Crilinian's eyes. "What's going on? What did you receive?"

"I didn't realise. I mean, I knew it was high, but..."

"What? What is it?"

The Cril Educator stood. His thin yet broad body overshadowed Dom's. "We already knew they're bigger and stronger than us, so it was no surprise to learn, prior to the Pretta forum, that the Kryon's average rating was higher than almost all our Defenders."

"We could have guessed that," Dom said, hopping off stage.

After grasping his pasty forehead in disbelief, the Crilinian's pale eyes, larger than any Earth human, gazed into the crowd. "Their lack of emotions were our Zordacian's only hope. It's what kept his EALF rating of seventy-five the same as the leading Kryons."

"And now?"

The Crilinian hesitated. "I have just learned the EALF of the Cril Kryon has climbed past eighty, and still improving as we speak."

Sam's jaw dropped. "But it can't be true. That's less than twenty points away from achieving their ultimate potential, something not even the Obzoovers have achieved."

"Who cares," Dom snapped. "I mean, what does that really show?"

The Crilinian stared up at the sky. "It means we're all doomed."

The old lady next to Sam stood and peered back at the

disheartened crowd. "Come on everyone. They're only numbers. Let's not put too much emphasis on it."

"Perhaps you don't understand," said the Crilinian, as melancholy draped his words. "The *Expert in the Art of LiFe* calculation is a measure of the physical, intellectual and emotional capabilities as derived from our Deoxyribonucleic acid, muscular fibres and brain wave stimuli. It is correct, and it is absolute."

"Maybe it's my lack of sleep," said the old lady, "but if we believe hard enough I'm sure we can beat them."

"Your faith is admirable, and would mean my work here is done. But this rating means the Cril Kryon could have combined their naturally elevated evolutionary potential with a supreme work ethic. If so, they will be better equipped to handle the Challenge than any of our Defenders."

The old lady leaned closer to Sam and whispered. "Don't believe everything you hear. If we trust our Defenders then they will feel our support. That's how we can help."

"You're right," Dom said, eavesdropping, "and who says that high EALF rating translates into running well on Elsh."

"Yes," Sam nodded. "Our two guys *can* do it!"

"Haven't you learnt anything?" growled the Crilinian, whose own emotions oscillated like a pendulum. "Just remember they chose the location of the race."

"You're so negative!" barked Sam. "You should be brave like us. It's your life on the line too!"

"Well maybe if your cousin had won the Massine Challenge the Kryon would not have Challenged your people."

"You can't blame Dom for this! He only represented the pro-Massiners to help this town secure water priority. Besides, the Pretta Chairperson said the Kryon would have found a way to Challenge us no matter what."

"Excuses are the cry of the weak. But then you are an Earthling."

"Hey. Don't talk to me that way! Are you gonna let him do that Dom?"

"No! But right now, I'd rather get some answers." Dom said, "Tell me Educator, what makes you think Sterling can't win. We don't even know what his EALF is."

"No Earthling has evolved sufficiently to race over two adjoining circuits, let alone win."

"But Ky just won without a scratch."

"That was a fluke, against lesser competition."

"But..."

"Since we seem to be going in circles I believe my work here is done. I just hope the Elders let me go soon."

Dom shook his head and turned to face the populous. "Our Defenders are also our protectors. Do not let your faith waiver."

Sam pondered his cousin's words, but while perusing the darkening sky his once hope filled eyes narrowed.

"Ah," announced the Crilinian. "My prayers have been answered. It is time for me to return home. Remember the Zordacian is our only hope. If *you* pray for anyone, pray for him." With a parting grin, he stepped to the rear of the stage, tapped his ear, and vanished.

Suddenly, a Façade link into Elsh activated, making the Tousol community aware of the impending countdown.

"Sam," Dom whispered. "Sam!"

"Oh. Sorry. What did you say?"

"Did the Educator mention any other Sterling?"

"You mean Ky's mother, Loush?"

"No. I mean Ahlis."

"Who?"

"Ahlis Sterling. She's Ky's sister and Loush's daughter."

"Nope," Sam shrugged. "never heard of her. But I think the Crilinian did mention how Ky's dad was once a Defender."

"Yeah, I heard something about that as well."

"Are you sure he didn't mention Ahlis?"

"I'm sure."

"Then what about Ky's flyat, Nibby. Did he mention her?"

Sam shook his head. "Never heard of her either. Why do you care so much about his family anyway? What's going on Dom?"

"The Grand Elder said two of the Sterling women hold a secret. Though not even shared with one another, it's a link that unites both Ky and Marc."

"And what does that have to do with you?"

"I don't know. The Elder simply asked if I would make sure the Sterling women are safe."

"Don't tell me you're going away again?" Sam fretted.

"Only if Loush is held up in Pretta," Dom said, tapping his transmission. "Wait here while I check."

"But you can't leave us," Sam whimpered. "This town's *your* family and we need you too."

LXVIII.

"Oh, thank goodness you're home," Ahlis said, returning home to see Loush standing under the hall archway. "Nibby and I are so nervous mum. We're so happy to see you. I can't stop shaking. What should we do?"

"I'm not sure," Loush said, having freed herself from the formalities of Pretta to rush home. "But after learning about those Hord creatures I feel we need to comfort one another."

"I wish we could comfort the Defenders," Nibby added, embracing Loush.

"We all do dear. But I'm sure they have enough help. In fact, I received a strange call from one of them, Dominique Sable, asking if I had arrived home."

"What's strange about that?" Nibby asked.

"Well he also wanted me to make sure you two girls are safe and to tell you that Marc Drayed sends his love. Do you know that Marc fella?"

"Ahlis does," Nibby joked, as the Façade flickered images of the darkening skies beginning to surround many human communities. "But best not to look outside," she added. "The Massine has arrived."

"How can we ignore it?" Ahlis said, covering her ears as a sudden crackle screamed from the Façade.

"You can't," Nibby said. "But for now, let's focus on the screen as it's trying to connect to Elsh, and to our Ky."

Moments later, a flutter of synthesised words rushed from the Façade and into the Sterling's lounge.

"Welcome witnesses. The Defenders are in their final preparations. Please give them the honour they deserve for they answer the Knowledge Base's eternal question: *what would you do to protect life itself?* For most, the question would never arise, but for the Defenders, it is a way of life."

Another chime sounded. The voice continued. "If the Hominidae win, Earth humans will be completely accepted as Nyrolacs...but if the Kryon win, all human civilizations will be annihilated – When the Challenge is over we will uphold the rules of the Knowledge Base governing this inter-species' challenge. So be aware that all Massines have now acquired their targets."

The hair on Nibby's neck stood as tension in her muscles crippled any movement. *Not again.*

"Isn't there anything we can do?" Ahlis pleaded, grasping Nibby's hand for a glimmer of hope.

Nibby nodded. "Believe in our men. No, believe in all human Defenders, like the Zordacian, for it's become apparent our choice in faith may be the only thing left we can control."

With the cloudy gloom of Massine surrounding all Hominidae, the finality that lay ahead became frighteningly clear.

LXIX.

The Zordac Defender's only memory of peace is what kept him sane through his rigorous training regimes, a process which had killed many before him.

Having been cursed with an un-naturally long life this Zordacian, who rarely spoke, had long since shut away the desire to receive emotional care, despite the echoes of what once was haunting his mind. *I'll always be with you,* speak the voices of his long-departed loved ones.

Prior to entering Elsh alone, and adding to his torment, the Elders had recently shifted his training focus from the more popular Defenders' Race to the vicious, yet seldom used, Zankar.

During this time, the Zordac Defender, who had found himself consumed with these one-on-one death battles, was visited by the Zordacian's only Grand Elder.

"You are Hominidae's warrior," affirmed the Elder. "We have relied on you to Defend us; to carry out many covert operations."

The Zordacian remained unmoved.

"Although the blood you stole from the Traveller shows her EALF rating has changed at an unnatural rate, it is you who are the chosen one, not her Earthling mate, for you have always done what the other humans could not."

The Defender's eyes leered angrily.

"Now you must do it again. You're the only one who can."

LXX.

Ky blinked rapidly and continued to rub his eyes. "Dad?" he repeated, as the thunderous roars returned, replacing the tranquillity of this imagery homestead. "is this Elsh?" he asked, watching the man move to within an arm's length.

Although boasting a similar appearance to Elric, Ky quickly realised he was mistaken, recalling Mr Regent saying these guides are members of a shape-shifting species who alter their appearance to avoid startling those unfamiliar with their true, more grotesque form.

Continuing to stare at the authoritative humanoid, whose lack of response reminded him that his translator had been disabled, Ky wondered how it knew to choose Elric to transpose into. Not that he had time to ponder, for in an instant his guide had turned and walked away, subtly gesturing to be followed.

Despite his legs wobbling in the chilly air, a bewildered Ky pursued his guide. But while each step allowed his strength to return, the dim surroundings sent shivers through him as Mr Regent's brief teachings came flooding back.

On the outer rim of the Goliath sector a giant star, known as Faru, is the light source to a pair of circling planets. Cril, the larger one, is home to both Human and Kryon civilizations. Though they live in close proximity, an ongoing feud has kept them segregated for over an Age. Of late, rumours emerged that the Kryon's desire for sole ownership of Cril was the reason behind the challenge of the Nameless; an astonishing thought knowing what the repercussions of their victory would mean.

But no matter their motives, while both species thrived on Cril, the unevolved inhabitants of its neighbouring planet, Elsh, were not so lucky. With Faru's light searing through Elsh's slender atmosphere every twenty Clicks the harshest period, lasting for fifteen of the twenty, repeatedly forced its occupants underground.

As Faru's rays shifted beyond the planet's rotation, a cold

darkness, lasting the next two Clicks, instantly cooled the burnt landscape by freezing the surface. Though the Dromes remained hidden, Elsh would quickly become inhabitable. As such, in the final three Clicks that follow, and prior to Faru's blazing heat coming full circle, the Challenge of the Nameless will be conducted.

Having already ended, the first of these three Clicks had guides scurry like buzzing insects in an attempt to complete the vital preparations.

The second, beginning just prior to Ky's arrival, would be dedicated to ensuring the race itself would conclude before Faru's heat becomes too great.

In spite of having sufficient time to exit Elsh during the third Click, it is in this last phase that the most brutal of all Dromes, the territorial Hord, are said to re-surface. For this reason, it's the aim of every Nyrolac to evacuate before this Click even begins.

Continuing to fall further behind his guide, Ky trudged through Elsh's strong gravity. As the intermittent roars became constant, and recalling that much of this new environment would be impervious to the Gravity Tunnel, he tried to ignore the discomfort of his heavy legs by examining his surroundings.

Though the misty dawn had trapped the temperate chill of the earlier freeze, Elsh's rotation around Faru forced the giant ringed planet of Cril, and its two satellite moons, to fade beyond the horizon, sullying any thought that the much-feared heat would be kept at bay.

Boom! crashed a metallic sound, transforming the roars into a unified chant.

I know what that is. Ky thought, enjoying the warm flutter which cloaked his body. And even after a stumble over a cluster of rocks had him silently begging for his guide to slow down, a movement from the corner of his eye kept him smiling. "Marc!" he shouted, seeing that his fellow Defender, led hastily by another overzealous humanoid guide, was also moving towards the chants.

Despite realising Marc was too far to hear, Ky regained his footing with rejuvenated energy. *The Gravity Tunnel*, he thought. *It's working.* But although he quickened his steps, his guide had stopped, preventing Ky's progress with one hand while raising a finger, to halt, with the other.

As they both froze, a flash whizzed past, stopping in plain view as a knee-high chubby wolf-like creature, with dirt covered scales plastered all over its body, had begun to spin with great speed.

"Look," Ky gasped. "It's a Drome."

His guide turned, raised both eyebrows and pressed his finger firmly against his own lips.

With a sense of urgency, the creature used two of its paddle-like paws and scampered sideways.

As Ky kept staring, he could see a third and fourth paddle tucked under its rear. "Oh, it's one of those harmless Rumies," he added excitably, recalling it looked like the only Drome Mr Regent was able to describe. "It doesn't look *that* friendly."

His guide groaned, incensed the Earth Defender was not quiet.

After hearing the strange human voice, the young Rumie froze, popped its narrow head further out from its body and paused to examine Ky. Just then, it coiled itself and sprung away on its hind legs, joining a group of other Rumies in the distance.

The group soon dispersed, leaving clumps of bushes in their wake. But upon closer inspection, Ky's eyes widened as he realised they were not bushes, but rather Rumie corpses, which draped the Elsh landscape. It was a stark reminder of the planet's unforgiving nature and even more reason for him to stay close to his guide.

The problem was his guide's confidence had also begun to dwindle for he knew something no one had revealed to the Earth Defenders. While the rest of humanity learned the truth, Ky and Marc would be oblivious to the fact that the Hord could intimidate other fearful Dromes into becoming their scouts. In exchange for sparing their life, these obedient creatures were forced to rush to the surface too early, enduring the harsh conditions, in order to inform the Hord if any Defenders had arrived.

Unfortunately for Ky, it was the Rumies who had been selected to fulfil this role on Elsh; a task at least one had been successful at completing.

LXXI.

If the Defenders are the soul of the race, the rhythmical chants of the onlookers had become its anthem. This synchronised tune, felt more by vibration than heard by ears, was being hummed during the humans' arrival into Elsh; a tradition the Earthlings happily adopted.

Feeling the warmth of this familiar tune, Ky began to move across the coarse gravel with uplifting purpose. But no sooner had he and his guide caught another glimpse of Marc than a deafening horn, crashing its way through the land, diffused the chants.

The wind had picked up, sending pieces of dirt into a rapidly swirling vortex.

Dark and heavy, a new and untimely drum beat had begun, one not familiar to Ky. He winced as numerous shrieks had him covering his ears.

Just ahead, Marc's guide looked back towards Ky's guide. The two exchanged a gesture.

As the unpleasant sounds ceased with a final thud, Ky caught up to both guides. "What's going on?" he asked, knowing his words were spoken in vain.

Hurriedly, his guide waved for him to catch up to the unaware Marc. But in doing so Ky passed into the belly of the Gravity Tunnel, enabling him to hear the hostile mantra which flowed through the air.

"Kryon! Kryon! Kryon!"

LXXII.

"Ky?" Marc said, clearing dust from his eyes. "Is that you?"

Ky grabbed Marc's shoulder. "Who else would want to touch you?"

"Um, your sister."

"Touché."

Marc paused, allowing their guides to pass. "Not quite what we expected eh?" he mumbled. "Elsh is different to anything I could have imagined."

"I know. And the Kryon chant…it's so creepy. I sure hope we get to hear *our* chants again."

Marc nodded, unaware of an elongated shadow encroaching over his own.

The wind eased slightly, allowing Ky to hear the groans of their guides hauling themselves up a steep sand dune. "We'd better get moving," Ky said, quickening his pace. "The countdown isn't getting any slower."

Marc didn't move. Hands on waist, and through gritted teeth, he tried to block out the discomfort of his pressurized arm band. "Okay. I'm coming," he said, catching up, as the pair trudged up the dune leaving the unwelcome shadow behind.

As the incline levelled out, and Ky felt the heaviness fade from his quadriceps, he stopped abruptly. "Look at that!" he said, peeking over the summit. "There are so many humans."

"Now that's a sight for sore eyes. I was beginning to think we were the only ones here," Marc said, panting. "And they must be our lanes," he added, pointing to the only vacant spaces he could see. "Come on. Let's catch up. Our starting bays should be on the other side of that wall."

"Um…I don't think that's a wall."

With their guides descending the dune, Marc stared, carefully scrutinising the open amphitheatre and the sea of Kryon that extended as far as the eye could see. "There must be thousands of them," he said, legs shaking.

"I'd say it's more like a million," Ky said reluctantly, walking behind his guide who had tagged onto another group of guides and their human Defenders. "But don't forget we have a million too."

Marc remained quiet for the longest time before sidling closer to his guide. "Do you think we'll survive this?" he said nervously.

The guide ignored Marc's plea.

Listening, Ky turned. "Don't worry. I'm scared too."

"Scared?! What makes you think I'm scared?"

"Come on. This could be it for the human race. You'd be crazy not to be. But if we keep reminding ourselves why we're here, to protect our people, and avoid eye-contact with the Kryon, like we were told, I'm sure everything will be alright. Even so..."

"Okay. Okay. I'm a little scared. Just stop your speeches and I'll feel better...Oh, and don't tell Ahlis I was afraid."

"Why not?" Ky grinned, his breath regulating. "Are you afraid she'll see your sensitive side?"

"No!" Marc said, winking. "Because then she'd think we're friends."

But as the chants for the Kryon elevated, any humour quickly vanished as the pair joined the last group of human Defenders in their march towards the two-thousand-kilometre-wide wall of giant Kryon.

LXXIII.

While the oddly shaped Kryon appeared to hoard the stadium's numerous starting bays, the finishing area two hundred metres further ahead was draped with an enormous Façade. Though most onlookers were now connected, it was the haunting chants of the Kryon faithful that echoed loudest.

Seeing that most guides, whose roles had changed to that of post-race medics, were already taking their place beneath the distorted Façade faces, each guide in Ky's group flung their index fingers in the direction of the few vacant lanes which remained.

Instantly, and without so much as a parting glance, the other human Defenders in his group separated, leaving him staring into Marc's frightened eyes.

Ky gave a knowing nod as he turned to pursue *his* guide. Though also wanting assurance, he knew the time had come to be alone.

Marc, trying to shake the feeling of abandonment, puffed out his chest and followed his guide in between two massive Kryon from the planet Yeminus. *Don't look at them*, he reminded himself, fixing his eyes on his guide, who was scuttling through the partially covered lanes and towards the other medics. But concerned these Kryon could encroach into his diminutive starting bay, he lowered his eyes timidly to the dirt below.

Though cloaked with an eerie silence, after smelling the Earthling's fear, the plans of these Yeminus Kryon had changed.

LXXIV.

Having crept past the rear of a number of occupied lanes, which alternated species, Ky noticed each of his human compatriots, sitting on bent knees, had clumps of calluses protruding from their exposed heels. He didn't like accepting the limitations of his own unevolved feet but was strengthened by seeing the same red arm band he wore choke the bicep of the other human Defenders.

Moments later, Ky halted as he watched his guide rush into one of the only vacant starting bays remaining.

He took a steadying breath and turned back to see that Marc had already vanished behind a wall of the grey coarse-haired antagonists.

Son.

Ky turned suddenly, but no one was there. *I can hear you dad,* he thought, *and I'm scared.*

Though he heard nothing else, thinking of his father had given him the conviction to glance up at one of his own bordering Kryon.

Following another breath, he took a single step into his lane. Despite feeling boxed in, he locked his eyes onto the giant creature.

Sensing a human stare, the Kryon released an almighty primordial roar as its outstretched body stiffened with violent force.

Ky's heart jumped and as he shivered his eyes instinctively shot out and up, towards the Façade.

Just then, a sickening shriek silenced the Kryon and diffused the Façade chants as it blasted from somewhere back on the other side of the sand dune.

Disoriented by the noise, Ky escaped his claustrophobia by glancing back up at the Kryon.

Though rising three metres, the average height for a Kryon, its one metre wide torso was at his eye level. Noticing clusters of protruding spiky objects beginning to wiggle in his direction, he averted his eyes. *Don't be scared,* he thought, glancing across at the other Kryon.

Even larger, this creature, layered with a leathery brown fur darker than the others, also had protrusions which immediately began to squirm at the incoming stares.

Don't be scared.

Scratching the ground with one of its three feet, Ky could tell this Kryon seemed much calmer than the others as its rigid skin tore up the surface below.

Although it was different, he did not realise it was customary for the Challenging species to place their top Defender next to those whom they had challenged.

However, Ky did notice that its three racehorse-like hind legs twisted around one another before joining into its disproportionately short mid-region. This torso also had three symmetrical sides with each containing bundles of spiky protrusions wrapping around a contractible eight-fingered claw.

Perched on top of the torso was a head almost as wide as its body. Although it was also covered with clumps of fur, covering most of its orifices, a small ivory unicorn-like horn, used for smelling, had begun to emerge.

Unaware of the Kryon's immediate intentions, Ky crept closer to the edge of his starting bay where he snuck a glimpse down into his lane. *Is that...?*

Interrupted by the violent squirming of one of the Kryon's claws, Ky glanced back up at the Kryon and was taken aback to see its sunken mouth, positioned below its horn, open wide.

What's that? He thought, noticing a black cloth, made from the same material which collared his arm, pinned inside its mouth. But as a slight breeze blew the cloth aside, revealing a single blood-shot eye, Ky was sprayed with an odour so putrid that he winced, instantly dropping to the ground. The spray, more awful than the stench of a de-composing corpse, was so strong that his body shivered uncontrollably.

Resisting the urge to gag, he composed himself.

Just then, a gong bellowed throughout the arena as the Façade's chants transformed into a roar.

With the smell fading, warmth returned to Ky's body. *No matter what happens,* he thought, rising to his feet, *I have to finish this race.*

Though he was happy to see the Kryon's mouth had closed, he suddenly remembered the black cloth represented the mark of the challenging civilization. *This is a Cril Kryon,* he surmised. But no sooner did that revelation become clear than he realised the surrounding creatures may also realise something; that he was from Earth.

LXXV.

Five hundred kilometres away, the Zordacian Defender had also squeezed in between two large Kryon.

Though his eyes sparkled with the confidence of the victor, an uncharacteristic drop of sweat fell from his forehead. But with the fate of humanity on his shoulders, the greatest of all Human Defenders knew he was ready.

My fellow man is weak, he chanted, recalling the multitude of bloody acts he'd carried out with ease at the command of the Grand Elders.

Like a wildebeest ready to charge, he scraped his genetically padded feet over the rubble. *There is no strength in numbers here. I need to win. I'm the only one who can.*

LXXVI.

The history of the Blorm was one created out of curiosity as Knowledge Base leaders first devised these destructive objects to see if a Nyrolac's EALF rating would change after an encounter.

At the same time as Elsh medics were following the order of removing all protective opaque blankets covering the Blorm, Ky's guide-turned-medic glanced at the Kryon's choice of robotic medics.

With the squirming shape-shifters released, and knowing how these robots mimicked the Kryon's own emotionless nature, Ky's humanoid medic also remained poised, staring back in Ky's direction and reciting the rules of this Challenge to itself.

1. Elsh's Blorm cannot be handled without proper equipment. Instant death may result.

2. Competitors begin when the countdown is complete.

3. Competitors who survive the first stage must wait precisely eighty-eight dats before continuing.

4. The first to finish the second stage is declared the winner if the margin is greater than five dats. Otherwise a Zankar between the two top finishers will determine the result. No physical contact is permitted prior to this point.

5. Avoid all contact with the inhabitants of Elsh.

LXXVII.

While his medic locked its sights past the mid-way platform and onto Ky's dwarfed silhouette, Ky stared down the half metre plunge, from his and every starting bay, into his lane.

Though initially trying to compute his take-off, he couldn't help but wonder if the drop was there to prevent the slithering wraith-like Blorm from detecting their victims too soon. Then, after hearing the Façade's roar ascending to new heights, with more and more faces joining, he retreated back into his starting bay to repeat his mantra. *Stay calm, I can do this.*

Trying to disregard his surroundings did not bode well for Ky. Forcing repeated half breaths into his lungs was essential as deep inhales were choked by the dense atmosphere. Following another breath, a sinister wind compelled Ky to turn and face the sand dune from where he came. He could see that beyond the peak which he and Marc had climbed, the heat of Elsh's daybreak was strengthening.

Squinting, Ky's eyes were drawn towards the undulating mountain ranges peppering the horizon. Although previously deserted, a shadowy outline, neither human nor Kryon, crouched.

As the silhouette of a jagged head and body sitting on top of thin long legs seemed to be staring back in his direction, a sudden shift in the rising rays momentarily blinded Ky. And when he had adjusted, the creature's shadow could no longer be seen, sunken beneath the slopes in order to camouflage itself from prying eyes.

Following another gong, he faced the arena. *Stay calm, I can do this*. His eyes shut and jaw relaxed. As images of his family flooded his mind, momentarily blocking any thought of the Kryon, Blorm or that mysterious creature, a full breath finally penetrated his lungs. The bond between his mind and body finally unified.

However, despite being ready, a blood curdling screech, rising from behind the sand dune, had every Nyrolac on edge.

LXXVIII.

Two million Defenders, spanning thousands of kilometres, wait in their imaginary cage as the countdown continues to tick away. Despite their outer poise, the shriek, which quietened the Façade, sends an eerie silence across Elsh.

A drum beat, louder than the previous gongs, sounds. Though more agreeable than the screech, an ominous feeling keeps the unease.

Ten dats remain.

The Human Defenders bend forward, pressing against the invisible starting barrier.

The Kryon do not move.

Ky grinds a bunch of rubble beneath his toes and lowers himself into his unique crouch position. *The Numerals*, he says, seeing a vision flash before his eyes.

Although only a fleeting image, he begins to feel the rhythm of Elsh.

Boom! Crashes another drum beat. Five dats remain.

Ky's body coils. His legs fill with explosive power. Although he places one foot behind the other, most other humans keep both feet together; their superior strength allows this more advanced method.

Boom! Three dats remain.

Boom! The Façade mutes. Two dats remain.

Every Kryon instantly changes position, as each takes a large yet measured step towards the starting line.

Boom! One.

The universe is silent.

B... They're gone! *...oom!*

With that sound, and as the Façade roars, a million human Defenders launch themselves forward, dropping into their lanes and driving themselves further and further ahead of their adversaries. Although the Kryon also take their first step, it is slow and deliberate, delicately gaining a sense of what lies below.

Like his fellow humans, Ky begins fast, blasting into the heart of the transparent Gravity Tunnel and in between a small number of unsuspecting Blorm. Despite his dexterity, the squirming chameleons further down his lane are alerted and quickly shift into place.

LXXIX.

Most humans, having evolved to find a balance between strength and endurance, continue to expand their advantage over the seemingly unhurried Kryon. But it's the long jumping grace of the Zordacian's take-off which propels him into the lead. While his initial six-metre circular step has the pull of the Gravity Tunnel at his mercy, the slightest of stumbles, when attempting to land in a tiny Blorm free area, begins a succession of uncharacteristic shorter steps; the fourth of which grazes his shin against a single sprouting Blorm. Nevertheless, his advantage over the nearest Kryon extends to twenty metres.

But while his adversaries' limbs, unaffected by the watchful shape-shifters, rotate in elegant unison, the Zordacian's refusal to decelerate, despite an awareness poisons are seeping into his blood stream, sees his stealthy movements begin to wane. What's more, a cluster of Blorm, camouflaging themselves halfway to the end of the first stage, decipher his new stride pattern and begin slashing at his elastic achilles.

Caught by surprise at the atypical action, and with another force tugging at his thoughts, he plummets to the ground, burying his face in the dirt. Though he tries to crawl, the tugging had heavied his body, preventing him from moving and giving enough time for the Blorm to reveal themselves, skewering his hide-like exterior from every angle. "Agrh!" he groans, still lying flat. But despite tearing away those preventing him to move, he fails to see another slithering rapidly towards him. Sensing contact, this new Blorm sprays an anaesthetic, softening the Zordacians normally tough rib cage from behind. Then, pushing inside and cracking through his breast plate, it brutally slices his heart in two.

Instantly, his eye's bulge and face shudders, as red veins spread over what was once the white sclera of his eye.

Paralysing venom continues to surge inside, leaving humanity's best hope lying motionless. *It can't be over,* he splutters. *I know how to cross the Blorm...and beat the Kryon. How can they be manipulating me?*

With his mind churning, and sensing the Kryon's pace only just beginning to quicken, the Zordacian feels himself once again targeted by something else. *Oh no,* he thinks, suddenly realising it's neither the Kryon, nor the Blorm, which had taken control.

LXXX.

Like all humans, Marc's initial strides explode off the dirt, leaving only dust in his wake. Though he begins faster than he's ever done before, one thought soon emerges. *Where are all the Blorm?*

Not wanting to dwell on his lane's scattering shape-shifters, he steamrolls towards the halfway platform. "Come on," he pants, seeing only humans in front, seventy metres in, "we may actually win."

His growing confidence, however, is met by a single leaping Blorm which scrapes his thigh, altering his steps. Instantly, he becomes sluggish, his legs heavy like tree trunks. Purposely slowing, knowing it will assist the negligible amount of poisons to dissipate, he begins to feel compelled to stop altogether. Aware of a pull, by something other than the toxins, he begrudgingly peeks behind.

The Kryon, and the source of this new burden, are closing. *Don't let them in*, he urges, pressing forward with a sense he can no longer outpace them.

Suddenly, a hidden Blorm cluster unite, spearing both his feet before quickly dispersing again, leaving Marc plunging face-first. Twitching violently, the screaming pain immobilises him, as those watching see a single row of one million unified Kryon swallow up, not just him, but every other fallen Hominidae.

Marc's bordering Kryon pass quickly, their single disfigured eye ogling his bloodied face. "Get out!" he yells, grabbing his head. "Get out!" Though trying to resist their silent demand for information, it doesn't take long for him to capitulate, relinquishing control of his thoughts. But despite circulating toxins, he refuses to collapse, instead clawing his way towards the safety of the half way platform.

But though the end of this first stage will provide brief respite from the Blorm, the real danger for all Defenders, as the Zordacian is discovering, is already assembling.

LXXXI.

Swiftly executing its three-movement slice, a lone Hord severs the head off its first victim. Then, after pausing to observe its artwork, it customarily devours the dead Zordacian's pulsating heart. As the creature retreats, waiting for the rest of its clan to surface, those watching know the chances of man-kind winning have just taken a fatal blow.

LXXXII.

Flushed with copious abrasions, Ky leaps delicately in between successive slashing Blorm. Though the end of the first stage is within reach, a lack of gaps in the vicinity of his next stride sees him land on top of a cluster of intertwined blades. Wincing, he resists the urge to press down harder than he has to. With minimal damage, his subsequent step hits dirt with force, allowing one of his sluggish legs to soar high while the other latches onto, and climbs, the elevated halfway platform.

Triggering his own eighty-eight dat countdown, he clambers with all fours to the centre of the rocky surface before sprawling on his back. Puffing erratically, his only thought is that a human is victorious before this temporary reprieve pushes him into the last stage. But moments later, one of the adjoining Cril Kryon, who brakes convention by forging ahead of its synchronous comrades, joins Ky on the platform, snapping any thought he has of safety.

Suddenly, he lifts his head and fixes his sight a dozen lanes away. "Oh no," he whimpers, spotting Marc crawling over the Blorm which are seemingly hacking freely at his limbs. "Come on Marc," he yells, attracting the attention of the Cril Kryon. "You're almost there."

The Kryon grunts, as if laughing at his plea, sending Ky's confidence into a tail spin as the giant creature moves to block his line of sight.

Refusing to make eye contact, Ky stares down, applying pressure to both feet before realising the cuts are deeper than first thought. Slowly, he squeezes out the poisons circulating near the surface of his skin. *Feel my strength Marc*, he urges, as the lethargy in his legs begin to dissolve in line with the dissipating toxins. With his breath regulating, and in spite of the surrounding groans and screams, his eyes close as he pretends his nostrils are filling with the most pleasant of childhood scents.

More time passes. In praying the remaining poisons do not reach his vital organs, a self-belief returns as he sees that, despite being slower than most of the human Defenders still in the race, his first stage took only nineteen dats; faster than he'd ever run before.

Sensing the Earthlings confidence return, an irritated Cril Kryon stomps one of its legs as its own focus changes, a shift none of the other Kryon had planned on.

LXXXIII.

The graceful line of Kryon quickly outnumber the humans slumping on the halfway platform. Unable to block out the mind sapping intrusions, it doesn't take long for any euphoria remaining in the psyche of the leading humans to be gobbled up as they prepare to leap into the last stage. What's more, the throbbing of their own stiffening bodies, and the sight of mountains of new Blorm, is giving rise to a simple conundrum; wait for treatment and lose the race for mankind or, when the countdown expires, jump into the pain of permanent paralysis.

Why aren't any Kryon falling? Ky muses. While frustrated, he accepts their tough exterior and methodical technique may be impervious to the Blorm. Watching on, a hush overwhelms many human Façade onlookers, distracted by a growing silhouette shadowing the sand dune.

Unaware of this darkness, Ky's abdomen tenses suddenly. His chest also tightens as heart palpitations accelerate. *Breathe,* he groans repeatedly. With twenty-three dats left before his invisible barrier into his last stage opens, the inner toxins have their way with him. His legs begin to tremble, then seize, sending him flat on his back yet again. "Agrh!" he shouts.

Flooding his thoughts, Mr Regent's instruction that the platform will lower to the Blorm's level once the countdown expires forces him to prop himself up with his forearms. "Get up! Move your body!"

Despite Defenders being taught to remain still, so the poisons will dissipate, Ky remembers how Dom helped Marc to overcome his Blorm-related fatigue back in the courtyard. Fresh in his mind, he does what the other human Defenders do not. He stands.

Immediately, his back stiffens as he drops back to the ground, lying frozen against the rough exterior of the platform.

Staring up, all he can see is the imposing figure of the Cril Kryon, still staring back at him. *This isn't my dream, or my fate.*

Refusing to turn away, the Kryon snarls with discomfort as the ill effects from its own unnatural burst of speed cannot be disguised.

Meanwhile, Ky's body curls in pain as he watches the leading Defenders launch themselves into the awaiting Blorm. *I have to do this,* he pleads, blood dripping from the corner of his mouth.

Three.

It can't end this way.

Two.

"No pain!" he shouts, silencing the roars of all nearby Kryon as he, plummeting platform and all, leaps into his own lane.

LXXXIV.

Of the two thousand human leaders who enter this last stage, only around one hundred of them persist past their second stride. The Kryon's unified mind manipulation, in forcing the humans to capitulate, is too great. What's more, the pace of those who avoid falling onto the piecing Blorm is no faster than an amble.

While the Cril Kryon closest to him waits for its own countdown to finish, Ky hobbles across the Blorm while trying to hold every ounce of poison at bay. *No pain!* he implores again, as fleeting thoughts of the Numerals wash over him.

But after seeing another human fall, he knows he can no longer hope for the Numerals, nor anyone else, to save the day. *No pain!*

Suddenly, his forward momentum slows dramatically. Although he is aware of all the nearby Blorm, he finds himself walking no faster than the trailing Cril Kryon, whose own countdown had just expired.

LXXXV.

Pulling himself up onto the small halfway platform, Marc, whose tattered body feels like it's been used as a piñata for knife wielding terrorists, rolls onto his back. He, like many others in the same predicament, face the frightening sight confronting the onlookers; the slithering shadow creeping slowly down the near side of the sand dune.

Peeking over the horizon, Faru's heat creates spot fires on top of the highest peaks, increasing the urgency of these indigenous creatures.

Barely enough room for him to lay flat sees Marc ease his pain by scrunching his torso. But sensing the shadows, cloaked by the landscape, swarming the entire starting area, Marc's muscles spasm as his breaths shorten.

Moving across the first stage, over the scattering Blorm and towards any Defender unlucky enough not to make it halfway, these creatures spew out a monumental screech which confirms everyone's fears.

The Hord is here.

LXXXVI.

Well into the last stage, the Kryon collective step over the Blorm with the confidence of the victor; their bloodstream clear of any poisons. Sensing it, and its trailing brethren, have already passed all but a handful of humans, the Cril Kryon's claw-like arms thrash about as its cerebral powers has the Earthling decelerate to a pace slower than its own.

Feeling the intense mental strain, Ky breaks his own rule and peeks behind to see a throng of Kryon closing in. He notices the Cril Kryon, leading the way, move within an arms-length. *It's in my head,* he cringes, grasping both temples as his intruder is revealed.

Despite the instinct to fight the invasion, Ky lets the Cril Kryon have its way, allowing his mind to become limp, as if mimicking his sluggish body. Even though this leading Kryon's stride has also been decreasing, due to its impulsive solo efforts, the giant creature knows it has control.

While the screeching Hord, having swarmed the entire first stage, begin ripping into the intestines of any Defender in their path, Ky, unaware of how his own efforts were impacting the race, grits his teeth and stares towards the finish. "Just-a-bit-more," he urges, able to hold the penetrating psychological attacks, demanding him to cease, at bay. But while he staggers to within twenty metres of the finish, the pain screaming through his head sees him stumble, enabling one of the quicker Blorm to skewer his foot's plantar fascia and for the Cril Kryon to draw level.

Though breathing heavily, Ky refuses to fall, instead narrowing his already blurry vision on his medic's deformed body. With any resemblance to Elric vanishing, Ky's eyes widen as he is jolted with the recollection of the Kryon's only weakness, giving him one last hope.

Despite knowing another Blorm attack may end more than just his race, he clenches his speared foot, pushing the deadly Blorm further inside.

Ky's tortured shriek screams through the Cril Kryon's head as the burst of adrenaline from the pain propels Ky's body forward.

Seeing the Earthling forge ahead, the Cril Kryon releases an almighty roar, forcing its way to the brink of Ky's sanity.

"Now!" Ky yells, purposely changing his thoughts as he relinquishes his protective shell that had served as a barrier to his emotions. Still maintaining its mental telepathy into Ky, this throng of unfamiliar feelings engulf the giant.

The Cril Kryon staggers as intruding positive emotions, oscillating from kindness to compassion, are too much for the mechanical Kryon to consume.

With Ky continuing to surge forward, the Cril Kryon withdraws all attempts to mentally conquer the Earthling. Using all three limbs, the giant's pace quickens. Though it is becoming susceptible to the Blorm, it draws level yet again.

But despite its long reaching strides, the Façade roars peak as Ky collapses onto the finishing area, and into the arms of his medic. "I made it," he wheezes, hastily wrenching the Blorm from his foot.

Numb with pain, Ky begins jabbering as he glares back down his lane. "The Zordacian! Did he win? Did we beat the Kryon?!" Although he can't spot his bordering Kryon, he notices a Numeral wisp over the wriggling Blorm he'd only just yanked out. "Did you see that?"

Though his senses flair, pain keeps him glued on all fours.

LXXXVII.

Eight-eight metres away, Marc's pain leaves him grasping the edges of the sunken platform with the hope the poisons will dissipate before the absent Blorm returns.

As a blood-filled cough splatters over his chin, his throbbing body drops, rolling flat on his back and leaving his weak arms flopping by his side.

Though his vision is cloudy, and the whispers of Ky long gone, he opens his eyes just as a shadow leaps onto his platform.

Despite seeing, what appears to be, a goblin's face stare at him, Marc could not lift his arms to protect himself.

Help me! he prays, watching the ghostly Hord creep closer. But with his words never having a chance to leave his lips, the once concealed creature props itself up on its hind legs, blanketing Marc with outstretched wings. Slowly, its sinewy body, encased by scaly battle armour, raises another of its clawed limbs. After waving it in a circular motion, as if purifying its victim, the drooling Hord freezes. Then, in a display of dynamic precision, its claw slashes across Marc's torso. The long tear splits his skin, leaving a gash the width of a human fist.

With his strength gone, a single tear wells. Unlike ascending this once high platform to avoid the Blorm, this time Marc knows there will be no escape.

LXXXVIII.

In Ky's periphery he sees a look of dread wash over his back-peddling medic. "Hey! Where ya going?" he mumbles, catching a reflection in the medic's eyes. And as a second Numeral flashes over the same Blorm, Ky is lifted off the ground.

Powerless, he thrashes his arms about while being thrown three lanes across.

Tumbling, he surrenders to the lethargy before coming to a standstill. Rubbing away any dirt, he sees the Cril Kryon slam each of its limbs on the ground as it stomps in a circle around him.

Gathering groups of medics watch closely as Ky groans; the cocoon of numbness, he'd cloaked himself in throughout the race, can no longer hide the pain of sliced skin, torn muscles and crushed bones.

Amid the Kryon's approach, Ky catches sight of his medic. Body stiffening, he scrambles on all fours in that direction as a splattering of mumbo jumbo hits his ears. But despite his own thoughts being lucid enough to hear the medic's panicked words, his quivering body crumples in a heap.

The nearby medics quickly retreat. And as a shadow encroaches overtop Ky, the familiar foul stench of the Cril Kryon fills his nostrils. Growling, the giant creature wraps one of its clawed arms around Ky's neck, squeezing him while lifting him in the air.

Struggling for breath, Ky releases pressure by forcing one hand under its grip, while his other close-fisted hand fights for one last attempt at freedom. But as the Kryon's blood-filled eye re-emerges, clearly incensed the Earthling has even survived the race, Ky is pulled flush against its coarse torso, sapping his remaining strength as both arms hang limply.

Though fearing his nightmares are finally coming to pass, Ky suddenly notices a green ooze squirting from its gaping mouth as the Kryon begins to convulse.

Unrelenting, the creature squeezes harder, its bludging eye protruding further. But following a colossal roar, the Kryon crashes to the ground, bringing the Earthling down under it.

Although one of Ky's arms is crushed, the other drops freely as his fist opens for all to see.

Gasps shoot through Elsh as visions of that Blorm, squirming away from Ky's lacerated hand, floods the Façade, informing everyone of what just transpired.

As Hord screeches drown out most noises, the nearby humanoid medics scream. "The Zankar is over! The Kryon has been slain!"

LXXXIX.

"How *dlosoe* you *lkuqwio qwejl* Blorm?" whispers the medics, still adjusting their translators.

Barely hearing his own thoughts, let alone the splattering of words coming his way, Ky, after being dragged free from under the Kryon, is placed in front of his own medic, who had taken the form of Elric once again.

"How did you pick up that Blorm?" his medic repeats, placing his arm carefully around Ky's tattered body. "How did you slay that Kryon?"

Though incoherent, Ky stumbles through his words. "Your eyes. They...they showed the Kryon coming for me so...so I scooped it up."

"Picking up the Blorm with your bare hands should've killed you!"

Ky groans, hardly any white in his eyes showing. "Did we beat them?"

"First, tell me why you picked it up?"

"It told me to," Ky mumbles.

"What did?"

"The Nu...the Numerals," Ky whispers, his eyes rolling back.

As other medics rush to assist, Ky's medic tries to process the events, recalling that Ky had flung one arm about erratically while he was being choked by the Kryon. But what the medic didn't see was the same hand, concealing the Blorm, embed part of the shape-shifter, along with all its poisons, in the heart of the giant.

After receiving a regenerative adrenaline shot beneath his ribcage Ky sits straight up, clasping his legs. "Did we win?" he shouts with clarity. "Why did that thing attack me?"

"The Crilinian Kryon attacked because you, and it, had entered the Zankar!" his medic says, trying to grab the attention of a more senior medic.

"What? How could that be?"

"Because *you* won the race, just ahead of that Cril Kryon."

With medicine disguising his pain, Ky glances up at the Façade. While hearing countless voices chanting his name euphorically, he sees his own image, in a split-screen replay, stumbling towards the finish. Next to the replay, his winning margin, and the reason for the Zankar, flickers.

Staring back down his lane he reaches for his arm band. No longer does it choke him. *Did I really win?*

"Ky Sterling," says the senior medic, rushing to repair one of Ky's more severe wounds. "Lay yourself down. You need rest."

"But how could *I* have won? What about the Zordacian. And where's..." Ky leaps to his feet, wobbly legs barely keeping him up. "...where's Marc?"

"Mr Sterling..."

"Marc!" Ky shouts, scrutinizing the corpse filled lanes.

"Mr Sterling!" affirms the senior medic. "Our time on Elsh is running out. You must be stabilized for travel."

"But Marc? He's still out there."

"The Kryon's medics are clearing the lanes. We'll soon know how your colleague faired."

After peeking up at Faru's shimmering heat burning the landscape, Ky allows himself to be helped onto a stretcher. "Are we going home now?"

"No. It's only this arena we need to leave. The few surviving humans are heading to the shelter, the only safe place left for us on Elsh."

"What do you mean, 'only a few survivors'? That sounds like

there aren't many of us left."

"Don't think about that. The threat to your species may be over, but Elsh is unforgiving. The safest place for us is in the shelter. That's where our departure will take place."

A high-pitched squeal rises from the horizon. Ky flinches, "The Hord...are they still..."

"They vanished when you won! Their mission is complete."

Ky appeared contemplative. "Then promise me you'll find Marc before...before this planet ignites. You must make sure he's okay."

The senior medic waves Ky's medic closer. Though the anaesthetic will be slow to wear off, the senior medic dissolves a sleeping tablet into Ky's forearm. "He must leave now, for not only did this Earthling beat every other human, but if the Numerals did show him how to pick up the Blorm, then *they* will want to speak with him."

Ky's nostrils flared involuntarily. "I don't want to talk to anyone," he wheezes, his words barely audible.

"Rest your thoughts," says his medic, taking over, "you may be more important than even we realise."

"Haven't we learnt anything from all this?" Ky whispers, as his eyes shut. "We're all important. That's why I need to find my friend."

XC.

Moments after the Cril Kryon was slain, the murky Massine, blocking the skies of Tousol, vanished.

"Do you think those devil clouds will ever come back?" Sam hollers over the cheers, as celebrations from his townsfolk drowns all normal conversation.

"No way," Dom grins. "Just look around at all the happy faces. The race is over...and we won. Our species, all our children, are safe."

"Speaking of children, do you think Drayed is okay? They haven't said whether he made it to the shelter."

Dom hesitated, resisting even a shrug. "He's strong, and the Hord will have scattered underground by now. So I have to believe that if Ky can fight a Kryon, Marc will be okay."

XCI.

"Did you see him?! Did you see him?!" Lenny shouts, bursting through the Sterling's entrance. "He did it! My little cousin did it! I have to tell the whole world!"

"You go and do that my dear," Loush says drowsily. "But first tell your parents we'll be over in the morning, after we get some sleep."

"Ok! Yep! Ok!" he says excitedly, running out while leaving the front door swinging in his wake.

Ahlis angrily grits her teeth and begins pacing. "But it's not over yet mum. How can we sleep, let alone go anywhere, when our guys haven't even made it to the shelter."

"I'm sure they'll get there any...any...moment."

"Mum!" Ahlis barks, startling Loush out of her droopy-eyed state. Though overjoyed Ky is alive, and that man-kind is saved, the exhaustive toll on Ahlis begins to show. Likewise, a sleep deprived Loush, slumping on the couch, can barely remain upright.

"Come on Ahlis," Nibby said. "We're all just as anxious as you to make sure Ky gets home safely."

"I know. I know. It's just that..."

With Ahlis' voice softening, Nibby reaches for her hand. "It's not Ky you're worried about, is it?"

Ahlis shakes her head. She ambles to the couch and sits in between the others. "Ky was amazing, but neither he, nor we, are in danger anymore."

"I'm sure Marc will be fine too," Nibby said.

"That's right," Loush says, propping herself up. "And we're going to wait here with you, no matter how long it takes."

"I know," Ahlis sighs.

"Wait on," Loush says, looking into her daughter's eyes. "There's something else, isn't there."

"What is it?" Nibby asks curiously.

"Ahlis?" Loush whispers.

"I've just been so angry he had to leave because...because..."

"What is it my dear? You can tell us."

With a deliberate pause, Ahlis takes a deep breath. "Because I'm pregnant with Marc's child."

"Oh my dear," Loush says, embracing her daughter. "That's wonderful."

Nibby smiles and grabs Ahlis' hand. "Wow. That's amazing. Looks like we both have reasons to glow."

"What?" Ahlis muses. "You too?"

"Yep," Nibby nods, seeing Loush dropping speechlessly back on the couch. "But Ky doesn't even know. So it seems none of us will rest easily until *both* our boys get home safely."

XCII.

Sitting inside the stone building, Grand Elder Esau turns to his long-time colleague. "I know we won. But your Defender is dead so why are you grinning?"

The Zordacian Grand Elder's smile widens. "It is true, we all saw the Hord decapitate him before consuming his mutilated heart. But I smile because it's how my Defender would have wanted to die. We both know he lived a tortured life, and is certain to have more peace in death."

"Then I wonder if he would have been surprised another human won."

"I'm not sure if he would have cared. The burden of being a species' best Defender is too great for anyone, just look what happened to that Cril Kryon. But I would like to think knowing there was another who could defeat the Kryon may have eased his pain."

"Hmm," Esau muses, "but that's not the only reason you're grinning, is it?"

"Ah. You read my thoughts because the same idea plagues your mind too."

"The second prophesy," Esau nods. "It seems it may not be superstitious nonsense after all."

"We've both seen *her* DNA change since their first meeting, and how *his* EALF grew in the same time frame."

"I know. But why are you so pleased? Uncovering this fact has come at great cost. Many Defenders, including my best Polmarian, have died."

"Well of course," revels the Zordacian unsympathetically. "The Kryon chose this battle wisely, knowing the Hord targets the strongest human from each civilization. But their instinct was wrong as the Hord themselves selected the wrong Earthling to slay."

Esau agrees. "Then let's hope Marc Drayed's sacrifice was not in vain for if the first prophesy is true, that *they* really are arriving as I had seen on Pretta's dome ceiling, then this second prophesy had better be true as well."

"This is why we have initiated our plan, part of which grants Kynan Sterling an audience with the Obzoovers. Knowing the Kryon are in possession of some kind of message from the Obzoover sends shivers down my spine, so let's hope this plan will finally enlighten us as to the real reason the Earthlings were challenged. If we can..."

Suddenly, the Zordacian Grand Elder places his hand to his ear.

"What is it?" Esau asks.

"Word has just been sent. The Kryon have not disabled all their Massine devices."

"What are they doing? We have to learn the content of their Obzoover communiqué."

"Wait!" pauses the Zordacian, still clasping his ear. "Massine activity has been detected."

"What! Where?"

"We don't know. But I suddenly fear the Kryons' secrets are going to kill us all!"

"I know," agrees Esau. "We need to know what's going on and we need to find out now!"

XCIII.

A group of medics rush Ky's semi-conscience body across Elsh's coarse rubble. Though only two carry the stretcher, a throng of others shield him from the hazy sky growing redder by the moment. Despite enjoying the pain-free euphoria of the sedatives, he senses the urgency may mean the silent killer of Faru's heat could be ready to pounce.

The racket of a large metallic trundle wheel, creaking like it hasn't been used in a generation, begins to turn. "What's that?" he wheezes, seeing his medic trot alongside while keeping pressure on his deepest wounds. Though no reply is forthcoming, the other medics come to a halt, lowering the stretcher to the ground.

Ky raises his head only to see a plethora of human legs continue their disciplined march. "I know you understand me," he enunciates, ensuring his words are audible.

"Welcome to the shelter Mr Sterling," says his medic. "This protective structure will keep us safe from Elsh's heat, along with any rouge Hord – at least for the moment."

With help, Ky stands up. But as the trundle churns again, his legs wobble. Grabbing his medic for support, it doesn't take long to realise they, and the wide platform below, are rising.

Ky rubs his eyes to see tens of thousands of surrounding humans stare back. "Who are they?"

"The survivors," says the medic, among the mumbling. "They, along with the onlookers, will pay you homage before we depart."

Ky scans the opaque shelter, a semi-circular dome spanning kilometres in each direction. "Do we have time?" he asks, seeing the Defenders, each with their own life-threatening wounds, being supported by just as many medics. "Shouldn't they be getting treatment?" Again, silence is the reply. Gazing up, he sees the Façade's blurry faces cover every part of the dome. "Can my family see me?" he persists, ensuring no tears flow.

"*Everyone* can see you."

Pausing for only a moment, Ky's eyes quickly widen as he scans the Defenders. "What about Marc! Is he here yet?"

"Mr Sterling," says the medic, lacking any emotion, "the Hord are relentless. They killed our Zordacian. In fact, most of our dead came at their claws."

"What are you saying? Is that what happened to Marc?"

An uncharacteristic stumble chokes the medic's words. "Yes. It is almost certain he was met with the same fate."

Ky stares into the Façade, "Agrh! It's not right. It's just..."

"Hey!" shouts a voice from below. "Stop ya screamin'. It's hurt'n ma ears mon."

"It can't be," says the medic.

"Marc?" Ky asks squinting. "We were just saying...I mean, is that really you?"

"Who else would tell you off after you just saved man-kind?" Marc coughs, dry blood staining his face as he hobbles up the platform's makeshift stairs. "You did it," he whispers, embracing a hesitant Ky. "You saved us all."

"It's good to see you," Ky says, pulling back to see sweat dribbling down Marc's forehead. "Are you okay? They said you were dead, that the Hord had taken you..."

Wincing, Marc lifts a discoloured bandage to reveal deep gashes across his abdomen. "As you can see, they were half right. But I've been pumped with some kind of morphine while their medicines are taking effect, so I don't feel too bad."

"Impossible," says Ky's baffled medic. "How could you have survived?"

"What?! Who are you?" Marc grumbles, squinting.

"That's my medic," Ky says, "and it's a good question. How'd you escape the Hord?"

Marc chuffs, more out of hiding his pain than at the question. "I can't recall much," he muses. "I remember being yanked from the halfway platform."

"You mean by the Hord?"

"I think so. I'm pretty sure I blacked out for a while, just happy the Blorm weren't attacking me anymore. But then I felt the pain, a tearing at my skin." Both Ky and his medic stare back at Marc's wound. "I don't remember much after that, except for a screech which startled me to wake just as the Hord was hurtling back towards the horizon."

"Ah," says the medic, "I know what made it stop."

"Really?" Ky says sceptically, hands on waist as his breath shortens. "And what would that be?"

"You winning."

"What?!"

"He's right," Marc smiles, pointing to a small bionic robot at the platform's edge. "That thing found me, hundreds of lanes from my own. And while it carried me here it forced me to listen to why I had survived, saying the Hord's purpose ceases when the Defenders' Race is over."

Peering at Marc, a defiant smile creeps over Ky's medic. "That *thing*, as you call it, is an Elsh cleaner. Their purpose is to empty each lane. And since they are only released when a winner is known, it appears Mr Sterling's victory has saved, not only our species, but you at a most opportune time."

"Of course," Marc teases. "That's what us Earthling friends do for each other."

"Very well. But I can't help but wonder why *you* were targeted, and not Mr Sterling."

"Who cares," Marc growls. "That doesn't matter now."

"Maybe not to you," says the medic, grabbing a transmission from the impartial robot, "but according to this, you were targeted by the Kryon because you convinced them you were Earth's best Defender."

"That's because I am."

"I'm afraid your self-confidence would not have sufficed with the Kryon, or the Hord, for only great mental toughness would have convinced them otherwise. Congratulations Mr Drayed, you too have contributed to saving our species by keeping the Hord away from Ky Sterling."

Though silent, Marc lowers his head sheepishly towards Ky and whispers. "Ah, who wants to be the best anyway? I'm just glad we're both here because there's something I was going to tell you, about your sister, just before we departed for Elsh. But since we're safe now, I think it can wait a bit longer. Besides, there's a ceremony about to start in your honour."

Ky squints inquisitively. Feeling a twinge of pain fighting through the sedatives, he lurches over as Elsh's heat starts to encroach into the Shelter.

"Ky?! Are you alright?"

"Step aside," says the medic, tapping the platform twice while injecting Ky with more narcotics. "We must begin the departure ritual. And though it's clear you both need assistance, I take it Mr Drayed is to remain on the platform with us..."

"Of course," Ky wheezes, supported by his medic. "He wouldn't miss a chance for all this adulation."

"Now hang on!" Marc says, as a voice, the same which greeted the Defenders prior to the race, speaks. "Nah, you're right."

"Welcome human Nyrolacs," announces the voice. "The Hominidae have won the Challenge of the Nameless and, as such, are accepted into the Knowledge Base."

Roars shoot through the shelter as the Façade shudders its approval.

Ky smiles and raises his arm, clenching his bloodied fist as high as it can reach. *This honours all of us.* Marc, seeing Ky's arm band partially hidden within his grip, tears his own off and follows in kind. As cheers fade, Ky opens his hand and shouts as loud as his fluid-filled lungs allow. "I hold this band to represent the unity of all Hominidae." The ripple through the shelter is swift as each Defender also raises their fists.

Ky's defiant act, witnessed by every species of Nyrolac, sends a clear message. From the time the Earthlings were forced to defend, to when he became victorious, Ky's efforts have done what Ages of advancement had not. *I love you dad,* he smiles. *Now we are united! Now we are free.*

But though he expects a sense of peace to follow, none is forthcoming as an eerie silence washes over the shelter. Ky's smile disappears.

"Safe passage to your home land is ready," says the crackling voice. "You must leave now as Elsh's environment will become unstable in precisely eighteen Ticks."

"Wait! Something's happening," Ky groaned, peering beyond the entrance to the shelter.

"I know," Marc says. "I feel it too. Something's making the

ground shake."

"I'm afraid it's not something," says the medic, noticing another ripple begin to move through the crowd, "but someone." In short time the Defenders closest to the disturbance begin lowering their fists. Hearing the sound of marching steps trudge across puddles of dirt and towards the platform, all medics instantly drop on one knee. "...It's the Kryon...they're coming for us."

XCIV.

"Why are those things still here?" Marc says, angrily gritting his teeth.

"I don't know," says the medic, standing with Marc's help. "This is unprecedented. They should have left by now. As it is written, contact between us is not permitted until authorized by the Obzoovers."

With the last of the humans parting, Ky steps backward only to see the Kryon surround the platform, cramming themselves between him and the other Hominidae. Before he can react, one of the Kryon elevates itself onto the platform, towering over the vulnerable Earthling.

Though the medic retreats, pulling a hesitant Marc back with him, Ky braces himself while keeping thoughts of his near death battle at bay.

Suddenly, the Kryon's horn recoils into itself, activating its translator as its low rumbling voice amplifies throughout the shelter. "I am the second of two Cril Kryon Defenders chosen to defend our species. From what we have just seen, I'm sure you remember the first."

Though unsure if he should reply to the rhetorical statement, Ky remains quiet.

Unhurried, the Kryon scans the Façade, knowing its presence would displease some. "We know coming here is not protocol, but there is something all the Hominidae, and you especially, must learn about us and our beliefs. A piece of information which has remained hidden within our civilization for many Ages."

Despite wanting to reveal the mystery, the surprise of hearing his adversary speak keeps Ky's words in his mouth. He can only speculate if this is actually the secret he'd heard his own Elders hypothesize about.

The Kryon snorts displeasingly as the discomfort from the heat creeps into the shelter. "It is this fact which had previously driven us to challenge many Nyrolacs. We always believed it was the only way to preserve our own species."

"That's ridiculous! No belief should make you kill an entire species, no matter what it is."

"Oh it is not a *what*, it's a *who*."

Who? Ky wonders as the whispers, and piercing glares, intensify.

Then, unexpectedly, the Kryon kneels and touches Ky's face with a gentleness that belies its demeanour. "We've spent a long time searching for you."

"Me?"

The Kryon groans as its foul odour strengthens, repairing its own wounds with each passing moment. "Yes. You are our secret. And after seeing how you defeated our greatest Defender it appears a new truth, something which will stop any further Challenges, has revealed itself."

"What truth?"

"Not many can do what you have just done. And though a great Defender can summon the Numerals, only a Candidate can handle the Blorm."

Joining the whispering, Ky too mumbles. "Look. I don't know who you think I am or what you think I can do, but I didn't control anything, especially the Blorm."

The Kryon huffs, as if laughing mockingly. "Don't be foolish. We have seen your thoughts. We know you gave instructions to the shape-shifters. It is the only reason you won and the reason why you are a Candidate."

"If you say so," Ky frowns, wondering if there may be more to his own visions than he'd ever thought. "Can you and your people get out of my head now?"

"There is no need for concern. Our entanglement terminated when the Challenge ended. But if an Earthling really is the *Masool*, then we too have been deceived."

"Candidate? Masool? Deceived by whom?!" Ky snaps. "You'd best keep your words simple. I can barely stand up, let alone try to interpret your language."

"Though your people will soon become well versed in Knowledge

Base tongue, I will explain. The Masool is the belief driving our actions. And it begins with a shared philosophy that a Nyrolac, known as the Traveller, will start a chain of events by turning a gifted Defender, such as yourself, into a Candidate."

Ky's heart skips. Contemplating, he tries to divert any thoughts of Nibby. "So where does the Masool fit in?"

"When a Candidate is found we believe our challenge may turn the truest of them, the one who can defeat us, into the Masool...the only Nyrolac with the powers to protect us all."

"Protect you from what?"

"The great battle. A looming clash that will, without the Masool, lead to the destruction of all Nyrolacs."

"That's crazy. If we're united surely no species can battle us all."

As the Façade whispers morph into murmurs, Ky scans the dead-panned faces jamming the shelter only to see his own medic talking to Marc.

Irritated by the onslaught of details, Marc shrugs off the medic and yells at the Kryon. "So who da hell are dese tyrants?!"

The Kryon grunts, ignoring the question. "They will not be pleased we are talking to you."

"Who cares," Marc persists, stepping closer.

"Yeah," Ky adds. "Why are you so scared of them?"

The Kryon grunts again. "We have seen their ability to wield Massine like no other, a power even greater than the strongest Obzoover. But now we have uncovered the last Candidate, we no longer need to be afraid."

"Hang on," Ky says. "If they are really that strong, why did they allow you to search for the Candidates in the first place?"

"Our theory suggests they were, and are, still preparing. You see, a long time ago the search for the Masool began after we alone stumbled upon their battle plans. But just as we were about to expose them they came after us. Though destroying many of my Kryon ancestors as a show of their strength, they allowed us to search for the Candidates so long as we kept their attack a secret."

"Why would they make a deal like that?" Ky says.

"Because we believe they too may need the Masool. We do not know why. In fact, we don't even know their reasons for waging this war, but it's only one of a few hypotheses which make sense."

"Sense!" Marc snaps. "None of this makes sense! I mean you, and this strange species, both want to find this Masool in order to defeat each other in some great battle. It all sounds like rubbish, don't you think?"

The Kryon grumbles, noticing speckles of volcanic lava burning the outside of the Shelter. "Our time here is running out."

"Fine," Marc puffs. "If you don't answer my question, at least tell me why you didn't send a message to the Obzoovers. They would have found a way which didn't involve killing species after species."

"If we said anything *they* would have destroyed us, and would have convinced others to keep searching for Candidates, just like they did with our predecessors."

Ky muses. "So what made you chose us Earthlings?"

"The time was right for the Hominidae to be re-tested. Though you humans are a volatile and fractured species, we hoped the idea of protecting innocent Earthlings would unite all your Defenders."

"But why go to all that trouble? You could have just told us you wanted to find a Candidate. It would have saved so much death."

"We are truly sorry for keeping it hidden, but we have no regrets. As you have seen firsthand, only when a species has to fight for its survival will a Candidate, and the Numerals, be revealed. It's just that no one, except perhaps *them*, would have thought an Earthling would partake in the Challenge, let alone win."

"You mean *they* thought we could win?" Marc says.

"It appears so."

"So now what? We're just supposed to believe in your great truth? That this clash has transformed Ky into your Masool?"

"No! He's not the Masool. He's just a Candidate."

"Either way, it all just sounds like superstitious nonsense," Marc says. "None of it may be real."

"You may not believe in legends, but only true faith can turn mythology into reality. One day your people may come to realise this."

"But I still don't understand how anyone can put an entire species at risk just to see if their faith is real," Marc says. "I mean, you killed many species just to save your own."

"Without the Masool we will all perish. That's what we believe and is something we are not prepared to risk."

Hearing the word *faith* sends a wave of confusion through Ky. *It should have killed me!* He ponders. *So why did I trust my instinct, the same one I felt from my dream, and pick up that Blorm?*

Ky suddenly realises it was not the Elders cry for faith, the same faith this Kryon maybe speaking of, which had him undertake the suicidal act. As his thoughts are drawn back inside the shelter he contemplates something that, until now, he had not dared to consider – that there really is a power inside of him unlike anything his Elders have ever discovered.

Sensing the truth behind this power and its link to the Numerals may soon reveal itself, Ky puts any further interrogation on hold. He calmly exhales and places his hand on Marc's shoulder, easing his friend's aggressive stance. "We should probably go mate, our time on Elsh is up."

"Yes," says the Kryon. "You need to repair your wounds. For the first time in an Age, we do not know what lies ahead."

"But why we should believe anything you've said," Marc maintains.

"If it is proof of our honesty you want, then you may wish to learn *how* we were also deceived…Clause one-hundred and twenty-one dash three dash twenty-one in the Constructor charter states if a member from the newest Nyrolac civilization defeats the Challenger, then a response in kind is to be carried out. Though *they* assured us you Earthlings would not participate we learnt the hard way *they* had tricked us; that *you* were always going to battle alongside your fellow humans." Sensing the Earthling's hesitation, the Kryon persists. "Because of your bravery much of my own species has just been targeted by Massine."

"But I thought *you* controlled the Massine in this Challenge," Ky says.

"Incorrect. The Knowledge Base does. And, as I speak, they are using it to annihilate many of my own kind. Why do you think the Crilinian humans did not want to help you in the first place? Though they have been shifted elsewhere their home planet no longer exists."

"That can't be right," Ky says, his voice filling with remorse.

"That's the risk we took."

"If that's true," Marc growls, his weak legs leaning into Ky, "then expose these bastards for the gutless creatures they are."

The Kryon glances up at the shaky Façade, sensing the fear overwhelming the onlookers. "It's not wise to get them mad as they have another merciless ally, and our successor, ready to obey their every request."

Ky furrows his brow, and is about to add to Marc's demand, when the horn of all the surrounding Kryon, except the Cril Kryon, reappear. Their Translators deactivate, allowing no more thoughts to be transmitted.

Though a sudden influx of Nyrolacs appear in the Façade, and despite Marc and the other Defenders being ushered away to commence their departure, Ky keeps his attention on the Kryon.

As is their custom, those Kryon who deactivated their translator bow and vanish by use of their personal Lest device, leaving their Crilinian leader the lone speaker. "Tell your Elders their fears are real for both prophesies have begun."

Continuing with meticulous clarity, the Cril Kryon whispers words Ky alone can hear. "Your Elders will soon learn that, even though *they* are coming, *our* task is now complete as all Candidates have been found. Confirming this is an encrypted Obzoover transmission we received, and could only be decoded, after this Challenge had begun. Though our Elders originally thought it referred to one of us, *your* victory indicates it may have been written about you."

Methodically, the Kryon lowers itself to the ground, as if deactivating itself from operation, before repeating the message:

Since we first saw you race we knew you would become the Chosen One. We are so proud of you, our creation, a concoction mixed with our own genetics which, initially planted in the Traveller, has ended up in you. If we are right, then you will fight for us, and we will no longer be fearful of the Nholl.